'You mentioned th
'It's all over the p
on all sides.'

'Really? Hmmmm. That's news.'

'There's the religious nuts – well, not nuts, the Archbishop of Canterbury's not a nut – then there's the scientists who believe it's some kind of natural phenomenon and the scientists . . . where have you *been*, Kevin?'

'Ah. Busy.'

'Ah-huh. Anyway. There's the UFO cranks and—'

'Which side are you on?'

'It's an epidemic. It's happened to famous people in public places. Jane Fonda saw one during her chat show on prime time TV. John Paul the Third has seen one.'

'Seen what?'

'Ah-huh. She said later she saw a Jackson Pollock painting. There has been some speculation. A lot of people think it's the end of the world.'

'Could be.'

Paul Voermans
AND DISREGARDS THE REST

VGSF

First published in Great Britain 1992
by Victor Gollancz Ltd

First VGSF edition published 1993
by Victor Gollancz
an imprint of Cassell
Villiers House, 41/47 Strand, London WC2N 5JE

'It is possible that. . .' from *The Notebook of Malte
Laurids Briggs* by Rainer Marie Rilke translated by
S. Mitchell, © 1982, 1983, published by Picador
Classics, 1988.

'Dear I know of nothing either. . .' from *In Praise of
Limestone* by W.H. Auden, Collected Shorter Poems
1927-1957, published by Faber and Faber, 1966.

A catalogue record for this book
is available from the British Library

ISBN 0 575 05282 1

Printed and bound in Great Britain
by Cox & Wyman Ltd, Reading

For Fiona

*I would like to thank all those who have helped me
with this novel.
They are:
Chris and Leigh Priest, Christina Lake, Judith Hanna
and of course my editor, Richard Evans.*

PROLOGUE:

from
Charms All O'erthrown

by MARTIN LEYWOOD

If I baulk and call the violence which crushed us that evening the act of a careless God, I should go insane. I wish Justice drove me here to let you in on subterfuge and betrayal but it's more a simple need to hold my aching head together. To survive. Like a man who feels the sand give way beneath his feet and the rip take hold, I'm all over the place, and filled with dread. This is not melodrama. As an actor I ought to know. The details of our story moe and chatter at me and I'll have no peace until I work them through. But I'm no Shakespeare. So I ask you to be patient when events sound unbelievable.

You see, it *was* murder.

Imagine, then, the killers as they plot our evening of liquid terror. On a pallid Sunday unusual for Adelaide in the spring, in a temporary office above a chip shop, somewhere within the Grand Prix line which cuts that city, two men meet. Unlike us they have nothing to do with the stage. Even our accountants dress more colourfully than this lot. Around their forgettable suits and faces is an air of the virtuous – the hint of an arch in one eyebrow, the slightly pulled-back shoulders – yet they don't quite fit the mould of Jehovah's Witnesses. They are men of action, but clearly some kind of élite. The plastic remains of a hamburger lunch are spread across the desk which separates them. The shorter and more cocky of the two licks the fingertips of his left hand; his right hand caresses the keyboard of what

looks like an old-fashioned PC with a small satellite plate fixed
on top as if he isn't paying the faintest attention to his partner.

The blond, taller, more reserved one is giving a briefing. This
concerns a play which will take place to the north-east of the
city, and especially one member of the company who is by their
lights planning a crime. But since all traces of the crime and
their own interference in the workings of an allied nation must
be effaced, all must suffer. For the Whole United Free World's
sake. Recall that phrase? Besides, although their instructions are
to use the top-secret device on the desk to neutralise the criminal
and his own version of the device by the simplest means possible
then get out of there, this mission will provide a lesson to those
foolish or twisted enough to follow a life in the theatre. Hadn't
the recent assassination attempt on the President been caused by
a play? It was a fact.

The blond one pulls a map from his inside pocket; the cocky
one puts the rubbish on the desk back in its bag and neatly ties
the top. The map is spread and they get down to business again.

'Here.' An area beyond some mountains is circled. 'This is the
target zone.'

The shorter man's lips move briefly. 'Heck, this baby won't
reach that far with only one operator,' he complains.

'That's why we're moving out to here.' The taller man points
to an underlined name not far from a salt pan. 'Once we've got
the tests done.'

The town's name is mouthed slowly. 'Real strange names they
got here. Aboriginal, huh?'

'Yuh. Think that will be close enough?'

'Bet your ass. Watch and learn, buddy, this will be totally
surreal.'

'Just so it works.'

'For sure.' He permits himself a knowing smile.

And so our fate was determined. The shorter one, the one
with the brown eyes and slightly rounded features, did a very
good job indeed. Of those who survived, few wished to talk
about what happened that night deep in our country's heart,

and they were not believed. Unlike the rest of this account, the above is merely a work of my imagination, but I know these two were the hired killers. As I lay in hospital afterwards these two Americans came to interview me. I thought I knew why. They promised a thorough investigation, then disappeared. Because I promised them to keep quiet for a month, 'so the perpetrators don't get wind of our enquiries', I let my best friend down when he tried to tell the world about these murderers. We fought; I have not seen him or heard from him since then. And later: no one had seen them come or go; there were no records of their existence; all knowledge was denied. Because I waited, and because my outraged version ranted of conspiracies, my story only raised doubts about my sanity.

I have been alone for some time now. I have written, collared, pleaded, threatened and lied. Journalists, scientists, parliamentarians, publishers, ambassadors, police: nobody listens and very few even remember the lives snuffed out. Here I sit with my kiddy's exercise book and pencil and strong black coffee before the endless mirrors at Pelegrini's, the place we'd often visit after shows. My eyes are red, but not from make-up. I can't remember when I last got up this early in the morning. Martin Leywood, pleased to meet you. You might recognise me from some old TV play – then again, perhaps not. I don't even recognise this ravaged face myself. My charms are all overthrown. But listen. Please.

ONE

When the little voice first came through clearly he was up to his ankles in duck shit. Kevin cast a longing look out the duck house door and up the slope to his own ramshackle place. If you're hearing things it's time to take a holiday. A simple thought when you weren't trapped in an acrid mess with a gang of ducks harassing you. So much work remained on the farm before he could break away for a long journey, never mind the jobs he'd have to cancel if he went. He hawked and spat, the duck dust by his calves went spinning; from her corner nest Hyacinth eyed him angrily. Kevin ignored her and tried to subtract what he owed from his bank balance as well as from the sums that were owed to him from recent landscaping. As if to deride his money worries a different voice spoke up, bright but echoed by headache:

> Get out, Mr Metalhead, get out and catch your friend.
> Write a note and run away, he's going round the bend,
> Get out, Mr Metalhead, one, two, three,
> Playtime goes until the bell and you – are – he!

Kevin chucked his spade at the door jamb. Ducks scattered. Hyacinth flapped and complained, then settled. The throb behind his eyes went away. He thrust his fingers into his lank black hair and held it out of his eyes and sighed.

This was connected with his last job in the theatre, he knew it. When half your best friends are wiped out in a not-so-natural disaster you do your best to get to the bottom of it. Nobody believes the disaster wasn't natural and the only other survivor who knows anything keeps mum, so after a while you find the accepted story more plausible than your own. It was after all a crackpot scheme; flash floods do happen in Central Australia, even if there's no sign of bad weather anywhere near you. Finished. Eleven years finished. Now this.

Kevin took up the shovel and held down the carpet of feathers and straw and faeces while he pulled out his feet. First indecipherable but familiar mutterings which cut off when you listened. Then a child's voice. He scraped his boots with the shovel's edge. Messages from his subconscious or whatever. Wasn't healthy to ignore your wiser half. He covered the area he'd cleared with fresh straw. There we go. Couple more trips to Sydney would do the trick. He might even drive further, past Newcastle to Paul's. Wouldn't *he* be surprised, the great grogan. Kevin quit the duck house, leaving the shovel by the door though he knew he wouldn't get round to the ducks again for another week.

But by the time he'd shed his clothes at the hamper in the kitchen, it was obvious that Sydney wouldn't be half enough. The other, garbled voice now came through as clear as the sunny day outside, as painful as a mattock by the earhole. It was Martin Leywood's voice.

> i could concoct a preservative for memory
> so that you won't be able to forget
> but imagine formaldehyde memories
> disintegrating in unlabelled glass jars
> anonymous & sickening & foetid as decay,
> you'd toss them out at the first opportunity
> & be glad to be rid of them.

Like an underwater stripper Kevin plucked and tugged at what he wore in a kind of slow motion which didn't get him anywhere. Previously, the voice had murmured while Kevin Gore relaxed, in the cool bath behind the house or in bed. It had been almost pleasant. Now he knew why. At the same time as it drove him spare the sound of the old bastard's voice was one he missed. What did it mean? As he undressed his skinny body he tried to nut out what his mind was telling him. Martin stood for the past. And the other way around as well, though it galled. With that much progress, he managed to pull his T-shirt up over his head. So what did the kid's voice stand for? The future, he supposed. He ripped half the buttons off his fly and from there it was easy. If he didn't go visit Martin, the one going round the bend, Kevin would be stuck with the memories he'd done his best to deny going putrid inside him. There.

He started up the stairs. He could ring Kirsten and leave detailed instructions for her on the dining table, then cancel his next two landscaping jobs with a few grovelling phone calls when he arrived. Family troubles. He smiled as he stepped into the shower. Martin had been almost family at one stage. The pump serving the upper floor rattled against the outer wall, another thing to be fixed. Fuck it. He soaped his stringy limbs and scrubbed his nails as if by his vigour he could rid himself of the sense of loss which rose in him afresh, eleven years on. It was this terrible feeling he had tried to deny when he had fallen out with Martin.

They had nearly come to blows. Martin, sitting smugly by the fire in his comfortable chair at his Fitzroy terrace, had simply crossed his arms and shaken his head. He refused to accept or deny Kevin's explanation for the accident that had crushed the play in which they'd both performed. He merely pursed his fat lips in a repressed smile and told Kevin enigmatically that everything would be put right in the finish. The grief and survivor's guilt and pain of love torn out had made Kevin clench his bony fists and make some wordless noise of rage as he stood there on the Persian rug, too wrapped up in himself to see that

Martin hurt as well. There was a cracked quality to Martin's knowingness. Kevin saw that now. Yet he had insisted Martin confront the secret scheme in which they'd been embroiled when it could have made the poor bloke madder still. That's what the voices were saying. He was partly responsible.

Kevin shut off the water and stepped out of the shower recess. He felt some satisfaction to have worked out the reason for the messages in his head, although the playground rhyme didn't fit completely yet. He attacked his dark skin vigorously with a towel and checked his face in the mirror across the room, contemplating a shave. He draped the towel over one shoulder and rubbed at the stubble on his sharp jawbone with one hand. He stepped toward the mirror. I should look me best, he thought. When he turned away he slipped on a plastic brush, and as he grabbed the sink to right himself he felt cold metal slice his index finger. He had seen the safety razor on the sink but he'd had no time to stop the act. He thrust his good hand out to halt his fall and flicked the cut one as if stung. Dark droplets flew across the room and on to the tiles.

He felt a slight throb of pain. He gained both feet and held his finger up to inspect the cut. He stared at the sliced fingernail and tip. After a while he looked at the small mirror above the sink: distorted, grey-green eyes inspected his, wide with shock, blinking rapidly in bursts. He began to pant; his jaw trembled; he pressed his good hand to his chest. Slowly, he dropped his gaze back to the tip of his finger. With an unsteady hand he reached for his finger and pressed the lower end of the cut with his thumb. The part-congealed droplet on his nail cracked as a new drop swelled beneath it, pushed it aside and ran down his finger across his callouses and cracks, to rest in the web where his index finger and middle fingers joined. Just a tiny drop of blood.

Yet he fought to stop himself from crying out.

It was an electric blue liquid with a pinkish opalescence. It could not be blood.

*

Kevin turned on the tap and thrust his finger into the cold rainwater. The stuff didn't mix. Voices, and now – I can't be going mad, I can't be. I don't *feel* insane. He laughed at that. Altogether too hysterically. He'd never been insane, so he couldn't tell what it might feel like. Of course, these things creep up on you. He had an uncle who'd gone crazy once, who had been found up the statue of Burke and Wills at three in the morning ranting about the snakes he saw on the ground. He had always been troppo. Used to talk about your essence as though it were a thing you could touch and never let you get a word in edgeways. Did Kevin do that? He had been a little anxious of late. Surely not that bad. Surely.

I don't want to lose my mind!

He stumbled from the bathroom to his bed and collapsed on to it, breathing through his teeth into the pillow. Sleep, he thought. Sleep cures all. Sheets pulled up over his head at first, he sank into a welter of unanswered questions and finally a restless slumber. He rolled on to his back and began to dream.

In his dream he saw himself get out of bed and go to the window. The top halves of the walls were missing, as if a giant had bitten the roof off. It was night, but there were lights below, spilling upward across his face. He knew the play being performed down there. He was supposed to be in it. Now he remembered he had dreamt this before. He saw himself raise his arms and call on the glowing bellies of the clouds above them. It began to rain. This is not how it's supposed to go, he thought. I was not responsible. Sparks flew from below, the sound of grating metal and splintering wood. He was inside himself again and looking down at the water, searching for heads. Thousands of wind-up butterflies and paper sycamore seeds drifted by amongst the suds. He felt a hand on his shoulder. He turned to find Martin Leywood, still in costume, the latex bits hanging off his smeared face, floating about two feet from the floor. *You did this*, he said. *Now you pay.* When Kevin held his hands up for peace he saw blue blood glistening under each fingernail.

NO! screamed Kevin.

He woke.

Midday sunlight bounced on to the ceiling from the tank outside the window, washing it with molten shapes. Kevin freed his hands from the damp sheets, stretching them high. A brown crust beneath one fingernail. Gingerly, he touched the split finger to his tongue, ready to spit – then sighed. With a forearm he wiped the normal sweat from his normal brow, swallowing his normal blood. 'It was not my fault,' he murmured sleepily. As he woke further he thought: It was only my fault if the flood was caused by us. What did they call it? Telekinesis. No doubt there was something in it, but why would a piece of theatre have that effect? Even if Martin and I had told the rest of the cast about the gadget the play would've gone on. Nobody would credit such a crackpot idea. He swung around to let his feet drop to the floor but they did not reach the rug. He lay there for a moment, accepting it.

No matter what he told himself, if he did not find out what really happened the night he'd last worked in the theatre this guilt would give him more nightmares; the hallucinations might get worse. There was no worming out of it. Kevin pushed off the bed on to unsteady feet, then made his way slowly down the stairs to the phone to begin to tie up loose ends.

'Haloo?'

Kevin ran away, up the rickety flight which by dint of patching and carpeting had served for years. A huge pair of navy shorts lay in a pool by the dresser; he leapt into them and struggled into the first T-shirt he saw. 'In the bedroom!' he yelled, pulling on some bulky socks.

Kirsten clomped up. Kevin sniffed his hiking boots, shrugged, and pulled them on as Kirsten's head appeared around the corner.

'God, those things are steep? You must have a hard time getting women up here, Kev.' She grinned, knocking her blond hair back over her shoulders, the sweat already drying on her plump cheeks. She was the teenage daughter of the architect who had recently built his summer house next door. She and her girlfriend were always 'just popping round' uninvited. Kirsten especially seemed to want to make real friends, partly out of pity, which annoyed Kevin as much as her obvious attraction flattered him. He concentrated on lacing his boots.

> Dear, I know nothing of either,
> But when I try to imagine a faultless love
> Or the life to come, what I hear is the murmur
> Of underground streams, what I see
> Is a limestone landscape.

Martin again. All right, he was going to do something about Martin and the business in Central Australia, but now his mind was using that voice to hassle him about his love life, or his lack of it. It wasn't on. He tied his boots savagely and sat back. He breathed out the pain.

'Kevin?'

'Oh. Hi, Kirsten. Only collecting what's left of me wits. How are you?'

'How are *you*?' She settled next to him. Kevin was at once aware of his rumpled, smelly sheets, altogether too intimate. 'You're sure you're up to the drive? You look like a mess.'

'Thanks.' He groped under the bed for his old leather duffle bag, looking at a Max Ernst print of the moon over a petrified forest.

'I'm sorry. Are you okay?' She eyed him maternally.

'Mm. Yeah. Funny dreams last night – must be those babies I strangle.' He gave a laugh.

'What was it?'

'Can't remember. Probably fucked me father and killed me mother. I remember wiping the axe on me pants after I disembowelled the little old lady, then I chopped her into—'

'Kevin!'

'I don't know what I dreamed. It could have been that for all I know; ache a bit now. Maybe it'll come to me.'

'That happens. Last week I remembered this dream I had three years ago. It was the strangest thing? I was in this vat full of cream and all these people—'

'I've gotta go. Sherelle's expecting me at four.'

'You'll never make it!'

'I'll phone her on the way!' He stood. 'I'm sorry. Come on; you can tell me about your dream while I tell you what to do. I really appreciate this. The house'll be open, okay?'

After he had seen Kirsten off he threw his bag into the station wagon's back seat then rushed about saying goodbye to all the birds and animals.

The dusty Volkswagen started first try. A few metres before the gate he stopped. He pulled hard on the handbrake, left it in gear, tumbled out, jammed the rock under the front wheel and ran back down the water-gouged track to the house. Following a few minutes' fumble with a dropped door he switched off the generator and sped to the kitchen where he scribbled a note to Kirsten about the quirks of the electricity supply then ran back up the hill, thin brown legs glistening with sweat.

As he swung the front gate open, narrowly missing the car, crashing the gate against his favourite flowering gum, he wheezed.

'Whoah, boy,' he whispered. 'A couple of minutes on three hours late isn't going to make a heap of difference to Sherelle.'

He dug his Champion Ruby and brass lighter from his giant pockets and sat on the Volkswagen's hood, rolling a thin smoke. Down the hill the turkeys went koolookoolookookook. Bellbirds rang. Ducks argued. A kookaburra laughed once, breaking off abruptly as if the joke had cut too close to the bone. It was a clear but not oppressively hot afternoon in late summer. Kevin Gore was terrified.

If other close friends could scare the bejeesus out of him, what might a visit to Martin do? Such a long spell of isolation didn't just wash off. A month ago he had barrelled down the snaky mountain roads to the sea, flapping his elbows, singing. Off to see Tracy Little, a drama school flame. That he never wrote back never stopped Trace: she still sent him gossipy invitations to drop by. Yet even the Littles' door had been a shock. A tough ceramic *machine*, dotted with sensing devices and nasty nozzles. After some small talk they had tried to sell him the Opposition's proposal to disenfranchise the first-generation 'Greenhouse Reffos'. He'd taken them to task, and during some heated argument it had emerged that their daughter had been raped by a gang of Salvadorean youths. These were the same tolerant people he'd known, distraught but intelligent and trying to cope with their fear. As if he'd dropped from the sky, they had finished up asking what advice he had, as an outsider. He had told them the truth: he had not really thought it out; simple solutions did not exist. He had wanted to scream, *How the fuck should I know?* He had made his excuses and left.

Distant friends had been easier. Yet he still felt like some old steam engine, not fitted to the smooth technology of the times, unable to match his old mates' speeds, nor designed for their niches, nor plugged into the same flows of information. Now, as he inhaled the strong smoke and dusty smells of his little farm, his lower abdomen juddered for long moments with uncontrollable fear of Martin. On the phone Sherelle had called him *mental*. Mental how? With what?

And another thing troubled him. Like grit in his sock not quite discovered, something about Martin's voice that morning distracted him as he slowly ground out his cigarette end and stepped into the car. On his way through the gate he stalled, rolling back toward the cliff above the duck house for a sickening moment before the battered Passat caught and he wheelspun past the gate on to the level bit. He got out without waiting for the dust to settle; his lungs paid for it as he closed the gate. Then, turning on to the road, he almost hit the only car for miles.

But the dust blew away and the feeling that he had not quite worked out the reason for the voices went out the window with it. The voices were his subconscious, telling him what could no longer be shirked. The headaches which came with them were psychosomatic. It was what the voices stood for which counted. The child: The Future, which he'd stymie with any more bitterness. Martin: not really Martin Leywood but The Past, what he had to deal with in order to close the circle and go on to The Future. It wasn't important what the voices said.

Or was it? Oh, bugger that, he thought. That way lay madness. And it's too nice a day to go mad.

Kevin was thrilled by the road ahead. He waved to his favourite, if diminished, beaches, glittering behind the trees. He even bared his teeth and waved at Grumpy Gordon the postie as he overtook his bicycle.

When the highway, now metalled, dropped away and the fishback blue of the Pacific rose before him, it suddenly occurred to Kevin why he had felt distracted. Martin's voice had sounded much older than he remembered it. All right, his imagination would compensate for eleven years. So it had exaggerated. He looked down at the hand which held the wheel, veering to the right side of the road, correcting.

That his index finger showed a fresh cut from nail to knuckle was not unusual. He often damaged himself around the farm. That he should heal up so quickly was.

He scraped at the remains of the crust of blood beneath his nail, browned human stuff, with his lower front teeth. He spat it out the roaring window. He looked down at the cut, up at the gently curving road, down, up and down again. By the time he reached the Victorian border he had decided three times the whole episode had been a hallucination caused by guilt, that the cut in his nail had been part of it. If he could imagine blue blood, a split nail was not so hard. Perhaps he had not cut himself at all.

The scar stood out against his skin and the brown steering wheel. The nail was smooth and shiny and whole.

'Tomorrow I finally do something about guilt,' he told himself. It sounded loud and false in the quiet car. He wound down the window and said it again.

A flat, straight freeway swept from Albury-Woodonga through comparatively treeless farms to Melbourne, under a blue sky. He resolved to stay as long as it took to do something real for his old mate. They had been so dissimilar, people used to joke about it. Close-mouthed Kevin, motor-mouthed Martin. There had been crueller jokes about Martin. No matter how time had changed things, he owed Martin a fair go, even if the prospect scared Kevin witless. Don't worry old son, he told himself, insanity's not catching. He tried not to ask himself who was the mental one.

He switched on the radio for some news and distraction. Another two major cities devastated by floods, the Australian government agreed to take more refugees from them in spite of the recent racial violence in Queensland; skin cancer was up by several per cent; the King was visiting for the signing of the new constitution, probably his last tour as Australia's monarch; some Argentinian Irishman had seen the Virgin Mary in his Wheeties; another bombing in the dope district, police were looking into it.

He turned the radio down. Police were looking into it. That was what they had reported eleven years ago when he had made the news with his accusations about the flood. But they hadn't even taken a proper statement. Kevin Gore had been just another Argentinian Irishman to them. Well, he'd get some proof together this time. On his own. It might take years, but this trip should get the show on the road. And then he wouldn't bother with the police.

As he passed a sign which read, 'Radar in use next twenty-five kilometres', he pressed his foot to the rusty floor, surging toward Melbourne past a convoy of automated cars.

Bugger that for a joke.

TWO

from
Charms All O'erthrown

Ordinarily, I could not be dragged to one of the Flagship Theatre Company's in-house extravaganzas by a team of bullocks, but my mum was acting in this show as well as a couple of good friends. Although my mother keeps him in Bundaberg Rum by her efforts, my father hates our trade and will not set foot in an auditorium which does not contain thick men pummelling one another, so it was up to me to show some support. This is how I came to meet Rob, and become involved in our misadventure.

It was the wettest spring in years. The Greenhouse Effect was then new to us and everybody blamed it on that. As I entered the foyer I hopped and shook one leg because I had just stepped into a hole where a bollard should have been, soaking my white silk suit to the knee. Thus, dancing and cursing on the cocos mat, I bumped into Enzo, who had come through the door behind me. A gangling, slicked-back yobbo in black leather, he loomed over me (and I am not short), and dripped.

'Mr Carmoni.' I nodded as I spoke.

'Martin.' He smiled grudgingly, showing his brown and yellow teeth.

I flicked the water off my camelhair coat. 'Still watching Mars?' I asked. He had the most fantastic twelve-inch telescope at his cottage in Greenwich, Sydney. He had even let me look through it once.

'Moons of Jupiter now. Look, I'd love to stay and chat but I've got a show to run and I'm late. See ya.' He dodged around me and took the steps up to the theatre three at a time. Enzo did not exactly like me, and I couldn't see why; Dave Abrahams, one of his closest friends, had introduced us. That was another thing I couldn't see: how one of the most acute businessmen in the theatre world had teamed up with a UFO nut, unless of course it was because Enzo was an excellent lighting designer.

Another familiar face, or rather bottom, greeted me at the ticket desk. Gillian Portman-Smith, the only person I knew with no enemies. She was rooting around below the counter through the envelopes of reserved tickets. After asking for my own complimentary pass I waved at her enormous behind and sang, 'Hi, Gillian!'

She found what she was seeking and rose. 'Hiya, Martin; look, hate to be rude and that, but . . .' She grimaced at me, bouncing her head apologetically like a puppy in a car.

'Yes, I know. I'll see you afterwards for a drink and a natter, all right?'

'Fab-oh. Check ya later.' She ducked under the gate and zoomed away, a billowing black silk locomotive.

Normally I am more popular than this.

Seeing no other acquaintances, I took my seat as soon as the door opened. I needn't have bothered to find such a good spot. The play was abhorrent crap. It made me squirm, embarrassed for my friends and mother. Fortunately, mum only had a cameo as the villain's in-law. Poor Sam Schuyler had to strut about as some Aboriginal bird spirit clad only in lasers (it *was* the nineties) amongst cut-outs of 'cave paintings'. An insult to any Koori. Most of the cast exuded that odour of discomfort which dominates such efforts.

Happy exception to this was a superb actor I'd noticed in several fringe shows. I wanted to cheer each time she entered. How she managed to maintain such dignity, I don't know. The massive Italian marble beak swinging back and forth alone would have reduced me to tears nightly.

Afterwards, a few fellow sufferers turned out to be friends, so while I waited for Gill we swapped critiques in the bar. Dave Abrahams, always kind, said he liked the part where they drove a tractor on stage because it revealed a deliberate effort at coarse theatre. My agent's boyfriend disagreed. Laughing, I turned to check out the crowd and saw Gill come up from the green room with Sam Schuyler on one arm and the actor I had admired so much on the other. Enzo Carmoni followed, disgruntled as usual. While everyone but Enzo hugged and kissed I quietly lusted after the woman I was about to meet.

Of medium height, she was broad-shouldered and obviously athletic. She had approached us with a dancer's wayward lope, though I had seen she knew how to walk in any fashion when she acted. Her hips were wide and powerful-looking; her breasts must have given her hell when she danced. And her throat joined her chest in a particularly elegant way. She had the kind of face many actors share: large eyes, a wide mouth and a nose too individual for a model. Her irises were green, splashed with dollops of uneven brown; she took me in from my mousy hair to the stain on my trouser leg with one sweep.

When introduced to Robyn Ho I made a few remarks about her performance which I hoped sounded forthright and not at all charming.

'Get off,' said Robyn. 'It's a piece of putrid old rubbish!' She rocked back in her seat and stuck her thumbs into her wide belt. 'Did ya like the bit where I get me gear off?'

I told her I thought it completely gratuitous.

'They're not *that* big, are they?'

Robyn looked down and I did too. I think I blushed.

'Ah, these white elephants,' I sighed.

Robyn shrieked with laughter. 'I don't know why I let them talk me into it,' she finished.

I leaned across the table, as much to catch the smell of Robyn's short black hair, still wet from the shower, as for effect. 'The dosh,' I whispered.

'Mm. And to see Rex Palmer's face as he undressed too.'

I laughed. 'Would you like another drink?'

'Thought you'd never ask. A black and tan please, Martin.'

When I had delivered my round to everyone and sat again, Robyn said, 'I really liked your work in *Hamstring*, Martin, old boy.'

'Thank you. You know, Mersey has written a two-hander which I think'd suit you very well.'

'A good part for you too is there?'

'Naturellement.'

'Hmmm!' said Robyn.

'Hmmm!' said I.

'Hmmm!' said Robyn. 'Let's talk about it.' She glanced at her watch. 'Blow! I've gotta go soon. Dave's got your number, hasn't he? HEY, DAVE! IS IT OKAY IF MARTIN COMES OVER ON SUNDAY? BIG BUSINESS!' Robyn shouted across the room. 'It's actually a meeting,' she confided, 'but you can come up after and we can go for a walk and talk; it's a fabulous property.'

Dave started to answer then reconsidered, looked seriously into the middle distance for a second, and walked over to our table. Dave, I thought, if you really are a friend of mine you'll—

'I don't see why he can't come for the meeting as well,' he said at an even pace. He found my eyes, suddenly the sharp old entrepreneur I knew and loved. 'Do you feel like discussing a hare-brained scheme Sunday, precious?'

He displayed his cheap dentures; his grey eyes knew what my answer would be.

Robyn grinned. I suppose at that moment I saw clearly I wanted to find out more about her. It was not merely a desire for her body which charmed me. She delighted in challenging work; probably her whole reason for wanting to talk to me was the part I had mentioned. Robyn's dizzy manner off-stage masked a fanaticism which she thought would turn people off. In a classless society people learn not to be too serious, a knack I have never picked up properly. Something English and élitist in me? Anyway, I grinned back at Robyn, a mirror to her look, I hoped.

Then, before running off, Robyn leaned across the table, quite careless of the glasses and debris in her way, to give me a tender and rather ambiguous kiss. I sat back and watched her move away through the thinning crowd charged with wild hopes as well as an instant revision of my ideas. I was still stunned when my mother tottered up to berate me for not sending a telegram and flowers on behalf of my father.

After an hour in the mortgage belt, another passing ferny gullies and wet eucalypt forests in the mountains (and getting lost), then half an hour on reddish dirt tracks, ranting along with King Sunny Adé and His African Beats in the spring sunshine, I found Dave's letterbox, a battered stage lamp neatly painted in white on navy: 'Abrahams'.

Still a way to go, if I remembered correctly. The property measured over five hundred hectares and unlike many of the other farms in the area it was not a cooperative. Dave and Pat had made a small fortune from advertising; in their retirement they had fulfilled a lifelong ambition, forming a real alternative to the production companies which rehashed West End and Broadway shows. Although my mother trained at RADA and was herself something of an institution it had taken me over ten years to start to earn a decent living, yet I did not begrudge the Abrahams' instant success for all my lack of acumen. They had shown courage to the point of foolhardiness from the beginning, and I adored their lifestyle. On my right was a huge dam stocked with blackfish. On my left a creek (which fed the dam) trickled down from forested hills. Wild orchids grew in orange sprays amongst the leaf litter, boronia and countless other small flowers waved in the fresh breeze, instilling in me a fondness for anyone who kept the bush this way.

And the house. Smack in the middle of an open-plan A-frame, the most fabulous wrought-iron staircase I have ever seen ascended in a riot of angels, demons and struggling mortals, a helical offering to the sky; it was sculpted as if Rodin had returned to do one last gig, just for Pat. She had designed the whole place, built most of it herself, brick by mud brick, from the Art Nouveau leadlight to the huge, counterfeit seventeenth-century fireplace.

As usual, the quiet gravity of the house distracted me. Thus, what with the hugging and kissing, a moment passed before I realised Robyn had not yet arrived. Ah well, I thought, she's a grown-up woman. She'll be fine.

'Oh, Martin?' Sarah Witchell strode up on immoderately long legs. She was the director of a recent hit miniseries, one of those rare sorts who bothered with theatre as well – exceptionally well, as it happened. She said sweetly, 'Robbie won't be here for a while. All right, mate?' Then she whispered, 'So you can relax,' and giggled. She left to join Gillian at the hommus.

Evidently I was that obvious.

I drifted around, first to find a drink and a satay stick then to find someone to talk to. I am not usually shy but Robyn's absence disconcerted me somewhat. Of course I had met most of these people before, seen their work many times; here was a very capable bunch indeed. It awed me. Kevin Gore, a small brown stick figure in oversized army shorts stood by the back doors, looking up at the trees. He and I had been to drama school together, back in the eighties. When I tapped him on the shoulder Kevin said, 'Martin, you old bastard,' and tried to rip open my cheeks with his stubble. Two people could not be more different: I am tallish, demonstrative, mousy-haired and rather too pink (in my twenties my regular features and big brown eyes landed me juvenile leads, which did keep me in pasta but taught me very bad habits); Kevin was the kind of kid they called 'prawn' at school, a hook-nosed Ken Rosewall of the theatre, diffident and tireless, able to tackle anything on or off-stage as far as I could tell, except romance. He stood apart. I was as close as one got.

'How was China?' I asked.

'It's a hard life. If it was worse before I'm glad I live here. We went down well. They have the most extreme sense of humour, they laugh at the oddest things.'

'Work?'

'Not a lot since. This should be good, but.'

Pat, the organiser and accountant, started making shooing noises then. We drifted outside, chatting. As I sat down I wondered what plans lurked in Dave's cunning head. Up to now I had been too overpowered by visions of Robyn to think about employment. Besides, I had just finished a short comedy for TV which had paid very well, so technically I was on holiday. Amusing myself with idle speculation, I looked around at the assembled group, now quite large. Say I wanted to cast and crew . . . *A Midsummer Night's Dream*. No, *The Tempest* would be right for this lot. Next to me Jenny Drape lowered her bulk to her seat. Ariel! ('Hiya, Jen.' 'Hiya, Martin. You still mooning about Anne?' 'Noo, do I look it?' 'Noo.') And Fred Carol for Caliban – his nose gave him a head start – and Kevin could play King Alonso with a little ageing and Pete Stanopoulos could be wicked Antonio and . . . In a few minutes I had us cast. I myself would play the handsome Ferdinand against Robyn Ho's exquisite Miranda . . .

Now, perhaps celestial music did lead us on. Not that Dave had a staff and his only book was *Towards a Poor Theatre*, but we should have spotted the flaws in his and Sarah's plans from the start. Perhaps the magic of the theatre was not his only persuader. Decide for yourself whether you would have followed them out into the middle of nowhere, I still can't tell. When our unruly mob had finally settled all over the garden furniture and empty beehives, Dave cleared his throat and said:

'Well, to clear up any doubts you may have about our immediate future, this is a paying proposition.' At which everyone laughed, since an ugly story (false) had circulated about wage problems with *The Idiot*, the musical. 'Pay starts today, if you accept this proposal.' There were a couple of cheers. 'Over the next three to six months we will mount a radical new production in South Australia, just north of the Flinders

Ranges.' The many wrinkles around Dave's eyes deepened as he waited for the words to take effect. (Or for something else.) His long legs, clad in white flannels, crossed and uncrossed. He leant forward, brushing silver hair back with one hand, and put his elbows on his knees. 'Over the past two decades we've seen this country's theatres taken over by dickless accountants. No offence, Pat, you know what I mean. If you can't prove from the outset that a show's going to be a hit you've got to mount some two-hander in a parking lot to do something original. You might think we might have dispelled such nonsense with *Gravity's Rainbow* but I want to go further, to present a show with even less reliance on publicity. A radical move, right now, to prove a point if nothing else.' This was wonderful, coming from an ex-advertising man, but so far it made sense. 'Okay, Sarah,' he finished, 'take it away.'

'Right.' Sarah stood, dappled beneath swaying wattle branches, yellow flecks alighting on her waist-length blond hair. She brushed down her skirt. 'Well, what Dave and I have in mind is to take a show out into an isolated spot, build a theatre for it and put it on without any hype of any kind. In fact, until it's up and running we're going to keep it a secret. Gradually, as the news leaks out, people will come. But there won't be any interviews, set times for performances, listings, no journalists or visitors from the funding bodies, nothing. Some people might come all that way out of curiosity, but everyone will have to be determined. This will be a word-of-mouth success in the purest sense. Not only that, our time in isolation will enable us to work up an original approach. *Good theatre is not made by hype.* That's what we're going to prove.' Sarah waved a typewritten cast list. 'Beginning tomorrow we'll be making preparations for a trip out past Arkaroola Station to mount a production of *The Tempest*.'

Guess who got Caliban?

Looking back on it, it seems the most ridiculous idea. And they hadn't picked me for Ferdinand!

Yet I agreed to do it. We all agreed. Was it little radios in the head? Drugs in the drinks? Pure charm? Regardless of whether Dave had any unnatural means of persuasion to hand at the time, I do have one theory: less than a third of us were children of the sixties. I have always felt a trifle envious of those who upped and went on an adventure, blindfolds and kaftans on, daffodils in hand. No matter how we have rubbished the hippies, I believe many of us who came later would dearly have liked something truly stodgy against which we could rebel, something bold and extravagantly foolish to do in the name of love.

THREE

It was like a piece of England. The native gardens cut off at its stone wall, wattle gave way to rose bushes, stringybark gums to birch trees and red river gums to conifers and maples. There was even a spreading chestnut in burnt bloom by the drive. It shed crimson petals on Kevin's Volkswagen as he parked near the entrance.

While he stood squinting at the bluestone of the old abbey reading the date above the chrome and glass doors, a man in an immaculate dinner suit strode by. He stopped as though he had just now noticed Kevin, turned to face his chest and said, 'You brought a tie to wear? I got an extra one if you don't I can lend you as long as you give it back no one never gives back nothin' around this place, just go off say they forgot next day, I say to Mr Anderson but he never does nothin' about it . . .'

He looked into Kevin's eyes, eager pools of flecked blue.

'You coming to visit?' he said shyly.

'Seeing a friend.'

He stared at Kevin for some moments, scratching his left shoulder with his left hand, then gazed up into the tree.

'See ya.' He spoke without looking down.

'See ya.'

Kevin started toward what he guessed was reception. The man in the dinner suit shouted something and strode away.

Sherelle had greeted Kevin on the previous night with a hug

and kisses at the doorway, though they had only performed together that once. She'd brushed aside his apologies for the midnight arrival, had heated a roast dinner and opened a bottle of Coopers Sparkling Ale (he felt flattered she remembered). She bustled, glowed, because she imagined he still worked in the theatre. Her husband, John, worked in a bank and they both played for an amateur company, above which Sherelle towered as a former professional who still got some directed extra work. John had kept his eyes on Kevin's knees. He had listened for a polite hour then retired to bed. A large, freckled, curly-headed man, he had blushed whenever his wife had clasped Kevin's hands in hers or held him by the shoulders, saying, 'It's good to see one of the old crew again. It really is.' Kevin had felt embarrassed too. At the first opportunity he'd told her about his landscaping business. He had not performed since *The Tempest*.

'Oh. Oh, really,' she had said.

She had brightened up quickly enough. They'd laughed about a few characters they both knew. Of course they'd talked around the unpleasantness. But she had soon followed her husband.

Because there were no signs, Kevin never did find reception. A massive nursing assistant shouted, 'Where are you going?' behind him. Kevin turned away from the empty office. He smiled.

'I'm looking for a man.'

'You and me both. Who?'

'Martin Leywood.'

'Ah. The actor. Follow me.'

The big woman led him further down the corridor. Neither spoke. Out another flash set of double doors they went, through a Japanese courtyard complete with wooden ramps, maples, stands of bamboo, a fishpond and a stone garden. He watched her hard buttocks rolling under her slacks. She resembled somebody – never mind. They crossed a new cafeteria. They skirted a broad couch-grass lawn. At last they stopped by what appeared to be a country dance hall in green weatherboard with

'Donview' painted in dun above the door, so out of place beside this cultivation and restoration that Kevin let a tiny laugh escape, a laugh so small and so near a wheeze yet she must have heard him for she turned a kindly smile on him.

'Just ask anyone; they all know who he is.'

'Thanks.'

'Ah – are you free afterwards?'

'Um . . . ?'

'Would you like to come for a drink?'

'Ah.' Kevin wondered why big women liked him. He did not look like anybody's little boy. She might be able to help, she might be pleasant company. God knew he needed that.

'All right. Why not?'

'*Por qua pa* indeed!' She raised delicate eyebrows and smiled as if to tell him not to take her too seriously. 'I'll meet you at the caff.'

Kevin nodded then went in.

Not everyone in this ward seemed round the twist. Still, he flinched when the sharp tang of men's urine struck him in the foyer. He asked two people about Martin without luck. They seemed more lost than Kevin.

'When they informed me I had a visitor I assumed it was my old mam.'

This came from behind. As he spun he saw the man strike a pose, arms open, smiling.

'Kevin Harold Gore.'

'Martin?'

It came out as a question in spite of himself. The man was shorter than he recalled, greyed, balding, with alcoholic pouches beneath his eyes and jowls, though he could not be much past forty. At least in a white Japanese suit, the previous decade's *haute couture*, he appeared, while rumpled, at least partly Martin Leywood. He listed slightly, leaning on his hickory walking stick. They stood and stood.

'Martin.'

'Kevin, you old reprobate. Come this way, I must lie down. Not long for this world, I'm afraid. Come.'

They passed a crooked man who held up his trousers with one hand and tugged a string of toy cars with the other. The cars were ordered by age, from the latest computer-controlled electrics to what Kevin guessed was a Model T Ford. He walked without the aid of his knees.

'The spirits say *neit so snell*! We are hurling, hurling, you bastards!' he shouted at their backs.

'He shouldn't be here,' said Martin, tapping the floor with his stick. 'This is only for – mild cases.'

'Like you?'

'Another mistake. My life is over.'

He turned to face Kevin, taking him by the shoulders, locking eyes. His stick slapped Kevin painfully on the hip. Martin looked away again, at the vinyl tiles.

'You must do something for me.' His voice cracked with what could have been art, although Kevin thought not. 'You see . . .' He let go of Kevin's shoulders, turned and walked on. He now spoke matter-of-factly. 'I'm going to die.'

Kevin stepped after him, stopped. He yawned: a long, shuddering breath. Then he followed.

Martin Leywood stretched out on his narrow cot, hands knit behind his head. He had not removed his jacket. It was a woody, light-filled room. Jasmine strangled a hydrangea below the window. Kevin could see a middle-aged Aboriginal man planted in the middle of the couch lawn, head tilted back at a difficult angle, mouth open. At which unseen events he gaped Kevin had no clue, but once in a while he would make come-hither gestures and laugh uproariously. Mischievous, as if he had played some vengeful trick on the world, he bounced a little. Kevin wanted to roar. He felt very angry.

'Didn't tell me you were sick,' he said.

'They wouldn't. A martyr is the last thing they want. Do you remember the song?'

Song? Did we have a song once? Kevin wondered.

'"When I had grown unto a man's estate,"' Martin sang,
'"With hey ho the wind and the rain 'gainst knaves and thieves
men shut their gates—"'

'Yeah,' said Kevin.

'"For the rain it raineth every day . . ."'

'Yeah,' said Kevin.

Martin mimicked his nasal voice perfectly. 'Yeah. Still the
same old Harold Gore.'

Kevin shook his head. 'No.'

'The country air, I suppose. You *seem* almost unchanged –
but then even in your twenties you looked and acted forty.'

Kevin glanced away. The man on the lawn beckoned to the
sky with both hands.

'Halleluja!' Kevin yelled.

'Don't. I'll have him following me around again.'

'Again?'

'It's good to see you. You could have prevented this—'

'I—'

'Had you known. It's not your fault, dear. I had been asking
for it for some time.' He gazed at the window. 'You know,' he
said, 'it's really quite surprising how many fellows are in here
for believing that something's coming or waiting for us or
amongst us already. Some of them have extraordinarily sophis-
ticated delusions, almost as clever as mine. I was talking to Dr
Cain the other day and he said the incidence of such delusional
systems has risen dramatically over the past few years.'

'Mass media. Snitheads.'

'No. The media's influence over such things is well docu-
mented. It peaked in the early nineties and has been decreasing
ever since.'

'The Mars missions.'

'True, true. Dr Cain says—'

'What are you dying of, Martin?'

'Liver's going, dear. How kind of you to ask.'

'What about a new one?'

'What, force grown? Ugh! I appear to have a startlingly original immune system, Harold. It won't take any old offal. Prime cuts, dear boy. Prime cuts.'

'You look fine.'

'Thank you, Harold, I know how I look. I daresay I still retain some of my striking spunkiness, but, alas—'

'What's all this Harold business?'

'Part of my – er – problem, dear. I believe I used to have friends; I call them by their middle names, sort of nicknames.'

Kevin stood and sighed. The Aboriginal man stopped laughing and began to dig in the lawn, tearing at the tough grass with his fingers. Kevin turned to the wardrobe. It was a gentleman's dresser, fifties style, in dark wood. On the attached chest of drawers, in front of the mirror and weighed down by a chunk of jade-bearing red stone, lay a manuscript. He heard a moan. Outside, a small thin man in pyjamas tried to drag the digging one away. They fell into the hole. Black soil quickly smeared them.

'Kevin.'

He glanced at Martin as the stout nursing assistant grabbed the struggling pair by their collars. They went limp at once.

'Kevin, I loved and admired you once. Don't be angry. Please, I could not stand it. Is it this place that makes you angry? Me? I'm sorry, it's just my way. You must remember that?'

The two patients were hauled to their feet.

'Have you forgotten?'

'I've tried very hard to, mate.'

'But it's our duty to remember, even now.'

Kevin laughed. 'Don't talk to me about fucking duty. Not after what you did.' The nursing assistant watched the man in pyjamas walk away while she brushed down the mischievous one, who stared at the ground.

'Please, it's my last request scene. Let me have the focus at least.'

'This is not some fucking play!'

'Ah, but it is; it's well past time we had a hand in its direction, too.'

Outside, the Aboriginal man caught an earful from the nursing assistant.

'Kevin, I let you persuade me to help thwart Packett and his plans. However much I regret the secrets we kept and what happened later, I do not regret our actions that night. I'm sorry I denied you. You must have read my version in the pamphlet I printed, and you know why I wouldn't speak about the device. I was deceived. But I've made up for it.'

'Lucky you.'

'Kevin, don't be so childish.'

'Are you really dying?'

'I am. Do you want me to swoon and cough weakly and flutter my eyelids?' Martin draped an arm over the bed's edge and placed the back of the other hand on his forehead. ' "Eh-heh! Don't worry about me, I'll stay here and take a few of Jerry with me before I go. You go on! Tell Ermintrude I'll be waiting for her and give the old sergeant a pop in the eye for me, eh?" ' He then died, with a liquid gurgle.

While not settled yet, Kevin smiled. They spoke of other productions, quick days when their only real concerns had been their craft and the location of the next Bolognese. Kevin grew more restless as the conversation wore on. He kept himself still and under a tight control, by old habit. Martin looked odd, too urbane, well-adjusted, totally smooth, damn him. Kevin drifted. He could remember now. It had been more fun than he'd recalled all these years. Even the pain felt exquisite now. He wallowed in it. His limbs hummed. Is this crazy, Kev?

'. . . this script. It's called *Charms All O'erthrown* like the prose version but feel free to change it. Change as much as you like, dear man.'

Why have I put up with this terrible guilt?

'You know the truth, you know how it should be. Of course it should be entertaining. We want people to watch it.'

'Yeah.' Kevin took the script. It was very thick.

The Aboriginal man stood alone now, rapt, face burnished by the afternoon sun, inclined back toward the sky.

It was bullshit. Kevin leafed impatiently through the green-covered script. The nursing assistant he had watched through the window would come soon and he wanted to get his ideas in order before she arrived. He got up to look at the shiny cafeteria. Machine-polished tiles. Soothing brown and green. Did the patients take care of the plants, the grounds? Kevin walked murmuring round the room. Why not ask this woman out? He wanted to get stonkered anyhow. The way he felt he might get dangerous, alone. A man, mouth full of cake or bread which spilled across his face, dressed in bright blue jeans and a freshly laundered blue canvas shirt, loomed smiling at the window, he raised his hand to touch the glass but stopped as if they'd told him not to smear it over and over so he knew this much and struggled with the urge to touch it still. I promised I would, Kevin thought. I promised. He could not judge the script till he'd read the lot and God knew he had nothing like an eye for talent. Always left literature to others.

'Check this out.' He thrust the open script of *Charms All O'erthrown* at the window man, who turned and ran, stiff-hipped and pigeon-toed, falling forward with cake spraying down his nice clean shirtfront. Your peers have spoken. Run!

He'd read it later, when he could concentrate. Dying or not, Martin rated that much.

'What's wrong with him?' he asked the tall, muscular woman as she entered, hair let down, make-up on, a cardigan over her uniform.

'Who? Oh, Patrick. Nothing much. Was arrested defacing a billboard and said strange things to the cops so they put him in here. The jails were full of rioters in any case. That was about seven years ago.'

'Hay?'

'He likes it here.' She sat. She puffed out an end-of-work sigh. With her chin she motioned him over. 'I'm Angie, by the way.'

Kevin paced, in stutters, to the door, then to her side. 'Kevin. Pleased to meet ya. So he's gotten crazier?'

'A bit.' Angie looked up at him, full of life and expectant, in spite of her recent exertions outside with the laughing man. She put him in mind of someone. Oh, he thought. 'He's mostly all there,' Angie went on. 'People come to see him for a bit of stable conversation. He watches the news, reads the papers. If you wanna know about the latest eco-disaster, he's your boy.' Oh, no, Kevin thought. 'What'll you have?' She got up and went behind the serving counter. Looking so much like her (though Kevin wondered if his memory lied) it hurt, she rummaged beneath it with one hand. 'Whisky, or gin?'

'Here? Okay, whisky.'

'Thought so. Soda?'

'Straight, please. Ice?'

'But of course. Against the rules, of course, but we have everything here.'

Kevin sat slowly. It can't be, he thought. In his confusion he blurted: 'Is Martin really dying?'

'Who? Oh, your friend.' She smiled. It was that smile which made her, more than ever, seem like the woman he'd lost. She laughed. 'Oh I suppose I shouldn't laugh: he is your friend.' She leaned against the counter and laughed some more. 'I'm sorry . . . No, he's not dying – but he's always going *on* about it! I think he really believes he is. I dunno, I'm not a doctor. 'Spose we're all dying, if it comes down to it.'

He couldn't hide. Finish up never doing anything. But there were other women in this city. No need to go out of his way to give himself pain. For that matter, why sleep with anybody? Not since his early twenties had he actually sought a one-night stand. It was never what he needed. It would be a mistake now.

Kevin took his drink and Angie sat opposite him. They raised their glasses, clinked.

'To self-delusion,' said Kevin. He took a sip.

'Bit never hurt anybody.' Angie made a moue of pleasure at

the whisky. All at once she looked nothing like Gillian Portman-Smith. Even so, he would make no passes at her. The whole idea was utterly out of the question. They could still go out and dance. What she did look like was fun.

FOUR

You've got to ask for what you want, her father used to tell the tribal elders. If you simply smile and bat your eyelids they'll walk all over you. Gemma wished she had a cigarette; they were useful at such times, when you had to get your thoughts in order and doing anything else would distract you. But she'd given up a forty-a-day habit three weeks ago and knew having one now would hit her like a croc in a swimming pool. For something to do she went through her list again, although every point had been memorised long before. This Schnarler could throw her off her questions anyway, if he chose. Everything depended on his good will. If he didn't trust her when she assured him he would never be named as a source, he'd smell prosecution and that'd be it. So get the assurance in quickly.

She glanced at her watch. She checked the videophone controls on the snit to make sure the number she had entered was the right one. She wasn't familiar with these devices, not owning anything more complex than a VCR herself. She looked across the room at the bar, with an idea that she should help herself to the Minister's whisky (he had said she should feel free), but decided against it halfway out of her chair. She sank back against the antimacassar and watched the pale pink numbers on the snit's chronometer change for a couple of minutes, then snapped out of it, examining the room to bring back her focus.

The town house of the Minister for Aboriginal Affairs

betrayed few signs of its use, aside from the two large acrylic canvases of dreamtime figures on either side of the flagstone fireplace and the government data centre at which Gemma sat. The late afternoon sunlight nearly opaqued the second floor terrace windows but still managed to bring the richness out of the predominantly dark wooden furniture. The room reminded Gemma of the other forcefully ordinary houses of politicians she had visited with her father back in the mid-eighties, as a gawky, freckled girl uncomfortable in a pinafore instead of shorts who knew well enough not to fidget while her father lobbied for the people who'd adopted him. She had not been brought along because her father couldn't find a babysitter; she had been a wiry little icebreaker, enabling her father to skip the formalities and get down to what he was good at: pressure. When Jack Stranger had died a whole nation within a nation had mourned. Gemma had been off at Bristol University studying drama at the time and hadn't been able to raise the money to fly home to say a proper goodbye. Perhaps that was why she had attached herself to this hopeless cause, Martin Leywood. He resembled her father, although he was only about ten years older than Gemma and his rather camp style was nothing like Jack's controlled explosions had been.

The snit chirped three times. Gemma rearranged herself in her seat and watched the videophone dial the long American number. A luminous mist filled the air above the viewplate while it connected. A Global Telecom symbol hovered while it rang. Gemma twirled a strand of bright red hair around one finger until she realised what she was doing. She clasped her bony fingers in her lap. Didn't want to appear the least bit seductive. The thought made her laugh.

'Hello – Ms Strange, I presume,' said the man in the wheel-chair above the viewplate. He was in his fifties, had the close-cropped hair of the military, and immediately struck Gemma as having a virtuous, clean-living sort of air about him. Sancti-monious CIA creep.

Nevertheless she answered politely. 'Ah, that's Stranger, Mr Schnarler. Pleased to meet you.'

'Charmed. Now, how may I help? This must be an expensive call for you.' He took hold of one knee with both hands and lifted, crossing one obviously paralysed leg over the other the way a ventriloquist's dummy might.

'No, Mr Schnarler, this is a government snit so I can assure you we are not being bugged and we have all the time in the world.'

'Well I don't,' he said archly. 'Let's get this done with so I can go out and play golf.'

Golf? wondered Gemma incredulously. 'Okay,' she said. 'First, I want to repeat the assurances I made in my letters: none of this will be traceable to you any more than any other source—'

'Hell, no one will believe you anyway,' said the former CIA agent. 'Shoot.'

'Okay,' said Gemma. 'I'll take it for granted that you admit your involvement in the plot to kill the cast and crew of *The Tempest* eleven years ago.' Gemma took a breath to go on.

'Plot? There was no plot. It was a covert operation in a friendly territory to protect US interests against the possible leaking of a secret weapon to foreign powers. For the whole United Free World's sake.'

'Fine. You admit to that?'

'Sure. Why not?'

A long prison sentence is why not, thought Gemma. Despite his relaxed pose the man must be worried about getting caught. And he must have a lot of bitterness against his old employer stored up to talk to me in the first place. The accident Schnarler had suffered had been Gemma's only piece of luck in a year's investigation. She had read the account in a back issue of a newspaper and guessed he had blamed the CIA for his nerve damage. Time for a bit more guessing.

'So. You are familiar with the effects of the, ah, secret weapon. The side effects on the users, I mean.'

'Yeah. Which is why we scrapped Project Thoughtboost back in the early nineties.' He stifled a yawn.

Thoughtboost? She jotted the word on her notepad without trying to seem elated. 'Right,' she said. 'Well, very similar events have recently started to occur at various places around the world.'

Gemma sat back and watched his shock as the implications sank in. 'Of course,' he said, rallying, 'someone was bound to come across the principle independently sooner or later.'

'I don't think so,' said Gemma. 'At least it's unlikely, because the people experiencing the events have not been picked according to any pattern as far as I can tell – and before you go writing this off as individual madness, there are two things which distinguish these – ah – visions: there's more than one witness every time; and they have a real, physical effect.'

'Then where do you think it's coming from, Ms Stranger?'

'You tell me, Mr Schnarler.'

'And what do you want me to do about it?' he asked, anticipating her proposal.

'I want you to find out if the CIA have made the connection yet, and if so what they plan to do about it. I hope to document the CIA's activity. It's the only way of proving their involvement with the original, um, covert operation.' Hope is the word, thought Gemma. She had only the money her great-aunt had left her to finance any jaunt to where the CIA might be looking into things. And not much time left to be going off to Argentina to investigate visions of madonnas, not for her thesis, anyhow. It could do Martin some good, but was she prepared to use her writing time for him, was she prepared to fail for him? She liked Martin, but when it came to it she didn't know.

'I said, what's in it for me, Ms Stranger?'

'Sorry. What's in it? The chance to wash some of the blood off your hands, Mr Schnarler.'

'Don't give me that crap.'

At the risk of the whole idea, Gemma could not resist a retort. 'Look, I know what happened. I know how many innocent people died in your covert operation. They may have been foolish – well, I'm trying to prove that they're not – but in any case, no way did they deserve to be executed for that! And I've met some of the survivors, Mr Schnarler. You've fucked up the lives and careers of some good people with your interference. I know you believed in what you did at the time, but I also know you no longer believe in the CIA and a lot of what it stands for. Go and have your game of golf, Mr Schnarler, and just consider it. You've got the chance to do some real good here. Set the record straight. Tell me you'll think about it? Please?'

'I'll think about it.' He looked sour, hard. Gemma decided she had blown it.

'Thank you for your time, Mr Schnarler.'

'Goodbye, Ms Stranger.'

He hung up. The air above the viewplate flashed white briefly, then cleared. Gemma fell back in her chair and blew out her tension. That was that. Finished. Her one chance. Her MA thesis. Well, never mind.

Gemma Stranger wasn't much good at tears. Her father had been able to bawl at the drop of a hat. She must have inherited the inability from her mother, who had the same pursed, held-in quality as Gemma in all the photographs she had seen. A stoic, red-headed Italian peasant line, almost Swiss in their laconic industry. Most of the women died young. Gemma was determined not to follow them, had taken up drama as a part of that. It doesn't seem to be working, does it, Gem? she thought dismally.

Mechanically she rose and went to fetch the large bag full of books and papers she carried everywhere, thin lips pressed tightly together. At the door, she surveyed the room to see that it was the same as she had found it. Dropping her bag, she went back to the snit and wiped the number she had programmed from the snit's memory. Where to now? She might as well go see Kevin Gore in the morning, find out what he had to say, if anything. His reputation for silence did not encourage her. Still, she had to go through the motions of interviewing everyone involved if her thesis was to appear credible.

Gemma went to the door, hefted her bag, and walked out into the stairwell. Descending, her sharp shoulder blades holding the wet patch between them away from her back, she trembled with anger, unable as ever to accept defeat.

FIVE

'. . . said he believed the light-lancing to be the work of the same group responsible for the Wagga Wagga tapeworm gene disaster. They have appealed to anyone who was in the area between twelve and two thirty last night to come forward . . .'

Kevin squinted in pain at the almost vertical summer's day which bounced cruelly round the annexe bedroom. While parts of his head felt as if they had been ripped out with rusty pliers the rest of him didn't feel too bad. The sheets slipped powderlike and clean over him as he snuggled back under them. They weren't his, were they? He was in Melbourne, Sherelle's. That's right. He had visited Martin at the hospital, then gone for a drink with . . .

He rolled over. There she was, large, soft, strong, and ever so faintly snoring. He hoped she'd had fun last night; bugger all came to mind when he tried to recall it. He frowned; the last woman who'd raced him off, in Sydney, the grog had been abundant with her too. And she had been large and gruff as well . . . Forget it, mate. Gill was Gill and this woman was her own person. If only he could remember her name.

'. . . finally, here's a piece of news from England. One Charles Hobbes of Nailsea in the south-west of the country hypnotised most of the staff and quite a few of the other patients at his nursing home! He convinced the nurses to go out and buy him jewellery, music software, customised robotics, a snit system and even a car. When finally stopped by an ex-policeman immune to his charms because his hearing aid was off, Mr Hobbes, a sprightly seventy-three-year-old, said he had been contacted by a little man from outer space living in a smartcard, who had given him his hypnotic powers as a reward for a hard life of toil in a chocolate factory. Well—'

Kevin sat up. Jesus God, it couldn't be! Then his hangover hit him and he dropped back on to the pillow, unable to think any further.

'. . . crew of the Mars Lander should watch out for this little man. They might make some dosh! Anyway, here's a smartcard that's making *this* lot some dosh. It's the Sang Froids with "Crunch My Goolies to Pulp".'

He turned down the radio, his mind awakening to turmoil. The woman beside him shifted in her sleep. Surely the story could not be about the gizmo. Yet it had all the elements: space, unnatural persuasion, a vision as well. He wondered what Martin might make of it. No. It was bulldust, pure and simple. That sort of crap came out of the English Sunday papers the whole time. 'ALIEN STUFFED MY SON DOWN THE TOILET AND USED HIM FOR GARBAGE DISPOSAL.' Don't believe it, son, that way lies insanity. Back to sleep.

But his mind would not let it go. Suppose it were true? Suppose this Hobbes or whoever was the ultimate by-product of what they had done in Central Australia? Not real contact with aliens, of course, but a lot more people having weirdo attacks. Martin had said the incidence of such things was on the rise. But why now, so much later?

The door chirruped. He rolled out of bed, landing heavily on all fours. To city men, used to alcohol and late nights spent in praise of late nights, to those who hardly saw the early morning except diffused through sleepiness, this kind of thing floated on habit. He envied and pitied them at once as he stood to search for the bathroom.

The door chirruped. He stopped short of a shout at the thought of the woman asleep in his bedroom. While he wrapped his skinny waist with one of Sherelle's enormous towels, he began to recall how tender and funny that woman had been, so he went to the bedroom door. Closing it, he smiled. Fell on me feet, he supposed.

The door bloody chirruped. The light which stabbed at him when he opened the door didn't give him a chance to see who stood there. She was short. Kevin stepped back to let her in, one hand on his forehead, the other on the towel.

'I'm sorry; I got you up.' She looked at her watch. Smaller even than Kevin, she made nervous flaps with one freckly arm as if she wanted to leave straight away. She paced to the right, dropped her heavy bag on the lino, patted the back of the couch and turned, perhaps away from his half-clad figure.

'No, no, come in, sit down. I was getting up anyhow,' Kevin lied, a great start. He crinkled his eyes at her, although he still felt a bit piqued at her interruption. He gestured at a stool, a seventies tubular *thing* all the rage again a few years ago. He put his hand on the white marble breakfast counter. 'Coffee?'

'I shouldn't. I've been off coffee for a week – all right.' She laughed: a goofy hiccough. The deep lines around her eyes deepened further. Finally, she looked at him. There was some kind of appeal in her eyes.

He crossed the kitchen area to look for the cafetière.

'Kevin Gore.'

'Gemma Stranger. It's very unusual, just to invite someone in without knowing who they are or why they've come.'

'I'm not from around here.' He shifted things around in the tea cupboard. 'Anyhow, I remember your letters now. So what do you want? And how did you find me?'

'Well, I'm not selling insurance or God.'

'What a relief.'

'I rang your home number and your girlfriend told me where to reach you. I hope that's okay. It's saved me quite a trip. I'm from Melbourne Uni?'

'Yeah, I know who you are and look I'm not interested. I've had about—'

'Please.' She heaved her bag on to the counter and fumbled through it. 'I've only got a couple of weeks to go before my synopsis is due, and I can't get another extension on it. I want to ask you a few questions' – she pulled out a thick sheaf of paper, then a fat blue booklet – 'about this.' She waved the booklet in front of her face as though she were a hawker at a flea market, as though it explained everything.

He opened the cupboards by the stove. What booklet? He didn't know anything about it. Yet it looked familiar (what beautiful breasts). This kitchen did have a cafetière, and fresh coffee too. He remembered that much from last night. Let her talk.

'I realise this is not a great moment to ask you questions. Maybe we can have lunch together. I mean, I'll buy you lunch. Your choice – anywhere.'

Kevin began on the cupboards below the counter.

'Um. What are you looking for?'

He snapped, 'The coffee-pot and plunger thing.' And went on looking.

'Ah-huh. Is this it?'

Kevin straightened. His towel threatened his hips and he made a grab at it. 'Yeah, thanks,' he said ungraciously. He took the infuser from her with his free hand then crossed to the power-point by the stove, where he put it down to tuck in his towel with his back to her.

'Shall I leave you to your breakfast and pick you up this afternoon some time?'

He turned. 'Ms Strange, I—'

'Stranger.'

'Stranger. Look, I don't want to answer any questions for your essay.'

'It's my master's thesis.'

'Whatever. It's something I've been trying to forget for eleven years and I've done very well at it so far.'

'Ah-huh. Didn't you visit Martin Leywood yesterday?'

Now he remembered what the fat blue booklet was. His own

copy had been bone-covered, run off and sent by Martin when it had been turned down by all the major publishers. In spite of the awful writing, Kevin had consumed the prose version of *Charms All O'erthrown* with a morbid fixity, then burnt it.

'The man has had a hard time. I hope you haven't been annoying him.'

'Oh, no. He loves to talk.'

'Yes, he does.' Kevin's tone softened despite himself. 'Then you've got the lot. I don't think you need to ask me anything.'

'So you confirm what he says in this?'

Kevin sighed. He said in an over-patient sing-song, 'How do you take your coffee, Ms Stranger?'

'Ah . . . black, no sugar.'

Here was a woman who had to think hard about how to have her coffee. Academics!

'Kevin, I'm writing a thesis on technology and Australian theatre; Sarah Witchell's *Tempest* is the most fascinating theatre story since *The Playmaker*.'

'Great book that was. Who wrote it again?'

'Thomas Keneally. It could change the face of modern theatre! And if it's *true*—'

'Wasn't there a film?'

'Fred Schepisi, nineteen ninety-three. Kevin, I'm only trying to do my job.'

'Where do you get off digging into the private lives of people still around?' She had gone quite red, in the face and just above her prominent collarbone. 'You could have at least waited till we were all dead, for Christ's sake. It wasn't enough that underneath the great loss to the theatre, as the papers called it – which is a hell of an understatement – that underneath there was a sneering, mocking tone which said we were bloody idiots to follow such a mad bastard out into the middle of nowhere? Isn't that enough for you? I don't care what you say about my friends or that after I'm dead, dead is dead and that's the end of it, but you're going to give us a hard time while we're still around and I'm not only gunna say nothing to you, I'm gunna do my *bloody* best to stop you. All right?'

Kevin was shaking. His voice had risen toward the end of his rant. Too late, he remembered the person asleep in the next room.

Gemma said in a small voice, 'I'll be dead too, Mr Gore, when it's safe to write about it. It – it was a – an innovative piece of theatre and that was one of the things I wanted to focus on . . .' The corners of her thin lips pointed down and the pockmarks from a past war with acne showed up vividly in her blush. A handspan of stiff red hair hung across her eyes but she made no move to push it away; her hands rested knuckle down on the marble by the dog-eared blue booklet, worn pinkies touching, moving apart, touching.

The kettle had boiled.

'Good morning.'

A tall figure with short, tousled blond hair stood in the bedroom doorway, yawning, wrapped in a sheet.

Kevin unplugged the kettle, took it to the cafetière. 'Um – Angie. This is—'

'Gemma.'

'Gemma. Ah – do you want some coffee?'

'No thanks, I just wanna wee.'

It was Kevin's turn for a nervous giggle. 'Be my guest.' He pushed the plunger down, too soon. 'I'm going to get some dacks on. Help yourself, Gemma.'

She nodded.

While he was searching under the bed for his underwear, Angie padded in.

'Hiya, mate,' she said.

Kevin found his boxer shorts. He turned in her embrace. They kissed. There was something absent in her lips. He reached up and kissed her again, with the same result. 'See ya soon,' he whispered.

'Take your time, Kevin.' Her soft blue look rested gently upon his face. She sounded sad.

Kevin put on his boxer shorts and a pair of jeans then left the room.

'Ms Stranger—'

'My friends call me Budge.'

'Budge?' He sat and poured some coffee for himself.

'It's a long story.'

'I don't reckon I – I don't qualify for that.'

'Then call me Gemma.'

'Gemma . . . Perhaps you can understand how we feel about it now. You can't be coming to me if any of the others have said anything about it: none of us wants to remember it.'

'I've had quite informative interviews with the other cast and crew. Everyone's been quite open with me.'

'Really.'

'Yes. But you and Martin are the only ones who can tell me for certain about the – unusual parts of the story.'

'And you've spoken to Martin. What did he say?'

'That everything he wrote in that' – she gestured with one small hand – 'is true. And that I'd have a hard time getting anything out of you.' She gave a rueful smile.

Kevin nodded. He found his tobacco and lighter in his jeans pocket and began to roll a thick one slowly on the cool marble.

Gemma said, watching him, 'He said you haven't seen him or even answered a letter for eleven years. He's been wondering about your reasons for visiting him. He gave me your home address.'

The tobacco had a snarl which needed careful teasing apart.

'He also said that your reasons were your own and I wasn't to bother you with questions concerning them.'

He rolled an exquisite cigarette, placed the excess back in his pouch and sealed it, stuffed the pouch into his back pocket and looked up. He took the brass lighter and snapped it open and shut while Gemma spoke.

'You see, all I need is the corroboration of a witness who saw everything and is not locked up.'

'He's in there voluntarily, now.' He lit the smoke, Gemma's eyes on every move.

'Yes. He seems to be very comfortable.'

The frustration, and beyond that the compassion, in her voice finally reached Kevin. She stared down at her empty coffee cup.

'Kevin—' Her words came sudden and loud. 'I think I may have some news which could help him, get him out of that place and – and *trying* again.'

'Yeah, what?'

'It's obviously not a great time to have a long discussion right now. Can I come back and pick you up, say, at one-thirty and we'll go to lunch?'

'I'm in stacks of suspense.'

'Right then.' She gathered her things and in a moment was gone.

Kevin listened to her car start as he finished his cigarette. He crushed the end, then stood.

On his pillow he found a note:

Dear Kevin,

    I had a really good time last night. Maybe we should leave it like that. If you do want to see me again you know where to find me.

                    Bulk Love,
                    Angie.

Sliding the french windows shut, he felt furious with Gemma Stranger all over again.

I'm supposed to go out and find a producer for this thing. The play was a bit better than the prose version for Martin had a good ear for dialogue, but it would benefit from some large cuts. Also, it might be advisable to change the names, to say it was 'based on true incidents' in order to get it on stage. It had been Martin's insistence on the absolute truth of his writing which had run him into walls back then. Enzo and Packett were dead, so they couldn't sue, but you didn't want to offend their families.

Kevin closed the script. He sat back, resting his tender head against the woollen couch. Even after all this time his heart had pounded when he had read the closing scenes, but he tried to calm himself, to bury his anger and look at the play objectively. It had an interesting cast, at least. Martin, foppish and romantic, the caricature of the juvenile lead. Robyn, talented, sharp, strong, but unwilling to get hurt in love. Me, a bit of a hard bastard, and one who could easily be suspected of being the criminal of the piece. Enzo, who looked like the classic villain but had no motives to be one. Packett, as a theatre critic, would get some laughs at least, and any crimes he was accused of would be welcomed by an audience. Dave, an eccentric father figure cast as Prospero in life.

Yeah, it could work. What about the plot? A production of *The Tempest* is taken out into the desert. However, the play is not being performed for the reasons given. Someone is fucking with the cast's minds. A whodunnit with a paranoid explanation? It does have a tragic ending, thought Kevin, yet the villains are never brought to justice. That wouldn't grab the theatre-goers. And even the innocent parties who survived might sue. Kevin looked up at the brick veneer back of Sherelle's house. She's putting me up in her granny flat and I'm going to drag that anguish out again, if I can. Our bloody pain wasn't unique because we had major parts, or because we have improbable ideas about a telepathic broadcaster being suppressed by the CIA.

Without naming her in his mind, Kevin's thoughts came to rest on his memory of Gill, next to him in the Land Rover on the drive from Melbourne to Arkaroola, cacking herself at something someone had said, Sam Schuyler possibly, her mop of blond curls tossed to one side as she laughed, that look in her bright blue eyes . . .

> Get up, Mr Metalhead, get up and save your friend,
> Get up, Mr Metalhead, it's closer to the end.

No! Kevin growled, throwing himself forward off the couch into a roll on the rug, just missing the coffee table, from which he emerged standing. He wanted to hit something. How *dare* the voice interrupt that memory! He felt a burning sensation at his temples and at his extremities. He had not felt this angry since, at sixteen, he decided that if God existed he was an evil fucker. Then, he had walked the night-time suburban streets hoping someone would attack him so he could kill them.

How many of his aggravations over the past eleven years had been based on self-pity? As far as Kevin could remember, Martin had predicted all that in their final argument. Martin had confronted his problems head on, while Kevin had withdrawn into the woodlands. Kevin could no longer tell who was better off. At least Martin was honest with himself about his conceit.

He stretched and yawned with a deep shudder, flapping his elbows. His watch told him Gemma was five minutes late. He went to look for a shirt.

SIX

from
Charms All O'erthrown

'Stop the car! Stop the *car*!'

Before he lost his licence, George Albert Leywood, descendant of dukes and earls as he would inform me when mellow, a broad-beamed meatbox of a man complete with hairy red neck and a distaste for hitching up his trousers, used to take me out shooting. We would tramp various dried-out pastures to the north of Melbourne, shotguns blazing at anything alive in pathetic emulation of our noble forebears. Or perhaps we captured the essence of the hunt; all I recall is keeping my eyes on my boots, wary of snakes or ankle-snapping rabbit holes.

I had finished the one about my father's gun and the farmer's toupee, Pete Stanopoulos had kept us in fits with the warnings his family had been given about the bush in the migrant hostels, and Robyn had amazed us with her account of a shark attack (she had doctored the victim then carried her three miles to a telephone), when Fred Carol, six foot five of gentle bisexuality and owner of one of the best singing voices in the theatre, cried out at a bird in a paddock beside the road. As might be clear from the above, while I enjoy the look of the bush I have no love for the prickly, stinging discomfort of actually being in it. Nevertheless I slowed; Fred had always been near during the time of my break-up with Anne, and in my inert period following the divorce he had bundled me off to singing classes. I would have done anything for the man, short of crawling in the stubbleland after some parrot myself.

I sat while the others raced across the empty road and under the barbed wire. We had not endured six weeks of preparation in order to experience the joys of nature, which could be sampled any time on video. Finally, I turned to look. Jenny Drape's curly energy was two tie-dyed buttocks between spent wheat fields on her way to a small dam by which a white speck waited, her quarry. I had to laugh. She weighed over a hundred kilos! How Fred had identified this dot as a long-billed corella, I didn't know. I was still not tempted to check it out myself. Then something caught my eye: only the inevitable turning vanes of a water pump, but coated with liquid gold by the light, the galvanised tower a criss-crossed ladder of sun. How many times had I seen these icons on film or trips from one city to another? Never before had I felt this compelled by its simplicity.

Out I got. In no way did I crouch or slow, so transfixed was I by the water pump. I soon passed Jenny. Fred, however, dear gentle Fred, grabbed my ankle as I went by, sending me face first into the dust. He offered me his binoculars. I submitted.

The long-billed corella is slightly bigger than the average galah and smaller than the sulphur-crested cockatoo, to which it bears a resemblance in that it is mostly white and has a crest. It is adorned with splashes of scarlet-orange, but it was not this which lead me to an interest. Like the corella (a far more common bird) it has a blue, naked eye-ring, larger below the eye. This makes it appear sad, the way a bloodhound looks dissipated and put-upon. Although I've never had much time for most humans my heart found, at that moment, a space for birds.

'So what do you reckon?' said Pete in his boyish way. His little red footy shorts and blue shearer's singlet were streaked with rust. 'Is this great, or what?' It was the beginning of a long series of exclamations from the curly-headed Greek. We had three days of driving before Arkaroola, and a good day after that, off-road. Fred was eventually forced to gag and bind him with jumpers, which he did with relish.

I was quietly moved, though not prepared to expose my feelings about the bird to Jenny's ridicule; I looked out at the passing flatness. Robyn had taken the wheel. She drove with the total attention of one not happy with it, which surprised me when I thought of her confidence on stage. (Later, by the camp fire, she told me about the accident that had taken her off the stage in New Zealand for a year and killed a friend, part of her reason for the move here.) After a conversation between Jenny Drape and Fred about his passion for birds, we lapsed into the silence of the road and rushing air.

'God, I hate the cops,' said Pete Stanopoulos suddenly.

'What's that in aid of?' asked Jenny.

Robyn eased off the accelerator, though the highway was empty and remained flat.

'Last week I was on the march against drag fishing in the Pacific? This hippy was making faces at the coppers lined up in front of the Japanese Trade Centre and one of them reached out and pushed his face on to the pavement. I mean he was being a dill, but he didn't deserve that. No one expected violence or anything, it just happened after that.' He shook his broad head, remembering.

'My dad was a policeman,' said Robyn, without taking her eyes off the road, uninflected. 'He was a country copper in New Zealand, but it's amazing how people's attitudes are different to you because of it, *Pakeha* as well as *Maori*. I used to use it at school; I'd tell anyone who gave me hassle that I'd get my dad to arrest them if they weren't careful. It worked.'

She laughed. We all did, rather nervously. Pete seemed abashed, and while Robyn knew how he felt she said nothing more for a few minutes. Then I caught her grinning at him in the rear-view mirror. I felt a pang of jealousy because she saw fit to toy with him instead of me. The one kiss had been all so far; we had been assigned to different parts of the city, because she was handy with a hammer and I with a photocopy machine. Now at last we were together, but I was afraid she had forgotten our good start.

I needn't have worried. Jenny began to tease me about my obvious fascination for the corella, my avowed disdain for the bush, even the kind of knickers I had packed (sensible white Y-fronts). Robyn joined in, becoming quite ribald. I protested, filled with secret pleasure.

When we arrived at the first night's camp, the other five carloads had already set up and Kevin Gore was preparing our supper, ably harassed by Gillian. Walking past Enzo's tent on my way to a splash in the river, I noticed a strange light, distorted shapes against the plastic wall. Already at work on the lighting design on his laptop PC, I supposed. But how could he be when we had not blocked the show out yet? The final script was still to be decided, since Sarah had told us we would improvise around the text at first. Ah well, they did say Enzo was an obsessed tech; lighting was his existence. That, and UFOs.

SEVEN

Riding into the city from Nunawading in the cool plush of Gemma's Triumph, Kevin noticed Gemma had changed out of the heavy boat-necked blue dress into a summery boat-necked blue dress. Her red bob sat still in the air conditioner's slight breeze while his own black shocks feathered at the ends. A damp towel was spread across the back seat, 'Yackandandah Swimming Pool' printed on it.

'Like swimming, do ya.'

'Ah-huh.' She looked fiercely at the freeway. Two syllables conveyed so much.

Kevin began the game he often used to play in cars or trains when his dad had had nothing to say to him, as usual. Stripping the concrete and plastic, the bricks and the steel away from the shape of the land, culling the alien plants, people and other creatures, he tried to imagine what the area had been like before the invasion by Europeans. Rolling hills covered in mountain ash, their branches hung with long strips of shed bark like rufous curtains, ascending from a rich green understorey of sassafras, blackwoods and tree ferns (about thirty years per metre). Or perhaps another sort of eucalypt lorded over this area, the messmate stringybark or the blue gum with its pied and knotty trunk: it was hard to tell when the very contours of the land had been chewed up and excreted into different forms. Definitely, a skinny creek would've run down that way, lined with red river gum and ferns, an overhung zone of cool shadow in the summer-dried forest (itself lit only by a shifting glare through the upper canopy and the odd narrow shaft, cooler than the present baking concrete). That bit across there would have been drier, lower scrubland of banksia, wattle, bottlebrush and tea tree. And there it might be regrowing after some burning by Aborigines, the normally tan forest floor blackened and furred with good-enough-to-eat green shoots, the gum trees' unkillable hides, too, covered with succulent green leaves.

His imagination easily populated the bush with green-backed rosellas, given away by their scarlet and yellow undersides as they swooped through the shadows, with yellow-tailed black cockatoos clothing the wattles they tore open for insect larvae, with a pair of stroppy willy wagtails persecuting a much larger kookaburra, with lyrebirds and fat ravens and currawongs and bellbirds. It was simple to picture a black-tailed wallaby browsing in the clearing by the bottlebrush, where little native bees lingered by the violent red blooms, a koala or three stoned up a manna gum, a couple of barred bandicoots that would fit in your cupped hands asleep inside a burnt and fallen log, a blue-tongued lizard, blunt and slow, searching for snails between a stand of bird orchids and the creek. But to people the landscape, which was fading fast as they approached their turn-off, to conjure more than an idealised image of a curly-headed man dressed in possum fur and holding a club, to produce more than a bloody nineteenth-century sketch in his living colour fantasy, that was nigh-on impossible – his image of an Aborigine came from a book. How many did he know? One, a lawyer customer of his, and him not well. I am an Aborigine's native gardener, he thought.

'Ha,' he said.

'Do you eat meat?' Gemma asked him.

'Ah-huh,' he mocked her earlier curt response.

They turned right, toward fashionable Brunswick.

*

Gemma became talkative as soon as they left the freeway. She asked him about his family and he lied, saying that they lived in Queensland so he never saw them. He didn't know why he lied; probably it had to do with his father having run off with a prostitute at the age of seventy and his mother dying from the shock. No one likes to expose a history of madness. She asked about his journey to Melbourne.

'Uneventful,' he lied again, then he changed the subject. He exclaimed at the growth of hologram-fronted boutiques, restaurants and so-called 'hormone bars' where factories had sprawled when he had lived nearby. This also was not exactly true, since it had been headed upmarket even then, but it was on the right track.

'Look at that! "Hand-Crafted Hardware, African Hardwoods Our Speciality." My God.'

Gemma laughed, that hiccough again, covering her mouth. Kevin thought 'Eeyore' was a better nickname for her than 'Budge'.

'Must sound like a right hick to you,' he said.

'No . . . yes!' she said and laughed again. 'I mean, I'm not laughing *at* you. It's nice to meet someone whose view isn't tied up with the politics of the area. This' – she waved at the cream-tiled street of restored and genetically engineered shopfronts – 'is not finished yet. It's part of a plan to rework the whole city. You see the funny struts on the walls?'

They looked like force-grown additions.

'Well, they're going to plant specially crafted trees on the roofs.'

'Roof gardens?' said Kevin, attracted and repelled at the same time.

'Not exactly. It's what they're calling a "verdant strata". Here we are.' She pulled into a narrow lane, the delivery bay of a shop. Kevin supposed she knew what she was up to. 'They want to cover the rooftops in as close as they can get to natural bushland.'

Kevin looked at her. A great gout of laughter burst from him which he tried to control with no success. He could not recall laughing at anything this way for weeks. He rested his head against the window till it passed.

'Yeah. Great if they can do it, but utterly berko, too. The state government was elected on almost that alone, so they have a mandate, if not the dosh.'

Around the corner a warehouse had been transformed into several shops using computer-generated shapes, mostly in ceramics. The result was a bit like a cathedral built by some clam-worshipping race, except where at random the architect had left bits of brick and steel sticking out. The restaurant, by the "mouth", was gently rippled white and polished wood, almost empty after lunch. They sat by the entrance.

He ordered a rabbit salad, she a marinara (the seafood here was metal-free, she told him). As Gemma finished pouring the Semillon she said, 'So. Is what Martin said in his account true?' She seemed not to doubt it.

'Almost every word of it. Cheers.'

'Long life and health.'

'Health, yeah.' He wondered at the amount of alcohol he had consumed lately. But it would help his hangover.

'Almost true?'

'The personal aspects are just his opinion.'

'But the weird stuff is true?'

'Every bit of it.'

'Ah-huh. So. You must have had a hard time.'

'A bit.'

'I'm sorry.'

'Nah.'

'Yes I am! I'm sorry I pushed you into the interview like this. You must have felt as bad as Martin, worse perhaps, because you pushed Packett, who—'

'I know what happened, thanks.'

'Sorry. But I mean, Martin is in a home because of his part. I . . . Sorry.'

'Martin was in love. He ran into a brick wall and got up and head-butted it again. That bloke never did know when to stop.'

'But your friends, the project . . .'

'*I was not in love, all right?* I haven't had a girlfriend for years. It was not my project, not the play, not anything else – I didn't give a shit. And grief, well, you get over that. You can get over anything if you set your mind to it. Some ways that's worse than anything, you do forget. Martin? He had a shock and it did something to him, I dunno. I'm not privy to anyone's bonce but mine, and I wonder about *that* sometimes . . . Where is the food?'

'And the stuff about the CIA?'

'You're not that much of a dill, are ya?'

'You said it was true.'

'I said I didn't necessarily agree with his opinions.'

'About the personal aspects.'

'About that too. And the rest is none of your business.'

'Sorry . . .'

'Here comes the food at last.'

'Did you read the Odd Spot in *The Age* today?'

'Hay?'

'A man in England—' She waited until the waiter, an emaciated Italian boy with breasts and a bone through his nose, had left the table. 'Thanks. A man in England says he received instructions from space which told him how to hypnotise the staff . . .'

Kevin had lost his appetite. He watched Gemma taste the fresh mussels and nod her approval, his chest as heavy as chain mail as the restaurant echoed each footfall of a passing woman in a too-red dress because he wanted to pound the table and speak harshly to the woman but feared what she might say, so he bit his tongue, he felt his ears pulling back with the tightening of his neck and he raised his chin, giving in, somewhere far, far away yet buried profoundly inside. He was sweating with a fever.

'I heard that story this morning on the radio,' he heard himself say, quite calm, really. Giving in. His temples burned and pulsed painfully, his limbs tingled as if he were about to vomit. He had an image of himself with sparks shooting out from his body, if he closed his eyes he could see them bouncing across the table, all over the food, he could smell ozone.

Up, Gemma looked, a forkful of pasta halfway to her mouth. She had put on lipstick since this morning. She appeared worried. 'More wine?' she said uncomfortably.

The words boomed at Kevin, clamouring through him:

'MOOOR WOOIINNNNE?'

She began to talk nervously, about the other strange things people were seeing, madonnas, one-hundred-metre-high glowing dachshunds, the faces of dead relatives sketched on roads. It was becoming too frequent to be put down as the usual scattered insanity of the world. Kevin could understand Gemma's words but they came at him in rushes, seemed to swoop around his head, go off and come back, louder in the midst of the next sentence. What was she saying now? That the visions may be the same in many cases but because of cultural and individual factors were interpreted as different objects entirely?

Kevin couldn't take it. He seemed to be moving away from the body which sparked and tingled in colours he could *smell* (giving in, somewhere inside), another man clutched the table's edge as he rose, fingers mottled, white and painful. Not Kevin Gore. That man obviously had difficulty breathing, therefore it wasn't him.

'Kevin!'

Nothing needed saying but he opened his mouth to explain the other bloke's actions and croaked like a startled cricket.

'What's wrong, Kevin?'

Why was she calling that man by his name?

Giving in, a deep surrender of his body.

It abated, for the moment. Reality rushed back in at him and he sat heavily on the carved wood. A troubled look from Gemma gave way to one of shocked amusement, then to careful neutrality. A pit of hatred opened in Kevin which he felt sure

she noticed. Lord, he had not felt so confused in years. Everything had seemed to open for him, however bleakly, around
forty. The childhood he could barely remember seemed to have
bent him into the sort of bloke who needed not much approval
to begin with. When he gave up the stage he had felt released
from an unhealthy thing he happened to be good at. Now, he
was frightened that she thought him mad, and he hated her for
it. Like a child.

'Kevin.'

'Sorry.' He forced himself to smile, to eat something. He
imagined he could see her recoil from his rictus. 'Sorry. Drifted
off a bit, didn't I?' He started in on his salad.

It surprised him that he wasn't afraid of madness now, just
that she might think him bonkers. The hate drained away in
that childlike fashion, as quickly as it had come. And her news,
it shocked Kevin, it confirmed what he'd heard on the radio, but
it was *her* and his sudden desire to be liked by her which filled
him with urgency.

Or was it? He liked her, thought she was very good-looking,
but was that why he had wanted to leave? Where had the
impulse come from? It hadn't seemed to be his own.

'. . . isn't that what it must be?' she demanded. He had been
carrying on with his side of the conversation automatically.
'People with no history of instability, no reason to lie, see things
that aren't there, things they feel speak directly to *them*? It *has*
to be this Thoughtboost!'

'I'm sure that in a world of over ten billion it happens every
day.'

'But think of how many other times it wasn't reported for
these six stories to come through on the one day.'

'Coincidence.'

'You're not listening to me! There have been more. And if
there are more tomorrow, what then? Soon they'll be a sensation
all over the world and people will want an explanation.'

Kevin nodded. 'And they'll find one. I've gotta see some
people. Thanks for lunch; it was great. I hope I was some help.

See ya.' He got up before he could see Gemma's reaction, and left. He was running a fever; what he had just felt had to be more than adolescent lovesickness; he was generating strong compulsions he was now sure were connected with the cut in his finger he'd thought was a hallucination. Stuff the consequences, stuff what anyone thought – it was time to find out where this led.

EIGHT

from
Charms All O'erthrown

It was this stark country that finally let me in on the reason
Sarah Witchell had picked *The Tempest* for her bold new
company's first run. This was Prospero's territory; spirits who
had lived here for eighty thousand years were still obvious in
every rock and tree. Robyn and I trod tenderly over the quartz
gravel toward a violent afterglow, as if this dreaming island
could wake and shrug us off. That afternoon, we had established
temporary digs in an amphitheatre formed by a sandstone
escarpment which traded hues in the gap between memory and
attention and was skirted by a clear stream, the lot of it solely
accessible by an hour's grind down a dry channel, beyond a
bullet-puckered sign which read, 'Floodway'. We had pitched
three tents on a crunchy meander, collected firewood, seen Kevin
and Gill off on an expedition to the nearest town for supplies,
then rested in our various ways. Fred had taken a group to the
top of the cliff to explore, Pete had started a footy match, Enzo
was showing Dave something on his computer, and Rob had
consented to a walk, at last.

For a long time we did not speak. The evening chorus was so
rich and strange this first exposure gagged us. The low whoop
of the crested pigeon, the soft whistle of the mulga parrot, the
low of the Malleefowl, the ticking and chinking and liquid
melodious pip pip pip hooee! I could not pick them out then,
and my memory might not serve now. They were enchanting.

When we did talk it was gentle banality about the weather and the trip up. I regarded her fairly large nose and sturdy Scottish chin against the red horizon and found myself at a loss to say anything more than, 'Mm. It's buckets of rain or not at all round here.' So we walked on until the purple above us turned to night and stars came out in mobs.

When she laughed I thought she was mocking my quiet agony.

She pointed. We were being spied on from the shadows. Past a group of boulders, beneath a stand of gum trees, a gang of grey forms shifted on spindly legs, some as tall as a man. We made our way very cautiously toward the emus, who cocked their beaks this way and that as they stalked about, their plumage swaying like soft grass skirts.

'Hello to you too!' Robyn laughed again and reached toward one, which stared with fierce orange eyes as though ready to snap. That beak would hurt.

'HUNGH!' it warned, and we jumped.

A game in a lingo far beyond what I might have tried on my own took us from then to suppertime. Their retreats were always followed by the hesitant advance of one or two, who discussed what we might do in a semaphore of head and neck. I took my lead from Rob. She wobbled her head with the best of them, showing the side of her neck, stepping back when they did. It was a queer, concentrated dance of hello, full of awkward turns and half-steps, in which Robyn appeared to be fluent. (She later told me she didn't know anything about emus, she had made it up as she went along.) I did my clumsy best. By the time the distant calls of our friends chased them away the birds had become curious about any rock or twig we showed them. As we walked back toward the firelight with our arms about each other's necks, I took deep draughts of pungent eucalyptus and thanked my lucky stars that I had not had the chance to speak my piece.

Bump in. Fit up. Pack in. These ancient rocks, once below an inland sea, had seldom if ever seen artificial lights. Certainly people had passed here now and then, several middens showed us that, but none with technology such as ours. We wore fist-sized capsules on our hips which Enzo suavely informed us combined radio mike, direction-finder, negative-ion generator (What? Out *here*? We laughed at the poor boy) and a musical instrument keyed to our movements, part of the computer that ran our lighting rig as well as several other functions which, he implied, mere 'talent' could never hope to comprehend. The mysterious Enzo. He kept to his infernal devices and we were everyone of us kept busy by Gillian's orders at this stage, the plastic jiggers didn't impede us so we forgot about them.

Gill worked us hard. Even old Dave carried and climbed. Sherelle Macaulay was like a monkey in the scaffolding; when Pete played Tarzan to her Jane and chased her across the proscenium arch we began to see the possibilities of staging the play out here. During the first tea break, Kevin laconically named our theatre. 'So it's come to this,' he said, scratching behind one jutting ear. 'Shakespeare in the Sand Pit.' Gill suggested some more original names and the cracks went back and forth, continuing some private joke about sand and genitals, but the name stuck. This was The Pit. After all, who would call their space the Nooldoonooldoona Laboratory Theatre?

The sight of so many rude mechanicals on a construction job which looked more like a repair of the cliff than an arena for magic and ritual probably amused any native Nooldoonool-doonans tucked into the rocks. We definitely amused ourselves. Fred, whose sunken features contrasted with his sweet falsetto, sang as he worked; it proved a surer way to find him than some lump of technology. That first long night of building, his voice rose out of a brief lull in the banging and clattering with a wistful tune which was to become our theme:

> When that I was and a little tiny boy,
> With hey, ho, the wind and the rain,
> A foolish thing was but a toy,
> For the rain it raineth every day.

Hey, ho, the wind and the rain,
For the rain it raineth every day.

The song for Shakespeare's clown. Soon we were all joined, Sam
Schuyler's baritone, Don McDonald's tenor and mine, Robyn's
contralto, even those with little voice at all added to that hymn
of resignation. Not many of us knew it all, so by the last verse
Fred and Robyn sang alone. We came back in on the final
refrain and as we spread the last few words to end it, something
extraordinary occurred. The halogen work lights dimmed on
their stands; out of the immense bowl of black which sucked
our vision upward came a cascade of lights, a meteor shower of
such proportions as I had never seen, wave upon wave of
brilliance, enough to leave even on our unadjusted eyes a streaky
after-image which lingered into our silence.

Then Enzo replaced the fuse and we slowly went back to
work, shaking our heads over the coincidence, not feeling much
like speech. They say it's great good luck to see a falling star.
We are superstitious in the theatre.

'I think you can do with a bit more . . .' Sarah made a face of
studied indecision.

Fred grinned tightly at the opportunity, his gaunt face transformed into something quite lovely for a moment. 'This?' he
asked, and tripped. His long legs flailed, but best of all he
appeared to hit the stage face first. At stage left I saw Gill and
Kevin wince.

'Well, if you can keep that up – yeah, sure, take it right over
the top. Do you want to go off with Jenny and work on those
scenes?'

'Do I?' Fred made smooching and slobbering noises in Jenny's
direction then checked Sam for jealousy, who merely rolled his
eyes.

'Okay, we'll get on with Caliban and Ariel if you two can get
along without Martin,' said our director.

'We can always get along without Martin,' said Jenny.

'Humph,' I said, thinking, *oh boy, me and Robyn!*

'On second thoughts we'll see how you and Prospero got on with that first scene again. Caliban, we'll need you here in a few minutes so don't go too far. Robbie? Just one more time, okay?'

One more time. I knew what that meant. I turned to exit for a coffee, stage right, then stopped, stunned.

We had been invaded!

A stranger in a beige safari suit stood by the 'boys' tent'. Definitely not one of us. He turned his slouch hat in fat pink hands, nose to nose in argument with Dave Abrahams. It was obvious why Dave was upset. This bald bastard had skittled our whole plan of secrecy! What was the use of coming out here if everybody knew about it? Beside me the action on stage ground to a halt as the enormity of this roly-poly figure's appearance sank in. The cast began to trickle out of the tent and out of the theatre to listen. Dave, his face red with the sun and his anger, jerked his head at us. He grabbed the intruder by the shoulder and marched him across to the prefab cabin beyond the stalls.

We stood around, looking at one another, at a loss. Over a month of preparation and two weeks of hard yakka had been wasted. The invader was a theatre critic.

'Jig's up then,' said Kevin.

'No. He's promised not to say anything,' Dave told us. He looked as though he believed it.

'How did he find out?' asked Jenny.

Dave gazed around the marquee, at all our faces, without coming to rest on any one. I thought, he doesn't want to give the name of the culprit. Still, he doesn't appear as haggard as he might, so perhaps it will work out for the best. 'I don't think it serves any purpose to name who, ah, blabbed,' he said. 'If they want to own up, they will. What matters now is that we work out whether or not we let Packett stay. While he's here, we can, ah, keep an eye on him. If he's chucked out, he'll not only be out of our sight, but also he'll undoubtedly be, ah, pissed off. Hm.'

'Ahmm . . . ?' It was a tiny voice we turned to, although he was a big man. Dressed in a red checked shirt and jeans, with the obligatory can of Melbourne Bitter in hand, he squirmed with guilt in the corner. 'I – I think it might have been me. I told my mum about it. I should have remembered at the time that she knows Packett's mum, but it only just came to me now. I'm sorry, I really am.' It was Robert, our assistant stage manager and designer.

'Ya great walloping dill of a man,' said Jenny, next to him, and gave him a hug rather too fierce to be entirely forgiving, thumping the top of his head with one fist.

Don McDonald asked, 'So what are we going to do about him?', gesturing at Robert. This set everyone off at once. Some told Don to shut his mouth, others defended Robert's natural mistake (if you can't trust your mum who can you trust?), most agreed something indeed must be done but not about Robert.

Then Kevin shouted: 'WILL YOU MONGRELS SHUT UP FOR A SECOND?' He finished, 'We've got some serious thinking to do.'

Gill grinned at him, one of those looks you would commit crimes for. 'That's what I was going to say, though of course with more decorum and natural style,' she said primly. 'Dave? I believe you had something more to tell us?'

The group was so large it took some discussion, but in the finish we let Packett stay on the proviso that he would not send any articles until some weeks into the run. Naturally, it wasn't that simple.

It began with one of those after-work sessions gathered around the front row to argue theory and history of theatre. Most of us hung around, relishing the chance to swap jibes with one of those who had dealt so many unfair blows in the past. Don McDonald, whose brand of English Marxism had annoyed enough people to have forced him out of the mainstream into stand-up comedy, carried a grudge. He mistakenly argued that Packett in particular and his paper in general (a respected

Melbourne daily) had distorted his efforts, and included some unfair allusions to Packett's recent messy divorce for good measure. Packett looked fragile, his sunburnt face twisted as he retorted, in bitter, short sentences. He became equally unfair. Jenny Drape put her considerable weight behind some facts:

'You used to walk out after five minutes! You found out what the rest of the play would be like using psychic powers, I suppose.' Stuff which left me cringed behind the dairy fridge she sailed through like a hovercraft. 'That's about as professional as a slug,' she said.

'My dear,' Packett replied, 'you know what that is: tommy rot.' His thick lips pursed in a smile, which faded as alarm at what had he had said filled his eyes.

We stared. More than one mouth hung open.

Let me explain. In Ballarat, in the late 1850s, a theatre manager named Charlie McGibbon made a secret deal with a Chinese family who had been decimated by the racial violence common then. They would mine the space under the stage in return for refuge there and a share of the gold. Improbable? Gold fever was high; other versions are more ridiculous. The Crown Theatre housed drunkards who did the usual things, notably the catapulting of faeces at the artistes. And no cheap ones, either: Lillie Lawrence for one braved the poo. I can't blame McGibbon for wanting to get out with some nuggets of his own. For a while things went well. The family Kwang did find gold under that there theatre, not a lot, but a living. Then McGibbon fell in love with a Kwang granddaughter.

One evening he left his post at the limelight to see her, confident the stage action would remain static, but after two steps a projectile hit the spotlight and the room soon filled with smoke. During the drunken panic that followed McGibbon struggled for the stage, screaming the girl's name. A fly weight dropped on him before he could reach her. The whole Kwang family died in the flames. McGibbon, dragged out by some well-meaning sot, whispered his true love's name until he passed completely away.

He whispered: 'Tommy.'

Ever since, her name has been as taboo in Australian theatres as that of the Scottish play. I have been told if you say *that word* counterweights will fall, or the lead will lose her voice, or the theatre will burn down. Who knows? Perhaps the audience will hurl turds at you.

For saying the T-word, Packett had to do some penance. I shook my head to think of him whizzing round widdershins singing, 'Oh God Our Hope' – he would certainly not recite a moronic rhyme or eat raw cabbage dipped in chocolate. I glanced across the aisle at Kevin, who gave me an exaggerated grim look, took a deep breath and began to whistle 'Blue Moon'. I took the cue and whistled 'In the Mood'. Others soon came in with different tunes. For the cure to work, we all had to whistle. Packett eventually was nudged into action by Gill. The moment passed.

But damage was done. Dave didn't look as though the earth would open and swallow him any more, but he remained extra-wrinkled. Don complained that he had been the only one to cover his eyes while whistling – *his* version of the cure. This startled a few people, but no one went so far as to begin again. We scattered with the feeling that we had not quite done all we could to clear ourselves of the curse.

It shames me to admit that it affected our work. It seemed the next morning everybody had the grumps. Sam bogged down a workshop on pagan spirits with fine points of theology. Kevin walked off stage mid-line, his face a portrait of taut sinews. Fred actually snapped at Jenny! Gill, after a conference with Sarah, announced a weekend.

Then the accidents began.

At a picnic arranged by Robyn and Fred, to watch some birds and have a swim at Nooldoonooldoona Water Hole, Kevin took a shallow dive too hard and cracked his head on the rock face at the far end of the pool.

That night those of us who'd eaten the chicken and pasta

salad came down with food poisoning. Poor Kevin also copped that.

And Robert, who is a renowned designer because he cannot stop work, fell down a trap door backward, five metres to the gravel below the stage, on to his back. Miraculously, he was unhurt.

We held a meeting. Packett took the blame, of course. He maintained a red-faced silence while Don and Enzo made some sharp remarks. Enzo was clearly only stirring, but Don surprised me: for a materialist he was very superstitious.

'What did Packett do? Poison the chook?' said Kevin. 'I didn't feel him push me in the water.'

We looked off at different corners of the dining marquee. Nobody had actually mentioned Packett's name yet. Enzo, leaning against the door frame, eyelids lowered, allowed the corners of his lips to twitch. Kevin proceeded to embarrass us some more. Packett had nothing to do with it and anyone who thought so was a mug; it was pure coincidence; these things came in threes anyhow. While we laughed, Enzo gave a single cynical toss of the head and left. The door frame wobbled as he ducked out. Leather trousers in this heat, I thought. No doubt he was off to the bio box, where he even slept. I sat by the flymesh window getting a headache from the sun and food poisoning yet unwilling to move. Normal breakfast chat had returned, but I noticed Don in the far corner with a couple of the musicians, laughing maliciously and rolling his eyes in Packett's direction. I heaved myself erect.

'What is this?' I asked them quietly. 'Where does all this crap come from, hm? This is the stuff, here . . .' I waved my hand around at the door.

They stared at me, no idea of what I was on about. My head felt like a squeezed sponge, so I made for the door. Turning to leave, I saw Dave had heard my incoherent little speech. An intense look of guilt and sadness passed over that craggy face, tears swelled but would not drop and returned to wherever it is that tears go in such a case.

It was another beautiful morning. I walked a wobbly way downstream with the vague idea of abluting my rancid body before it got too hot. My mind was, however, stuck to the memory of Dave's face, and I ground to a halt a few metres from the door, towel-less and witless. A shaking Packett slammed out of the marquee, bowling past me.

Dave did not strike me as the superstitious sort. From the beginning of these accidents something had upset him deeply, I saw that now. It could have been the presence of the theatre critic. But I did not think it was. I racked my aching head for what I might have said to trouble him just then.

I began to find out the next day.

That night Robyn and I discussed the situation in private. We walked toward the place where we had met the emus, beside the creek too fresh and clean to have a European name. A few stars were already kindled above. Without haste, a wallaby hopped out of our way behind some bushes. I gave a sigh of pleasure at the new rhythm imposed by this wilderness I had underrated so much. Hand in hand, we kept silent for a while, normally hard for me, but growing easier, here.

'So what do you reckon?' Robyn asked at last.

Not one sign of human life, from here to the horizon. I knew what Robyn meant but was tempted to rave about nature. 'I don't trust Packett,' I said.

'Could be sending articles out by crow.'

'It's not that . . .'

'You don't go in for flyweights and whistling in the theatre and that, do you?'

'No.' I kicked at a clump of spinifex. 'I don't actually know if it's him. There's more to this . . . Packett's really got Dave worried.'

'I should think so.'

'No. It's more than that, I – maybe it's me, I dunno.'

We walked on for a while. The feathered secret agents did not show at the boulders. It was completely dark by now, and growing chilly. We stopped. I turned to Robyn, taking both her hands in mine. On the mild breeze came a waft of smoke and laughing conversation.

I sighed. 'It was probably wooziness from the chicken, but I have the feeling there's something going on here, something we haven't been told about.' I shook my head. 'It's probably just silly.' I appealed to the soft grey area of her face.

'Trust your instincts, Martin. I certainly will. I'll keep my eyes open. *I* thought Dave was having an affair with Enzo.'

I laughed. 'They do spend a lot of time together . . . No. Enzo's as straight as they come.'

We stood that way for some minutes, taking in one another's smells. I opened my mouth, closed it, opened it again.

'Robyn,' I said. 'I have another instinct.' Which I suppose sounded all right, but in truth I was a moil of conflicting emotions all of a sudden. Nevertheless, I took Robyn in my arms and bent to kiss her.

'Martin,' she said, a touch desperately. 'I do like you a lot.'

That stopped me. She took her chance and kissed me lightly and broke away, crunching on the gravel as she spun and walked back to camp.

It seemed a long time before I followed. On my way back, I reflected on what was instinct but unrecognised and what was not but which I thought was instinct. There is no perfect guide for telling right from wrong. I had just been taught a lesson by Ariel.

Back at work the next day, Sarah watched our first run through without stops with a guarded turn to her lips then stood and gave us a dressing down. Partly show, but it was what we needed. We sat and took it like naughty children. She strode back and forth on the stage, waving her arms and swinging the long blond hair out of her face and picking the eyes out of the half-hearted performance we had given. Even taking into account that some of us were still delicate from the 'weekend', we had been crap. We nodded. We made resolutions to do better the next day. We enjoyed Sarah's performance. It brought us together again.

A number of us were assigned to help Robert rig Ariel's web lines, the nymphs' and reapers' machineries. The manky ones were given the rest of the afternoon off. The group scattered, talking about the play, delicate but positive.

I hung around to watch the work. Robert, who knew I was not up to physical labour, handed me a can of Melbourne and I put my feet up in the third row to watch the comedy of Gill supervising Kevin in the part of rigger. None of the other lackeys got such a hard time from Gill. Those two must like each other a lot, I thought. She harangued him and belted him on the behind when he dragged his feet, which was as often as he could. Gore's impassive face made it all the funnier. After a cooling gulp, I nursed my bitter; I rolled the can across my forehead as I chuckled. We began to lose the light, shadows slipped across the stage. From his nest in the tower, Enzo snapped on the worklights and instantly there were serpentine shapes about the framework, and more on the fossil-laden stone backstage. The fireman's poles were hung, rocking horses were installed on the cliff face, a curved ramp for the skateboards was fixed from floor to cliff – almost everything ready to go at last. Robyn's web, though, would probably be hung tomorrow since tea would start soon.

No. Ariel's Tarzan ropes were brought out by Gill and after several tosses were hoisted into the grid. Pete Stanopoulos, our golden wild man, wanted to show off to Sherelle and Gill, and Gill, because Pete really could do it but mainly because the web did need a test with a heavier weight than Robyn's, bowed and said be my guest.

Pete wound a calf around the soft rope and climbed. I had to admit (to myself, anyway) he looked good with muscles rippling, although how his huge thighs did not split those little red football shorts I never fathomed. He swung. A bit like Johnny Weismuller on Valium he worked his way from upstage right downstage to the centre and back upstage left in a shallow 'V', then, turning, he swung back downstage and without apparent effort grasped the skimpy harness Robert lowered for him. There was the merest click – Pete appeared to float. I applauded. Sherelle, Gill, Robert and Kevin joined in. People emerged from the dining tent. Pete waved as they cheered.

I laced my hands behind my head and contemplated Pete's singleted torso in a swallow's thrust into the dusty shafts of remaining sunlight. The dust rose like smoke.

Hang on. I flung my legs from the bench and scrambled to my feet.

It *was* smoke.

NINE

First (sparks appeared at the edges of his vision whether he closed his eyes or not) he was determined to work out if what he heard inside his head, felt in his limbs and at his temples, saw coruscating over the tram seat beside him, meant one of the visions Gemma had mentioned or one of two other possibilities. He might be insane or it might be something else, he did not know what, but he would make a start on finding out when he got home with a simple operation, not the kind of thing for the kids to try at home themselves, he thought and giggled, then realised it was his fever talking, he had to maintain control. He had felt a bit like this when he'd passed his first audition – he remembered as he rode home on the wide-open tram with the air rushing past the mums, pensioners, commuters off early, students and him, Kevin, a man with a special secret he bet no one would have guessed in a million years to look at him, something they might envy once he found out what it could do, which *made* the bloke who looked to be a railway worker by the tan on him – although he'd felt a little apprehensive to leap like this into adventure, it had made him feel unique.

At his stop he bounded from the tram and purled across the road and along Sherelle's street, hurdled the white wrought-iron gate, stopping only to pant at his door, fumbling for the keys. My wheeze is gone! he thought as he raced through the flat to the bathroom where he flung open the shaving cabinet (the mirror on it flashed his wild eyes at him, swinging past) and grabbed his safety razor, unscrewed it, plucked away the grimy blade, wiped it between his thumb and forefinger, thought what does it matter anyhow?, and pressed it to his wrist.

It dented the skin but did not pierce it.

Kevin Gore gritted his teeth, which made the humming louder in his head, like the crystal set his father and him had built when he was little and the old man still bothered with him, all it had produced was such a hum, he took his eyes off the words 'Fuji-Gillette', and bent his head away so beams of afternoon glared through the frosted window directly in his eyes, looked back down, drawn by a desire to see his own body at what might be the last moment whole and in good order before he disappeared to join the universe again in blithe unconsciousness – and pressed, down.

A few minutes later he decided he was not insane, or if he was this was a doozy and worth a chase to see what else he might come up with. It was not a vision, either: his last had been eleven years ago but he did remember that they didn't repeat themselves this way. Those were one-offs, even if they did have real consequences, more like what Gemma had been on about over lunch – giant dachshunds, strange fires and such.

The fever seemed to grow more distant, if not to die away, the humming too; while to either side there was still a crackling pool of light, he could probably live with it, if it didn't spread across the centre. He rubbed his wrist in the place he'd cut it, toying with the little ridge of brand new skin, poking at it with his thumbnail to see how it reacted (just like skin), blinking down at the pool of liquid in the bath. He went into the kitchen, rummaged till he found a plastic bag, returned and knelt and scooped some of the electric substance into the bag, none of which would stick like blood but rolled off his hand like jelly, then he squeezed the gruesome parcel to get rid of the air and thumbed the pressure strip across the top to seal it. Kevin's special secret. He shoved it in his pocket as he dashed across the kitchen on his way out to the car.

*

As he drove, almost of itself the pastureland on the suburban edge receded before a kindling-dry expanse of heath; this was his childhood travel game again, but played against his will, perhaps, or driven by some impulse he didn't understand as yet. The tender native herbs (no bracken here) swept back into the foothills of the Great Dividing Range like a grass fire in reverse, cows and barns and haystacks and chic commuter villages evanescing as they grew back, stands of spiky myrtle and tea tree scrub, peppermint gums and stringybarks accompanied them; here, unlike his previous fancy of a fern-filled rainforest, was a dry, unromantic landscape, a bare bones place to live. Even the determined Australian Impressionists had had eyes too European to paint this kind of harsh light very often; it dried out the mouth to look at it.

Also opposed to what he had imagined earlier, this country was inhabited, that man had straight black hair, army surplus shorts, his skin the luminous brown that comes from extended labour out of doors, rather like his own . . .

The man walking away, down the hill to the stream, disappearing now amongst the river red gums and the rushes – he felt sure it was himself.

Although he knew he'd built this inside his mind, Kevin had to fight the urge to stop the car and pursue the man. It would be avoidance. When he had called from the service station (she might have been out, a waste of a day, and, yeah, she might appreciate some warning), Pat had sounded truly pleased to hear from him after all these years and he had felt a lot of warmth himself, so he'd be blowed if he let what was really cowardice at these mysterious compulsions divert him to a paddock in search of fantasies. Ah, but he could *smell* the walk into the past, citrus and eucalyptus rising in the heat, he could hear the crackling underfoot, feel the shock of the cold in his balls and spine as he slid into the water after such a parching walk.

He almost missed the turnoff to Pat's.

*

No need to reinvent the countryside up here, lots of the cooperatives banned pets and shooting, allowed most of the land to regenerate itself, but it took wealth to purchase land within commuting distance, more to keep it up: Kevin passed two retirement centres where, on lawns crafted not to grow past rolling height or to turn yellow, the aged majority lived apart from a world of daily accidents and 'natural' disasters. Lots more dwelt in similar places up in Queensland.

After half an hour's speeding down a winding gravel road, Kevin skidded to a halt beside the letter box with 'Abrahams' painted above its hand-cut slot. He backed, then turned into the drive and cruised past rusty Saab remains. Iron sculptures partly finished were dotted along the scenic view: bits of Dave lay everywhere.

Pat was squatting in the herb garden as he pulled up, attacking the weeds with vigour for a woman pushing eighty. Her elbows pumped, the weeds flew. She looked up with raised eyebrows, though she must have heard his car. When she recognised him she beamed. Without apparent difficulty, she stood and walked toward the car, rubbing her hands together to shed the soil.

Kevin felt miles better just to be here.

'Pat.'

'Kevin.'

They joined hands ring-a-rosy style and looked at one another for a while. Pat had a large, high face, more open than ever, still firm though incised into chunks by time. Her brown eyes regarded Kevin with gaiety and the mischief of a woman flattered. It refreshed Kevin to be with a woman who made no assumptions about what he was or had been but accepted him this way. He kissed both her cheeks and she his.

'I'll put the kettle on. Or would you like a beer?'

'Tea's fine, thanks, Pat.'

The place was wilder than Kevin remembered it. And not from the neglect of a woman left alone. Boronia, in brown and yellow and green, left its exquisite scent on his legs as he followed Pat into the house, which was almost covered now in coral vine. Inside, more tribal art than ever cluttered the wide A-frame, her sculpted iron staircase rose into the cool dark with as much muscular grace as he recalled.

While he stood in contemplation of Dave's sculpture, Martin's voice rang through him, more familiar and almost more excruciating than he could bear, yet *older*, even older than the real Martin Leywood:

> **Is it possible that we have had thousands of years**
> **to look, meditate, and record, and that we have let**
> **these thousands of years slip away like a recess at**
> **school, when there is just enough time to eat a**
> **sandwich and an apple?**
> **Yes, it is possible.**

Kevin shuddered uncontrollably; he half turned and dropped one hand on to the bentwood chair beside him.

Pat was eyeing him with some concern, but she said, 'You've got a farm yourself now, I hear.'

It steadied him to have to answer.

'Southern coast of New South Wales. Near Lily, which is near Tathra.' He took a pace and sat, feeling furious with himself and helpless, thinking, If this is not just guilt speaking in Martin's voice (and the other) then it's connected with the visions or why would I start to go berko (or whatever it is) when Gemma told me about them? And the blue blood is connected with the visions, too. His mind made lots of links, but the damn things broke . . .

'I'm glad they stopped the woodchipping around there. Were you involved in that?' She turned on the kettle.

He could not keep his eyes off the dull black spiral, which depicted an evolution from crawling boneless things to soaring, airy spirits. Flocks of birds arced away, clouds of insects and troupes of apes; humankind occupied the central support. But should they? Kevin wondered.

'No way,' he answered, aware that he had taken too long to

do so. 'I've stayed pretty much out of everything for a fair old while. Made some scones though.'

'It's funny, I went the other way when Dave died.' When Kevin failed to react, she eased herself into the chair opposite, saying, 'I threw myself into good works left, right and centre till it got dangerous to m'health.'

They began to fill each other in on the past eleven years. Gradually, the confusion and anger were suppressed by warmth and gratitude. Kevin discovered he could speak naturally, even at length about the days he hadn't mentioned to anybody, because Pat spoke so simply, openly. She laughed so much! Her grief obviously ran deeper than his own yet she encouraged him to compare his largely unexpressed feelings about Gillian to her loss of half a century's love. He watched her in the rich colours which slanted from the kitchen leadlight and tried to feel decently ashamed of the comparison and couldn't – she'd never allow it. Kevin smiled, sitting back.

Then, as if it had waited in ambush, the heated compulsion which had driven him since the lunch with Gemma Stranger slammed back into him, bringing an acute unease about the plastic doggy bag of blood against his leg. Abruptly, he clenched, secretive, desperate, impatient; he bit down, again utterly furious with himself for being this way at Pat's. You bastard, he thought, but there was nothing he could do when, as Pat went on about her recent film on the life of a prostitute in the opal fields at Cooper Peedy, he saw his hand reach down a sparkling tunnel urged on by faint chants of a children's rhyme about a game with hankies to jerk his handkerchief out of his pocket, so 'accidentally' tugging up the bag with it.

('Sorry,' he said, and bent to scoop up the bag. 'Me suntan mixture. Nice blue, isn't it?' And when she agreed he could have kissed her, never mind that he'd been forced to fish for this confirmation. She could see it! Blue!)

The kid's voice and the sparkling died away once more. As soon as possible he outlined his plans for Martin's play.

'Yes,' she said, nodding slowly, 'that'd work. We dearly love to hate Americans here, and especially now they're blocking the money for the dykes in Bangladesh. But you'd never have the connections to find the backing any more, would you? I think I can help you in that department.'

She stood and broke into a smile that sloughed the years off her, springing as it did from a little girl who had always skipped gaily through life. Whether or not she had really been such a girl was beside the point; she had long ago decided which little girl she should have been and, knowing what a sham most adult behaviour was, gave herself quite artlessly over to that child as the day saw fit. Where was Kevin's cheerful brat?

He didn't have a clue.

'What we need is some wine, red wine. Serious scheming always calls for a bottle at least; I have just the thing. I bottled it eight years ago and it should go very well with tea. You are staying for tea, aren't you, dear?' Her eyes shone flirtatiously from the deltas of skin around them.

'Guess I am, Pat,' said Kevin. He pushed his chair back, looking forward to a meal prepared together. Should he tell her what had been happening? No, there was not enough to give to anybody, yet. He stood. Never mind the fever, the blue blood, voices, Gemma's visions; if he took it day by day it would turn out all right.

'That one wants to be an actress,' said the man with the moustache. He looked more cricketer than producer.

'So she's making coffee for you.'

'Great coffee though. And great head.'

'Don't get much of that where I come from.'

'What: head or coffee? Ha ha! Where's that again?'

No, total fuckheadedness. 'Near Tathra. Southern coast of South Wales.'

'Ah yeah.' He sat. 'Yes. I have some friends there. They reckon land prices have reached their limit.'

'I wouldn't know. I've been there for a while.'

'Bought up early, ay, mate? No one's made you an offer?'

'Not yet.'

'You'll have to sit on it a couple of years then. Wait for the sea level to drop.'

'I'm in no hurry.'

'Smart way to be.'

'About the play . . .'

'Pat. Yes. Well I've read it. You know, Pat used to be a very astute lady. Dave – he would have made a pile out of all that if the crows hadn't come home to roost.'

'You think that was it, then?'

'Hay?'

'Interference.'

'Oh, no. It was an accident.' He essayed another laugh. 'Just a figure of speech. No, what I don't get is: what's in it for you? For Pat too? I mean, bottom line. That's what we haven't talked yet. Aside from some of the estimates you've got here, we haven't talked money at all. What do you want from this?'

'It's a homage. It's way overdue. I guess it's also a statement about art and idealism—'

'No but – are you trying to make a comeback? Or are you trying to form a partnership with Pat?'

'What? Producing?'

'Yeah.'

'Would I be coming to you if I were?'

'I dunno . . . If we do this – and it's going to take a lot of rewriting and some real money for the effects – there's going to be such a stink—'

'You think they'll take notice of a piece of theatre?'

'I'll make sure they do. I mean, look at those vision things; they're all over the news, right?' He pushed a tabloid across the desk at Kevin. The headline story concerned a young Spanish girl who had seen an electricity tower come to life and admonish her about Spain's involvement in the European Bioethics Pact. 'This is the silly season here but the *Europeans* are taking all this seriously!' The Spaniard was already the centre of a small but noisy sect. 'Mate, people will swallow anything.' Kevin stared at the sidebar about the growing number of strange sights cropping up around the world while the producer went on: 'If we do this, you and the writer and, to a certain extent, Pat – you're going to suck up the publicity. Where do you want to take that?'

'Hm?' Kevin looked up. 'Some public discussion would be good. I'd be prepared to put up with that.'

'Tha's great! But you don't have to play it that way with me. I mean – bottom line – what do you really want out of it? What direction do you want to go? Film? You know there isn't a whole heap to be made as a literary agent in this country. If that's what you're after, unless you're dealing with—'

'John?'

'Yes, mate?'

'I don't think you – I – this is a one-off. It means something to me to see that it's done but I'm not really interested in the theatre any more.'

'That's what I'm trying to get at, mate. I mean, obviously this is a vehicle for something else. It's *designed* to cause a stir in the media. What is it you've got your eye on? For *afterwards*.'

'Landscape gardening.' I really couldn't tell you because I'm following compulsions against my better judgement, groping my way away from madness and voices.

'Landscape gardening. Look. If you're not prepared to invest in a trusting situation, why have you come here? Mate, I'm not a confrontational sort of guy, but that's the bottom line in this business: trust. If you don't tell me what you're really after how can I market it properly? That's ninety per cent of the scam, quality marketing. I've gotta get the straight line so I can do some strategic planning, have a word in the relevant ears.'

'I don't reckon your relevant ears are working properly, *mate*. I said the story is *true*, in the details. The people involved meant something to me – *mean* something to me. I'd like to see some discussion about the issues involved, but I don't hope for anything else. Certainly I don't want to use it as a stepping stone. I fully expect it to be ignored and to go back to my own

business when it's finished.' Except that there are other compulsions lined up behind this one, I can feel them even if I don't
know what they are. It's follow them or go mad.

'Kevin, I'm afraid if you won't be honest with me we can't do
business.'

'John, if you won't listen to me I'll take the script and go.
Thanks for your time.'

As Kevin picked up the script he saw anger in contest with
surprise on the man's craggy face. He felt sure the producer
would decide it was a bluff. Pity to disappoint him.

To regard himself as merely a vehicle for the task at hand helped
sustain him through the weeks of driving around the city, phone-
calling, arglebargle with producers, walking and, of course,
waiting about to see people. Glorious summer mocked his
efforts, a season not too hot or rainy for a change put smiles on
the faces of police people, songs in the mouths of tram conduc-
tors and sex in the eyes of strangers, but heightened the feeling
that Kevin's feet knew which paths to tread – and they weren't
telling his stubborn head at all. He was left lost in the bright
streets. The newspaper banners often screamed about visions
such as Gemma had mentioned and Kevin tried to ignore these,
but even the normal headlines concerned subjects with which he
hadn't bothered himself in years; it was sometimes as though
society had reconstructed itself during his eleven years in com-
parative isolation merely to estrange Kevin Gore. He visited bars
in the evenings, found the bands and talk had grown incomprehensible in his absence, yet stayed, again on automatic, an
ability sometimes vital when, as an actor, he had lost the feeling
for a part and going through the motions helped trigger a true
response.

He found, though, that each time he relaxed into the new role
people looked at him as if he'd exposed himself, especially when
seated across the desk from producers – once, mid-rant, he
realised the fop he had taken two weeks of patient courtship to
see actually feared that Kevin might strike him, perhaps he had

seen the fever which had returned after the visit to Pat's (she'd seen the stuff in the bag as blue, thank God, but she couldn't very well feel the humming which went right through his bones at times) in Kevin's eyes. The grimace of alarm and the body tensed for flight under the Thai shirt said nothing else, so Kevin subsided, dumb with the idea he had been so vehement; he apologised for getting off the track and tried to go on, doing his best to assume the air of cynical bonhomie the administrators used with one another, and while the man relaxed visibly, his eyes remained glazed with suspicion. Kevin delivered the proposal devoid of enthusiasm, by rote, and left him striped by the thin venetians in his cool office. He tripped down the side steps of the restored Palais, back into the unsettling sunshine and walked across the road to the beach where he ate a stunned lunch.

Another potential backer for Martin's play threw Kevin out of her office with, 'I only saw you because you said you were a friend of Pat's', combing the curly red hair which hung across her eyes with purple fingers, one elbow propped across the desk (a real hamburger) as though she'd had the mother of all hard nights. 'It's an insult to read such crap and now you want me to believe it too?' She shook her head and reached for the joint burning in the sesame seed ashtray in front of her (the desk mooed softly), breathing, 'No,' and something else unintelligible.

'From the way you were talking before I wonder if you have read it,' Kevin rejoined, stung.

'That's it. Get out.'

Her eyes looked red and hateful in the midst of the caked-on white and purple lines; scratching under a tasselled nipple with one fingernail, she waved him out with the other (purple-banded) arm.

Moo.

The cafés outside in Brunswick Street were filled with plants and flowers in shades fashionable a decade ago. Kevin let his feet take him where they willed, but when he saw Gemma sitting alone in the back corner of an empty seafood spot, snipping items from a curled mass of news printouts, he went in to ask her advice. She looked genuinely pleased to see him, though as he told her of his efforts she approached a wince, then sat thinking for a good minute.

'I don't know,' she confessed, 'I'm just an ivory-tower type, I've never really met any of these people on a business level.'

Kevin must have looked despondent because she sighed and asked how many backers he had yet to see.

'Two.'

'How many have shown any interest so far?'

'Two.'

'Try a bit of obvious razzamatazz, perhaps; these are party goers you're dealing with, they're naturally attracted to a good time. If you look like you're a fun person to be around it will give that kind of aura to the whole project.'

'It's not exactly a comedy.'

'No, but it's not exactly lighting up dollar signs on the inside of their eyelids either.'

'It did with one but I persuaded him that wasn't what it was about.'

Gemma grabbed her forehead. 'Oh, God. Look: Martin's not precisely a comedian but he can be witty when he wants to. Couldn't it be seen as a piece of fun with a twist in the tail because it's based on fact?'

Kevin admitted it was possible, Gemma said she would meet him after the last one, on Friday, for a drink. She would call. Kevin left her to her flood of new data. As he walked out he glanced back, and silently thanked his feet for bringing him here.

Of the final two, the first not only left every part of him with the impression of having visited the right place, she also showed real interest. For half an hour before his appointment at Borovsky Studios he swam laps at Sherelle's local pool in order to feel as fit and relaxed as most of the producers looked. He dressed as if going to a fairly casual party and did not bother to

shave, but wore his best shoes and his granddad's gold watch
and a belt bought especially for the occasion from a flash buckle
boutique. He tried some showbusiness at the interview. The
woman laughed appreciatively. She told Kevin, yes, she agreed
there were light, even comic moments throughout, but at bottom
this was a serious piece, requiring careful thought as to who
would work on it if it wasn't to be trivialised. Kevin Gore
emerged into another lovely day surprised that one of the largest
studios in Australia should be so sincerely positive and direct.
They usually make movies son, he reminded himself, so don't
bolt for the mail.

Sure enough, on the morning of his final interview he received
a letter – his first reply – regretfully informing him that a stage
version of *Charms* would not in their opinion succeed but that
the idea had merit and they would therefore be delighted to
consider a treatment for a low-budget feature film.

Maybe this'll satisfy Martin, thought Kevin, folding up the
envelope and shoving it into his trouser pocket as he rose the
forty-three floors to see Caroline Walsh, a former actress and
his only contribution to Pat's list of contacts. Because he and
Caroline had once been lovers (for three weeks) he looked
forward to the meeting and, although he did not expect her to
treat his proposals more seriously than the others had, he did
believe she would break the bad news gently. As this was the
last one, Kevin felt a sense of abandon: this detour from his real
task (whatever that was) would soon be over.

So it drove him utterly spare when the voices made him
appear stupid in front of Caroline; he strengthened his resolve
not to listen to them, but then they nagged and pontificated with
such mind-numbing pain he was forced to excuse himself; he
staggered to the toilet and sat, waiting for the spell to pass. This
went beyond the fear of insanity: he just wanted it to stop – and
why was it always in silly rhymes?

It had started with a stray remark about how he didn't expect
to change the world with the play. Sweet words and agony:

The Goose, the Calf, the little Bee,
Are great on Earth I prove to thee,
And rule the great affairs of Man,
Explain this riddle if thou can.

He returned from the toilet resolved to plead with the voices if
need be for long enough to finish the interview. He had never
spoken back to them before, aside from expressing the desire
for them to end, for it seemed to lend them credence as people;
however, as he sat, smiling his best carefree one at the indulgent
and still-beautiful producer opposite:

> i could concoct a preservative for memory
> so that you won't be able to forget
> but imagine formaldehyde memories
> disintegrating in unlabelled glass jars
> anonymous & sickening & foetid as decay,
> you'd toss them out at the first opportunity
> & be glad to be rid of them.

All right, yes, I will listen to you! he shouted inside. Just let me
get this over with and I'm all yours, honestly – please, *please* let
me alone for a minute . . .

Silence. The pain in his head began to fade.

'. . . very good job on this.' Caroline Walsh picked up Kevin's
prospectus and dropped it gently on the blotter. 'For someone
who hasn't been in the business for a long time and never really
did any administration.'

'I had some help,' Kevin said.

'Yes.' Caroline smiled fondly at the reference to Pat. 'The
problem is,' she went on, looking Kevin in the eye in a way
which begged forgiveness for the decision she had been forced
to make, 'I can't afford to stage this. There are some good ideas,
but the script needs so much work, the cast is huge and it jumps
all over the place.'

Kevin nodded.

'It might make a better film,' she said, tilting her head thoughtfully, her earring touching her bare shoulder.

Caroline gave him a shortlist of familiar names (including Borovsky Studios, asterisked) then smoothly ushered him out, her wide, expressive mouth managing to leer and frown regretfully at the same time; before she kissed him goodbye she made him promise he'd ring her to make a date for a few drinks and a chat about old times, the lingering way she brushed him with the insides of her forearms as they broke apart suggested more than that, yet he realised in the elevator down that he would never see her again.

While he did care what came next, this strange fever had reached a stage past aggravation where every object (chrome ashtray full of sand, marble fascia, heat-sensitive carpet which displayed the fading footsteps of those before him in the foyer) stood out as if against a blank white backdrop; he revelled in the searing clarity, freed, freed into another stage in the development of this madness or whatever it was that bespoke a lessening of all this bullshit; explanations would come soon, he would be off again soon but now the time had come to revel in the excruciatingly superb weather before he headed out again, into the future. No, he didn't think a night with Caroline Walsh was part of it . . . no. *Never mind!* At last he felt in tune with the grins on everyone's faces and he grinned back for all he was worth.

What an absolute *rip-snorter* of a day!

At the pool, the voices sounded so far off he barely made them out against the shifting liquid sounds and shouts around him, as if whoever spoke inside his head had given volume up for clarity. His headache had not faded, though. It beat between his ears; it gave no pause. It didn't matter if the voices spoke or not. At first he worried that the pain wouldn't *ever* stop; he could not bear it and walk and talk as well. Drugs had no effect on it. Only floating, full alignment, eased it some. As he'd been taught in drama school, he breathed into the pain, contained it, and became more troubled by the questions raised now the voices spoke out clearly than by the prospect of continued agony.

Why should his blood be blue? It took performance to provoke the strange effects he remembered from *The Tempest*, and he had not performed for years. This was repeatable as well, and visible to others later on, as his experiment with the razor and the bathroom and the plastic bag had proven. No, what flowed within him really was electric blue. And why should this coincide with the visions fast becoming more than summer madness (or food for Gemma's thesis) round the world? Those had disturbingly familiar qualities ... He had no doubt the voices were no invention of his own, yet if not his then – whose? Martin, the old show-off, could never have resisted blabbing on and on about a psychic power had he possessed one.

As Kevin thought this, afloat upon his back in the bit of pool reserved for play, the voice said:

Call me Oscar.

He didn't have time to convey the rest of his instructions and explain too, Oscar told Kevin, but naturally he must be told. It would come to Kevin that night in a 'hypnagogic state', before sleep, as Kevin's own theory.

Like the notion of steaming on with Martin's plan to stage the play he wrote? thought Kevin. You were behind the urge to go ahead with the bulldust with producers when you knew I didn't have a hope in hell! Weren't you! What was that *for* if it wasn't a favour for a crook and rather silly mate?

Make no mistake, my old friend, the voice of Oscar tried to reassure him above the hiss within his head and as if from down a tunnel yonks away, **your theory will be correct. Everything you have done and will do is necessary, no matter how bizarre it might appear to you at the time. Now brace yourself.**

And while the water (which smelt of roses) was almost warm, Kevin shuddered, a gross, unnatural wracking that passed right through him several times like some pathetic animal's throes of death and, just when he thought it might have stopped, it slammed him once again with carnal violence, then bled away as nervous twitches down his limbs into his hands and finally his fingers, until he drifted, still, staring numbly at the painted letters, 'SHALLOW END – DO NOT DIVE' upside down, and at the empty blue above in a state more vacant than he had ever felt and yet utterly prepared for action.

Trust me. Please do not question my sources. Hindsight rules. Follow instructions to the letter.

With a rush of commands the voice that had seemed like Martin Leywood's made an urgent outline of Kevin Gore's course for the following months. How the instructions he had to obey would join up with his electric blood and with Martin's script and with the visions beginning to plague the world and visits to producers and *The Tempest* so long dead, Kevin could not think. He did trust Oscar. Not even out of the curiosity and sense of adventure which he thought had led him since his shortened lunch with Gemma. It was because he sensed his path would clear up what he'd left to fester in him all this time, the canker at the base of his intolerable fever: as a child he'd believed, mistakenly, that his father had been bonkers, and because of that his greatest fear was madness. If he didn't follow what this Oscar said it wouldn't make him any less insane; if he went along with it, it might just solve itself. His crazy uncle and eccentric father had built a fear of a family madness that had to be demolished. Fine, he would give up completely on Martin's play – that was necessary but over. Okay, he would do exactly as the voices told him. Yes, yes, *yes*! He would commit the crime.

TEN

He had been reared by the biggest landfill in the state so whenever he saw wilderness like this he half expected a hole full of garbage to be there when he looked around. Sometimes, as a joke on himself, Jay would spin his wheelchair suddenly to catch the gaping pit of old appliances, papers and nameless chemical gunk before it vanished. But this was Arizona and miles from any Dead Zone. The odd cactus, spiky grasses, and tough desert pines spread across the quiet, flat land beyond his golf course, the vapour trail of a test flight sliced pink across the blue above the distant mountains. He was about as far away from the last century and his father's glory days of opportunism disguised as liberal concern as he could get. Jay Schnarler was openly rich, celibate, retired, and bitter.

He wheeled away from the golf course under the power of his own arms down the path past the Bangladeshi gardener (whom he did not pretend to acknowledge) to the side patio, where he dismounted and swung easily on the bars to the bath. There he soaked, free from gravity and the need to be strong. After a simple meal of bean curd, vegetables and rice he rested in the induction field by the broad windows at the rear of the house, reading Balzac's *Splendeurs et misères des courtesanes* for the seventh time and glancing up at the glow of Phoenix now and then and rubbing his eyes, which still troubled him after the laser hosing he'd caught in Syria on that last CIA mission.

But it was another operation which scotched his pleasure at the machinations of Monsieur Vautrin. A minor thing, really, compared to wartime intelligence in a hostile country. He was used to the eyes, he could deal with the eyes and what he saw now as his overreaction to what was, after all, just a job. In his retirement he had worked it out, he thought. He had taken the same line as his mother had when she'd left his father to go back to her high-minded family on the north-west coast. Principles were principles, right or left. It was a rebellion against both his parents to work for the CIA in the first place. Yet the whole time he had actually been following his mother's trail because he had seen the CIA as steadfast defenders of democracy, of course from the opposite side to his mother's family. When the debacle in Syria had revealed the CIA's real concern, feathering its own nest, he had likened it to his father, who had been instrumental in creating the toxic Dead Zones at the same time as beating his breast about them and living nearby (but not too near) in order to 'share the suffering of the people' he supposedly was out to defend. Syria had been one vast Dead Zone, made that way by the CIA and kept that way in the guise of helping against the supposed villains. For the money from arms and drugs. Now he saw himself as freed from the need to make any point about his father's hypocrisy and wealth or his mother's principles and relative poverty. They were both dead anyway. But things he had done nagged him. The doctors said that theoretically he should have been able to walk again and scratched their heads; Jay attributed his disability to his Christian Scientist upbringing, which would have equated his problem to Error, curable by prayer and correct thinking since the wicked things he had done in his life were nothing before the power of Love. Jay did not believe in God, but he did believe in conditioning. It did not matter that his father's hokum about the Love of God had been insincere; it had sunk in. And so things like the Australian operation, Thoughtboost, and that Stranger woman's appeal offered the chance to ask God for the right path. Pure doodleflap, really. Tempting doodleflap, however. He was a cripple, yeah, but he was comfortable, rich enough through inheritance never to confront his state if he didn't want to. And strong: his arms were like damn tree stumps. And this induction field meant he could relax in midair all day if he chose. And he didn't give a shit about walking because he would have to go out and face the fucked-up world if he could walk.

He could also stroll through the desert at sunrise, feel the gravel churn beneath his soles, run if he wanted like he had done as a kid on the edge of the landfill with no busybody housekeeper growing concerned about him if he stayed out too long, run down the interstate to the diner for an unhealthy breakfast of ham and eggs and a stack with maple syrup all over it and eat in a booth or at the counter like anyone else without being not-stared-at, hitchhike to Phoenix and get himself laid by some sweet boy who did not have a thing for guys in wheel-chairs, some kid who would have been revolted by the thought, so full of shoot he could have picked any guy in the bar but had picked *him*, Jay Schnarler, for a night of sweat and nosing the pungent cracks, and the next day he could strike out home, go singing through the National Park and end the day with his sore feet up on the end of the couch and a beer in his hand, able to read this damn book without straying off in a hundred different directions to a past financed by drugs and powered by violence for its own sake, just like the terrorists they were supposed to have been against.

Jay told the lights to switch themselves off, tossed his book across the room and rocked forward so he'd be in a suitably devout position for prayer. He floated, hands clasped before his chest, eyes on the hard-edged stars, calling to a God he had put in its place at the age of nine.

And the Lord spoke.

For sure, not in so many words, He was more powerful, elemental than that. It was not the namby-pamby God of Love of his father's Christian Science, either; here the Lord of the Old Testament gave him a lesson in flames and blood, a warning of what Godlessness might bring about. Somehow, the actors in *The Tempest* had contacted the Devil.

Satan strode across the sky beyond the window on soles of cracked volcanic rock, lava seeping through the gaps in them, glowing round the edges as if the Devil's whole insides were of molten excrutiation. His face, too, showed the fallen Angel's pain, plumes of sulphurous gases spewed from around his widened eyes, from his flared nostrils as well as from that gaping pit with lips pulled back in rage and anguish filled with the naked and writhing Damned, his mouth. Here was the Evil spoken of by Jay's fundamentalist grandparents sketched incarnadine against the black of night. Horns and all, the once best-loved of Him rampaged past Jay's house famished for yet more unbelievers to scoop and swallow so that he might fill his armies against the coming day of battle with the Lord.

Jay knew he was prime fodder for the Devil. He stared up at the furious visage with its igneous jowls and mockery of a broad and noble forehead, at the muscular chest as wide as Hoover Dam, and the obsidian thighs which rippled sensuously with every massive, electric pace, and his mouth opened in a scream that although it made no sound set his own head alight with a ringing pain he could not escape from hours after his vision had passed. Jeremiah Schnarler, for the first time in an often dangerous life, knew terror.

As the Devil disappeared over the mountainous horizon Schnarler slewed sideways in the induction field so that the impregnated pads strapped to him, which by repulsion kept him afloat, passed beyond the field's influence and he dropped to the carpet with a painful thump. Never mind, it was nothing compared to the pain in his head. He dragged himself behind the bar and lay peeping around its corner at the speck of angry red, panting like a cornered gopher, until it dwindled to another twinkling star, then nothing.

Schnarler bore down on his fear and tried to prise the whole vivid horror open to winkle out its meaning. If, when he and Rolf had used the Thoughtboost device to destroy that

Australian theatre company, some message had been sent after all (that *was* the purpose of the device and what he and Rolf had used was a side effect) – who knew where the message had gone? So, what guys around the world were seeing in their breakfast cereal and so forth and what he himself had now witnessed was a prefiguring of the havoc to come. No one would be prepared for it because the damned CIA was obsessed with secrecy. Schnarler was one of the few who knew the complete story and the only one who could see where it was going. It was up to him to do something. When the CIA woke up to what was happening around the world their only concern would be for their own survival: they would eliminate anyone who could not be trusted with the truth, who was likely to be believed when the public looked for an explanation for the visions. Of course that meant Schnarler, but also Gore and Leywood. And Schnarler would need them both to corroborate his own story.

Lying on the carpet, his cheek pressed to the teak panelling of the bar beside him, Jay Schnarler planned a trip to Australia. Tomorrow morning would not be soon enough. But he was confident: at last he had a clear-cut evil to fight; at last the Lord was on his side.

It did not occur to him that he had seen anything but the Devil.

ELEVEN

from
Charms All O'erthrown

Between the floorboards and up the rake it seeped and curled like vagrant dreams of the continent below, so beautiful an effect in the dying light that for a second I admired, dumb. Then the flames leapt up so quickly I found myself on stage without knowing how I got there, yelling, 'Fire!' too late. People hurtled in all directions, Robert swung and flicked the centre webline at a frantic Pete who missed it each time, iron specks from Robert's drill work shot sparks through the flames in green and blue which lent a festive air to the scene. I decided I was useless gawping here and ran to help form a bucket line from the creek. As I took and gave the buckets and billies and foodbins my eyes were fixed on Pete. He lashed at the fire with his feet, still not reaching the line, in a kind of dance with the inferno which now reached out to take him.

He glowed.

This was not from burning or Greek ancestry. Like molten gold his body gave a flat reply to the flames, his clothes lit up like stockings over a lamp, the only dark parts were his hair and eyes and teeth. As if he clasped the cheers of some spectral crowd to his breast he reached out into the air again and again in slow motion, a kind of ecstasy on his face. My hands snatched bucket after bucket and my mind asked with dull repetition to match, *why doesn't he jump?*

Who else saw Pete a-glow? Whites showed in the whole line's

eyes, which could have been just the fire. Kevin had a steady
bead on Gill – who was firing bursts from an extinguisher – so I
hoyed him, gesturing up with my chin. For once his deadpan
face let rip: his mouth fell open; he twitched; he glanced back
down at Gill in a state of alarm.

Then it rained! Not enough to matter to the fire, though; the
shower came and went as fast as inspiration. Droplets spattered
Kevin's neck and made him jerk again. The sky was utterly
cloudless! When we turned back to Pete the fire was gone. I
wept with relief to see him slumped forward into Gill's embrace,
the harness's cord a tangle on his back. Steam ascended around
their feet.

'Keep going!' Kevin shouted to the others in the line. 'It may
not be out yet!'

We poured water on the stage till it gave off no more steam.
Robert, Gill, Dave and Sherelle carried Pete away. As soon as
Kevin let us know it was over I dropped my bucket and ran to
the kitchen tent after them.

Pete lay on a trestle table, which wobbled. He shivered,
hyperventilated; he tried to rise. Gill gently pushed him flat.

He looked untouched.

'Ught!' Pete's eyes snapped open, wild, they darted around.

Gill whispered, 'You're all right possum.'

'I . . . Did I black out?'

'The cream!' young Sherelle announced, pushing through the
door.

'I feel fine,' said Pete, in a simple way. Again he shivered, and
was calm.

'There's enough for most of you; it'll do until the flying doctor
gets here,' Gill told him. 'We'll have to cut your clothes off.'

'Me *shorts*! No! I feel okay!' On to one elbow he rose,
pushing Gill back when she placed her hands on his shoulders.

He really was okay.

Kevin, Robyn and I sat by a camp fire on the other side of the
stage from the kitchen tent. With the sky still perfectly clear, a

starry mass helped calm us. Our backs froze and our fronts roasted, as usual. Now that the fuss had died away, the native beasties ventured forth and we were soothed by small hopping footfalls, occasionally a pair of yellow eyes at the shifting light's perimeter. Whichever spirits dwelt in the rocks had decided the one to cop all the smoke was myself, also as usual.

A crunching approached, a silhouette so broad it could only be Gill – or Packett.

'Speak of the critic,' said Kevin, though no one had mentioned him for some time.

Humph, went Packett as he dropped to the other end of Robyn's log.

The fire crackled. We listened.

Said Robyn: 'Maybe it'd be better for everybody if you went home.'

'That's bullshit, Robyn,' said Kevin, pleasantly enough.

'He's quite right, Ms Ho,' Packett said. 'Whatever occurs here is not my responsibility. This company ought to be taking the proper precautions where fire is concerned.'

Kevin snapped, 'I said I don't believe in this superstitious crap but that doesn't mean it's open slather on the company, Packett.'

Conciliatory, I put in, 'Perhaps it would be better for everyone, regardless of the truth, if you did leave.' My sharp tones, however, surprised me.

'I shan't argue with that.' His orbits, underlit, looked more worn, more piggish, than usual. 'But as to the truth – simple carelessness. The stories about Stanopoulos are . . .' He trailed off and stared for a moment into the fire as if hypnotised. 'They are the result of superstition.'

'Virtually everyone saw what happened,' I stated quietly.

'It might have been electrical, I suppose.'

Really, Robyn? I thought. She looked dejected, her muscular forearms cradling her breasts, shoulders hunched.

'That was no electrical fire,' Kevin said. 'Enzo checked the wiring under the stage, what there is of it. No shorts, nothing even touched. There was hardly any fire at all.'

Packett's port-red lips fell open. 'But the flames went right up to the rig!'

'Then you did see Pete!' I said.

'I saw him.'

'You saw everything,' said Kevin. He seemed about to spit.

'I don't know why you don't go home.' Robyn's voice convinced me, for a second; her conviction seemed grounded in a rational set of apprehensions. Then I thought: she can't be so superstitious, it must be the group she fears for.

'I should think that was obvious, Ms Ho.'

'I have a name. It's Robyn.'

'Robyn, I am a journalist. You for one are worth coming to this God-forsaken place for, alone. In only, what – two years? – you have come from nowhere to—'

'I came from New Zealand.'

'—you came from nowhere to become the most sought-after actress in the country. And not for nothing, too—'

Robyn was neither amused nor flattered by this alcoholically smooth rubbish: 'Look, everybody knows you hate Dave's guts, Packett, so why?' ('My name is John,' he said.) 'Why do you want to do a hatchet job on something that's gunna die in the bum anyhow? For fuck's sake just leave us alone!'

Looking off to one side, Packett took a deep breath. He glanced up, fearfully it seemed, then made a decision. Contempt filled his words, recklessness; he suddenly sounded more drunk than before. 'I do not dislike Dave. We have known each other for years. I have not arrived with any preconceptions of . . . of any kind. When I believe . . . a piece of theatre to have merit or to be of *any* possible interest, I attempt to explain why. Over the past years Dave and I have disagreed about the direction of Australian theatre . . . Or rather *I* have believed in a direction for the theatre and Dave has *attempted* several directions at once. This . . . Well, obviously I cannot outline my point of view for you in one evening,' he finished condescendingly.

'He's stuck the knife into anything and everything,' said

Kevin. 'Do you blame it on your wife or is that why she left you?'

Pause.

I sat dreading the counterattack. The smoke tormented me but I refused to cough. I looked at Robyn; she wore a look of profound, perhaps fatalistic despair: an effect of the firelight, perhaps. When the tirade came, it started soft. It convinced me Packett had gone utterly mad from frustration, the barbs of vengeful actors, from gin, his marriage break-up – whatever, it seemed to have no connection with reality.

'You poor bastards . . . You follow that Froot Loop out here into the wilderness.' He was sucked down into himself, the outskirts of his mass held no life, were completely still. 'It's one huge conspiracy . . . As usual the talent are the last to know what's going on. Everybody else knows but you, that slimy Enzo, Sarah bloody sexpot Witchell, the tart. I'm not exactly sure what it's about but I mean to find out. You crazy hippies, he's fucking around with your minds – he should be *stopped*! I'm sure it's drugs . . . I know a thing or two about sweet *Dave* and his doings in the sixties. There's a file on him, I'm sure, there's a file on the lot of them. This is not *theatre* it's a bloody parody of art a bloody joke but it's not funny when innocent people get hurt, you think it's me . . . it's not and I can prove it. I should stop him. I should smash his bloody drugs, burn 'em all . . .' Now he trembled and every part of his body wobbled as he ranted: 'I *shall* stop him!'

He tilted forward, rising to his feet; I braced for a stumble into the fire or past it on to me, but he thrust one boot out and propped on it.

Humph, he went. He turned and lumbered away.

'Well, well!' Kevin raised an eyebrow. 'What did that mean, kids?'

Robyn gave an exasperated wail. 'Why don't you just set fire to everything and be finished with it, Kevin?' She launched herself into the dark and strode off in a fury. So that was it: she reckoned it had been arson, care of Packett.

We rested our ears.

The light breeze shifted; I escaped the smoke. Kevin dug his Ruby Champion from his shirt pocket and began to roll a 'greyhound'.

'You did that on purpose,' I said.

'Well, it was no bloody accident. The word is "calculated". And whether or not he did anything before he's going to do something now. And we're going to catch him, cobber, and get rid of him.' He gestured with the half-rolled cigarette. Tobacco flew off into the fire and caught.

'I guess that's why Robyn was mad at you.'

'She wants him to leave and she thinks she can just ask him. Or could. So, let's go.' With some finality he licked his thin smoke shut.

'Go where?'

'Some place near his Portable Palace, then when he comes out to do his dirty work we turn on the lights and nab him.'

'A stake-out.'

'Too right.' He lit up.

'A bit melodramatic, dear.'

'It will get us shot of him; I can't think of a better way.'

'We could simply ask Dave. What happens when we get back to Melbourne? What's to stop him writing what he likes about us?' I caught a whiff of aromatic tobacco on the nervous wind.

'That's the beauty of it. We can threaten to have him arrested if he writes a word. He couldn't tell much of a story without describing his part in it. I mean, Dave – you know him, he always gives you the benefit of the doubt, he'd be too nice. We could offer Packett the right to document the rehearsal process as a peacemaking gesture, after he's sobered up, but he knows he'd be ruined if he went to court. I mean, a critic can't go round sabotaging shows on the strength of some hard words and suspicions. He'll be so humiliated he won't say a word.'

Kevin grinned, a sight which made me realise why he didn't often do more than smile faintly in mixed company.

'What do you think he's going to do?'

'Something illegal, I'm sure.'

'He didn't have anything to do with the fire.'

'Noo. I don't know what happened there.' He stood and stretched his whole bony person, pushing his elbows back like wings, fists clenched. 'But maybe we might find out a bit about that tonight.

'Let's go,' he said. He started toward the dining tent, stopped, dropped his cigarette end and scrunched it out with that characteristic thrust of the hips. He had a glint in his eye; he always looked happiest up to no good. 'Well come on, ya gutless grogan!' He sounded like a schoolboy getting his courage up for a prank.

I stood and followed.

TWELVE

Kevin Gore rose early the next morning. After a short swim at the local pool to clear his mind, he sat drinking sweet black coffee, elbows and stringy forearms on the bar, thinking. He sat very still. He felt fine.

While the galahs left their roosts to feed and the starlings shut up, the day grew warmer. Sherelle emerged from the house to hang floral sheets and pillowcases on the hoist, transforming it into a large tent. Gore remained at the bar. Doves called. He got up only to make more coffee. Now and then he rolled a thin smoke.

Beside his makings, ringed by coffee and covered in tobacco crumbs, a large sheet of paper showed his effort at a man's face. Curly hair ending in long muttonchops, stubble, deep-sunk eyes, heavy eyebrows on a thick bump of bone and a very large, pointed nose. He wore a permanent scowl. There was also a drawing of a car's engine in cross-section. Made with more precision than the face, it was hardly to scale. But it would do.

At eleven forty-five Gore went into the bedroom and dressed in a new, conservatively cut suit. Into the pockets he dropped his car keys, bankdisk, wallet, a blank envelope, a scrap of paper with bus times on it, and a comb. He rummaged through his leather duffel bag until he found his granddad's gold watch. Thirty-seven years of service to the railways. After winding it and setting the time by the radio alarm he strapped it on. Then he went to the mirror and stared at himself for a few minutes before leaving.

The suburban bank was filled with lunchtime trade. He queued and kept to himself. At the counter he deposited the cheque from his last job and withdrew every available dollar: two thousand. From the business account he withdrew four hundred and sixty-seven more. Using his disk he obtained a cash advance of seven hundred dollars, his limit for daily transactions without approval. Almost all the money was in two hundred dollar notes. He thanked the teller, smiling faintly, then left.

The Collingwood Café was run by an Indian-Fijian refugee, a very tall man who carried his fat in neat packets. Two Lebanese boys played an ancient pinball machine in the back corner, pounding it with their small fists, shoving it from side to side, yet barely able to see over its top edge. Outside the traffic growled continuously down six lanes.

Gore leaned across the counter. The man had his back turned, frying orders of barracuda, shark and chips. A stack of potato cakes sat beside the fish, ready to go.

''Scuse me.'

The café owner gave the chips a shake and turned. He had an open, friendly face. He looked like a kind father.

'What can I do for you, sir?'

'I'm a friend of Oscar's.'

The man looked down, ashamed.

'He told me you might be able to help me. With a car.'

'A car.'

'Which nobody owns.'

'Property is theft.' He smiled shyly at his own joke, reached over to a jar full of pencils below the counter and wrote a phone number with an area code on a corner of white fish and chip paper, which he tore off and slid across the marbled laminex.

'Ask for Max. He should be able to fix you up.'

'Thanks.'

'Don't mention it.'

Gore went out to his car. He drove to the public phone by the railway station and tapped out the number. It was a brief conversation. He wrote the address and directions under the phone number, his own lazy scrawl cheerful against the tight, spidery Indian's handwriting.

And you're not so happy either, he thought. Mr Metalhead.

He checked the car (it would be safe, parked by the cop shop) then caught the next train into the city.

When he arrived at the industrial estate on the north-western outskirts of town he found the address given eluded him. However, he did not ask directions but sat for a while consulting his hopelessly out-of-date street directory in the shade of the only tree in sight, a paperbark. Eventually he decided that the streets which previously had numbers were the same ones which bore the names of Aboriginal dreamtime wanderers. This was Numbat Man Avenue, therefore he wanted Two Lizards Drive. Those at the other end of the phone must have had the same street directory as him . . .

It did not bear thinking about.

The car was parked next to an almost-completed factory. It started first try. He checked the brakes and compression, not bothering with the gearbox but noting that the old Ford's steering was close to perfect. In the glovebox were papers which said it belonged to a George Shearing. Gore slipped an envelope with one thousand dollars in it under the factory's side door.

Driving through the city on his way to the north-east, he realised that the car would take an off-hand inspection but a closer look would reveal it to be largely well-disguised rust. He drove carefully.

In an unofficial dump in the hills beyond suburbia he parked the car amongst the burnt-out shells of several others and threw some corrugated iron, weedy chicken wire and ashes on the roof; he placed a large metal pipe across the bonnet, locked the doors and steering, and walked away toward the nearest railway station. He hoped kids would not discover it before his return.

A few days would be enough.

*

That night he cooked a simple meal and went to bed early. Undisturbed sleep came quickly.

The next morning Kevin Gore spent shopping in town. He visited the Centre City Pharmacy (still the best place for make-up), several footware shops, an electrical goods store, and finally the State Library. By the time he reached the enquiries counter he felt sticky and worn-down. The pleasant spell seemed set to break; temperatures had risen into the forties; humidity would begin to climb soon; for now a baking north wind parched the throat and kicked dust into the eyes as the trams whirred by. Kevin felt like nothing but a beaded glass of beer in an air-conditioned pub. However, a busy afternoon of waiting lay ahead and he had to set up a purchase for tomorrow after this, else he might, he had been told, have to wait until next week.

Which would be cutting it fine.

The man who emerged blinking from the labyrinthine stacks appeared to enjoy playing the unworldly librarian. Sporting a sky blue pink bow tie and the John Lennon glasses unavoidable last century, he met Gore as if happening upon a sea slug of rather distasteful habit in his teacup.

'You want to look at the Blake collection.' He turned away from Gore slightly, eyeing him over the top of the glasses. There was something missing behind those eyes.

'Songs of Innocence.'

'And who, might I ask, recommended me to you?' he asked in a friendly way.

'Uh, a man I play billiards with. Oscar, his name is.'

'I see. Come this way.'

Gore was led in silence down a corridor and into a room which could have been any size, since he could not see past the shelves housing untidy piles of dusty books. After many turns down this narrow path into forgotten history they reached a clearing where the busts of men once famous poked out of cardboard boxes or lay sadly on their cheeks.

'Here.'

Gore stopped. The librarian with something missing went to

the corner where he pulled aside some thick quartos, then lifted three boxes which had held Skipping Girl Vinegar and Velvet Soap a long time ago and laid them carefully one beside the other to his right. Beneath them was a stack of yellowed newspapers, the top of which he peeled back to reveal a long, new box.

He gestured at it with a slender white hand. His eyebrows questioned.

Gore crossed and knelt. He lifted one end of the box and pulled it open. He drew out its contents, laying them across his knee.

An antique. A two-four-three Husquevana with a free-floating Seiko barrel. There were no sights of any kind.

Gore removed the small magazine. He released the safety. He flipped the bolt up and back to look at the rifling. It had a jewel-finished Winchester action. A hunting rifle.

'Of course it ought to be stripped down, but it should prove true.'

'Sights?'

'Yes. American. And what kind of cartridges do you require?'

Gore told him. Since Oscar was gagged by an ominous static, he had to trust what the voices said: he'd think of the right items on the spot. The librarian got everything from the appropriate dusty nook. And each new box – each accessory Kevin could never have imagined he might buy here, from this bloke he'd never met before – brought relief. It meant he was not insane. They were real, cool and heavy in his hands, and had only come to him through Oscar. The name seemed to open doors to weapons and cars and who knew what else in an underground Melbourne Kevin could never have believed existed. It'd take a fair amount of research to find this one little cache, he thought.

The librarian received the envelope Kevin gave him with a small, tight smile, and committed the address Kevin came up with to memory without apparent effort, as if he rented out and picked up weapons the whole time. Perhaps he did, thought Gore.

It did not bear thinking about. Kevin left. When he stepped out on to the oven-like street he saw that peak hour had already begun. He walked briskly to the nearest pub for a short glass of bitter, which he downed in a few gulps.

It tingled as pleasantly in his throat as it had ever done before. Why shouldn't it?

The man with the long curly hair ending in muttonchops, with the pointed nose and wild simian eyebrows, bounced into Commonwealth Industrial Gases as if listening to the personal stereo knocking at his hip. This the shop assistant remembered later, as well as the beer pot barely covered by his orange T-shirt, as well as the boil beside his huge nose. Which was a beauty.

He even remembered the colour of the hairs around the moron's bellybutton, ha, ha. Yes, they were the same ruddy colour as his curly mop, maybe a tiny bit darker, so it couldn't have been a wig on his head. Yes, he was an observant fellow. Always glad to help the police with their enquiries. Call again if you need anything else. Thank you.

The man who bought the liquid helium and various fittings, who loped in with intense eyes elsewhere (on drugs, no doubt), who had the appropriate papers (or at least good forgeries) and signed his name George Shearing, looked several kilos heavier and many centimetres taller than Kevin Gore.

Despite its sloppiness the operation stood up all right under scrutiny. Provided the scrutineer had the operation's safety in mind rather than discipline for its own sake. The boys and girls always broke for lunch at the same time, but did so at different places on each occasion. Probably more from a desire for variety than anything else. Their movements in general showed little predictability. This resulted from horseplay instead of adherence to procedure.

Most of it did not matter to Gore. It did provide alleviation from the boredom of watching others work. What exhausted him most was the need to concentrate on details without an idea of what might prove important later. Although 'Oscar' had given him enough information, Kevin was nervous. He followed at a safe distance, dividing their journey into convenient sections which he examined using different modes of transport for each and – twice – different appearances. One day he followed them by tram, another by bicycle. He even chatted to one of them in a pub after work.

Without pumping her he found out quite a lot. The amount necessary would be carried on almost any day of the week, so the figure he had been given for a Friday was probably correct. Why wouldn't it be? thought Gore dressed as George Shearing as he strolled past the armoured car. Everything else had proven true. The woman – Ros – whom Gore had shouted a beer at the HIV bar cast a glance at the ancient hippy standing in front of the videophone display window.

That was the bloke who tried to pick me up!

Gore could see the look of recognition flit across Ros's face. He also saw the desire to greet him, and the stifling of that impulse by the armed flunky persona, in her reflection in the window. Gore concentrated on the recorded message being played over the videophones. You were invited to scrawl your message over an image culled from TV, in this case the King of England in tears after a vision had converted him to Catholicism. Though confident Ros had not penetrated his disguise, Kevin felt chilled, deep below George Shearing's belly.

Now all he had to do was wait. Cooped up in the flat, the humidity, at tropical levels already, maddened: it threatened to break, yet thick day followed sticky night without so much as a patter of rain. Kevin couldn't remember it getting so bad when he was a kid. He took to spending most of the morning at the local pool, which was programmed to cool as the day grew warmer. He read no papers, watched no television, listened to no radio and spoke to nobody. In that way it felt a lot like his isolated childhood: he'd hear talk on the street of, say, the army being brought out in India over sightings of Shiva and Krishna, or see an executive weeping in the milk bar. Then he didn't have contact with the world because his father banned it; now it was Kevin who wanted to keep his mind free. The effect was the same. The more excluded he was from major events, the less he wanted to know. Especially about this. He visited cinemas in the afternoons (at least they were cool) and went to bed early.

He felt contented and secure in this separation. If he could not see the world then the world might not see him. He read a little, children's books from the local secondhand shop, but the humidity restricted his reading to times when he could not sleep, and dulled him even then. Partway through the second week he grew bored. Some constructive act was needed. He knew of a place where he could test the rifle without arousing suspicion. He was tempted to accept Oscar's judgement on the matter (had 'Oscar' been some underworld figure?) but that would be taking trust too far. He'd go after he'd stripped it down and put an oily rag through it. The walk would do him good.

Weapons and precision camera engineering have a great deal in common. Gore was looking at the countertop of rifle parts thinking about the similarities of camera crews and hunting parties when the door chirped. He shouted, 'Coming!' while he wrapped the various bits in their yellow and grey stained bags and stuffed them into cupboards and drawers around the kitchen, sweating. Lucky he had just baked a quiche to take with him; it would mask the smell of gun oil.

It was Gemma. Her broad, slightly pink face was shiny with perspiration. She carried no bag this time but still wore a boat-necked dress, possibly a different one. It, too, was moist. Kevin, shocked by unbidden fantasies about the feel of her body against his, of his lips against her ear, her collarbone, the smell of her hair, stood in daft surprise. He wondered how many boat-necked dresses she owned, and whether they were all in shades of blue. He wondered for the seventy-seventh time why her friends called her 'Budge'. He wanted to smooth the deep lines of her forehead with his tongue!

'We had a date. I just called by to see what's become of you.'

What I've become. Gore stepped back and let her in with a nod. *I'm still not quite sure what's become of me.*

'So. How's it going?' They stood awkwardly by the door.

'What?'

'What. Ah-huh. The play?'

'It's not.'

'You can't get the money?'

'No.'

'Well – I came to make you an offer. I have some I inherited and I haven't got any aim of settling down. I might as well invest it – I might even get a return! It's – it's yours if you want it. If someone else takes the plunge they might look on it with different eyes.'

Kevin started to answer, then stopped. He had to appear interested. He got up.

'Coffee?'

'Thanks.'

'How much?' he asked as he crossed to the cupboard where the cafetière lived. She wouldn't recognise the bolt – besides, it was wrapped in a rag. Completely, he hoped.

'Thirty thousand dollars.'

Before he could stop it hope shot through him. It would cover the wages bill and more besides. The nerves he had stomped on clamoured for release, and he shuddered, despite the heat. 'How long—?' Then, in a quieter voice, 'How long would it take to get it?' he asked, which he regretted, but he couldn't think of anything else to say.

'About ninety days.' Gemma leaned toward him, squinting as if to see better. 'I could give you a letter saying you've got it, which'll be good enough for the powers that be.'

Kevin opened the cupboard. 'Yeah, I suppose so.'

He took the brewer out slowly. He closed the cupboard, then put the brewer down on the counter. Her face remained puzzled at his reaction, only that.

'Gemma. Thanks for the offer . . . I couldn't take the money.

You've read Martin's writing. It — well, it doesn't translate well on to the stage. Everyone who might have taken it up has already refused it. I'm going to see Martin this afternoon. We've had a try, it was something between him and me. We were quite good friends back then, but we've both got to live in the present. I've shown him that I do care enough to try. It's all I can do; I reckon it'll mean *something* to him.'

'But you can rehearse for a work-in-progress with what I've got, then with all this stuff in the news nowadays you're bound to get backing for a full-scale show!' The flush on her face and slender neck had deepened.

'Thanks. I really appreciate the offer, but Martin'll be cut up enough after *this*. I'd destroy him if I raised his hopes then dumped them: nobody but you will connect what happened to Pete and that with this vision business . . . And besides, thirty thousand doesn't go nearly far enough these days.'

'Oh. Well. I just—'

'I know. It's very kind of you to offer. I mean it's more than kind. I mean — you're amazing.

Kevin put on the kettle to hide the double meaning of his words. They talked about some of the movies he had seen. He asked her about the university, her professors. They drank the coffee, sweating. She started to tell him about the visions people were seeing and he changed the subject, saying he'd ring her to make another date for a drink. She left.

On his way to the car he met Sherelle. Fortunately he'd already packed the gun. He told her he was off for some country air. He had a few people to see, and if nothing came of them he'd go home for the weekend. He thanked her profoundly for the use of the granny flat. She was apologetic about not popping in to see him more, but her amateur company was doing *A Streetcar Named Desire* and she was Blanche.

'That's all right,' Kevin said. 'We'll get together for a drink before I go, I'm sure.'

In a pig's eye, he thought. Two sessions of lying were enough.

*

On the morning of the show Gore opened his eyes on the most muggy day he'd met this side of Darwin. Regardless, he dropped out of bed on to all fours and began a Salute to the Sun, to limber up for the 'performance'. Sherelle's garden looked exhausted. A gull, panting, walked past the window as if the air, heavy with temperature inversion, was too thick to fly through; it eyed him suspiciously, then waddled away, plainly without patience for the antics of humans.

The old alchemy necessary for a successful show had begun its demands the previous day. Suddenly a plain meal of steak and rice and lightly steamed vegetables became *vital*. Sleep with the sheets tucked in *just so* was all that would do. He had ignored the nervous impulse to switch on the television: he didn't want a 'hangover'. A bowel movement before bed was a positive sign. This morning: coffee and plenty of toast, eggs and bacon would allow a light, easily digestible lunch later. He did not want a belly swaying about during the show.

At seven a.m. he began to apply the make-up. By eight fifteen he was George Shearing without the hair, stomach, elevators or clothes. In the new grey suit he went from bungalow to car – a risk of two metres – carrying two bags, one light, one very heavy. He left the Volkswagen at Malvern Station and proceeded by train out to Dandenong, the end of the suburban line. By bus it was forty minutes to one stop past the dump where the Ford was hidden. At ten forty-five he set off for the city centre again.

This, however, took longer than it would normally, since he turned left into a track which looked unused, to complete the disguise. George Shearing stopped to pick up a lunch at a wholefood takeaway in Hawthorn. There he blended in with the unkempt mob in the streets, and it was a short drive to the South-Eastern Freeway. He lingered over lunch, sitting in the car in a busy road used by few pedestrians, then drove to the busiest petrol station in the area for a full tank, paid to the exact amount in cash.

It was three p.m. by the time George Shearing made for what

Gore imagined was George's penultimate destination: a service road by a brothel overlooking the middle of the South-Eastern Freeway. The area was hardly frantic during the day. His was the only car parked by the plastic barrier. Some things never changed in Melbourne, only the locations. There had used to be factories here, then a government attempt at cheap inner-city housing had been sold. Several chains of brothels had bought houses here and it had been declared an official red-light district. Sweatshop to knockshop, thought Gore, looking into the car's mirror to check his make-up for damage.

Fine. The traffic was building up for peak hour. In twenty minutes it would be alive but far from impossible. Gore flexed his feet and toes, part of a Japanese yoga routine, to keep himself alert. He placed the make-up remover and towel ready in its bag on the passenger seat. He unfastened the end of the long cardboard box containing the rifle and positioned it so he could remove the gun stock first in one stroke to where it could be thrust through the window cleanly. He looked at his watch. He sweated and waited.

It was a good thing he had tested the gun. Its inaccuracy had shaken him. If those directing him through this could get that wrong they might have gotten other things wrong too. It was a short step from doubting their judgement to branding it delusion. And if Oscar was crap (feverish, he'd accepted Oscar, with his crime and that, in order to stop the *insane feeling*, and now it had subsided he shied at any thought of the outlandish theory supplied 'as his own' which said this would solve *all* his personal problems, in the finish) then there had to be some other reason for pent-up rage and this result of armed robbery. During the twenty-minute wait he thought about his life and realised he had plenty of good reasons to go insane. His father's silence for one. Kevin had worshipped Clarry Gore and in imitation had hated his mother. He had developed the same angry pauses and inflicted them on his mother in the same way. And yet Clarry's reasons for hating his wife Susan had never been spelt out; the man had been as silent with his son as with anyone else. The small, leathery railwayman had been so silent it wasn't even clear that he *had* hated his wife.

Although he had been through this before, Kevin felt his sweaty discomfort intensify as he flushed with guilt. He could smell the linoleum kitchen, see it dingy and green and fly-specked yellow, his mother turned away to look out across the other cheap weatherboard houses as she pretended to busy herself at the sink, hiding her hurt from her truculent son once again. It needn't have been that way. She did tell me, over and over, and I never listened. She died, and I never wept.

His watch said four twenty. Gore drew out the gun. He took aim using the door as a rest, the leather strap wrapped about his left hand and wrist. Then he relaxed somewhat. Nothing yet. By four twenty-four he was getting worried. Perhaps they were caught in the traffic somewhere. He could not afford to be seen with the gun just yet. Almost absently, he began to hum the Fairie's Lullaby from *A Midsummer Night's Dream*. But he was Puck, the trickster . . . Ah, never mind that it wasn't his song, that the rest of the cast hadn't arrived yet. He was warming to his part and they certainly wouldn't be miffed if they missed out on the action. He began to sing.

The armoured van sped into view and he sang with all his soul, the adrenaline and the other performance hormones − or their equivalent in this renovated body − surged. He sang to his prey with the soaring joy and mischief of Puck, fool and practical joker, servant and fairy. The rifle barrel followed the van's engine as Gore/Shearing/Puck squeezed the trigger gently, the sights' crosshairs centred where the armour-piercing bullet would find its way to the distributor. A simple shot with this engine. There was a sharp crack, the rifle kicked but Gore followed through, ready for a second shot.

None was necessary. Still singing, Puck pulled the rifle back and dropped it on the passenger side floor and leapt from the car, keeping his eyes on the slowing armoured van. God knew what the guards were seeing right now. Bunyips, angels on pinheads, perhaps. Not enough to make them crash, anyhow.

Puck swung the two cloth bags over the railing and ran down the bushy verge to the emergency stopping lane. This was the most dangerous part, when passing motorists might notice a loony on the road and have their snits call the police, but Puck capered along the road, the upper half of him swaying, he sang, a one-man corroboree of sleep:

> Philomel with melody,
> Sing in our sweet lullaby:
> Lulla, lulla, lullaby; lulla, lulla, lullaby:
> Never harm, nor spell, nor charm,
> Come our lovely lady nigh;
> So, good-night, with lullaby.

It was pleasant for the voice to be his, at last. He reached the van, unzipping the heavy bag. He pulled out a crowbar and opened the passenger side door. If the guards were not asleep it was too late anyhow . . .

They were out.

Gore climbed up, reached across and unclipped the keys from Ros's belt then ran to the rear door. Inside, the guard lay on his side, snoring. Suddenly, it grew almost dark. Startled, Gore looked up. Dark clouds bellied over the city. Very dramatic, he thought, and climbed in over the guard. He unzipped one bag and drew out the apparatus attached to the helium canister and fixed it to the top of the safe. He switched it on. Then he took out a sawn-off sledgehammer, removed the helium outlet and struck at the acid-proof, drill-proof, laser-proof, explosive-proof safe. Which shattered, beading a little like a car windscreen. Gore removed only the notes. Then he turned to go, but something grabbed him by the ankle.

The guard was awake. Gore ignored the clutching hands and grabbed the revolver on the guard's belt. This did not come easily since it was a buttoned-down pouch. He tugged, at the wrong angle. It would not come, and the guard was waking fully. Desperately, Gore wrenched at another angle. The gun jerked free and out of his grip. It flew out of the back door into the angry twilight.

The guard continued to hold him fast. There came a groan from the other guard. Gore struck at the hands with his fist. It was enough to loosen the grip. The guard bleated and Gore slithered on to the gravel at the freeway's edge.

He stumbled to his feet and up the grassy slope at the same time. The air had chilled. He did not have long. Perhaps it was already too late. The bag with the money in it was like part of his arm. He swung it over the freeway barrier then fell over after it. He got up and ran headlong into the closed car door.

It stunned him. He grabbed the handle and pulled, forgetting to press the release.

'Shit!' The first drops of rain struck the back of his neck.

He opened the door and threw himself in.

He turned the key.

It did not start.

He pumped the accelerator. It did not start.

A police siren sounded in the distance, faint in the growing storm. He had flooded the carburettor; there was nothing he could do but wait. He toyed with the idea of an escape on foot. He cursed himself for an idiot.

The siren grew louder. Others joined it.

THIRTEEN

from
Charms All O'erthrown

White Primus light spilled through the gaps in Packett's small marquee and we could hear his wheezes and the scuffle of crêpe against canvas as he bumbled about inside, so we retired to the nearby Boys' Room where an effervescent Pete, declared fit by a flying doctor (who'd been sworn to secrecy) and clearly relieved he still had all his bits, trounced a few dollars out of us at poker. In shock and enthusiasm, a mild Greek accent emerged, making him sound more boyish than ever.

'I've never felt anything like it.' He wore the blue truckie's singlet and red shorts and his nearly hairless torso radiated nothing but *joi de vivre*. 'Man, it was like tripping – the fire made m'muscles buzz when it touched me. And I heard voices!'

'What kind of voices? What did they say?' asked Don.

It makes me laugh, looking back on it, that this rabid communist dinosaur should have shown such interest in the supernatural. I was too anxious for laughter at the time.

'Americans! They were fucking septics! It was like one of those shuttle take-offs, you know?' He formed a megaphone with his hands: 'Kchshsht – stepping up DBT kchshsht – eep!' He laughed. 'But the main thing was the fire. The voices were really soft, like through a wall – the colours! Man!'

Pete babbled, spurred on by Don's questions. We sipped our beers while most of the others (Robyn had retired, thank God) went from merry to loud. Kevin snaffled a seat by the tent flap, from which he could observe Packett's abode.

I play a terrible card game because I am the kind of actor whose presence is large despite himself, an asset when immersed in a part but when the script is life my whole body is the mirror of my soul. I bite lips and blush and squirm – in short, I broadcast what I hold. Kevin's only sign of our little intrigue was that he smoked each slim cigarette to the end without letting it go out; my nervousness decimated my control so utterly I won nothing and lost a great deal, even by my standards. When Kevin gave our agreed-upon signal – a huge yawn – I all but fell off my chair. He tossed me an amused glance as he turned to go. Indignant, I sighed as casually as I could and said yes, sleep sounded just the ticket, wondering what people thought of this terrible piece of impro, hoping they were too drunk to notice.

It took a while for my eyes to adjust to the darkness, during which I stumbled several times as we skirted the tents in pursuit of the journalist. Kevin would silently outpace me without difficulty, so that I would find him waiting for me to bump into him at each turn, making impatient gestures. I made obscene ones.

We followed Packett around the perimeter of our tent city to the back rows' scaffolding supports, where the audience would enter The Pit. I looked up at the 'Gods' (not really, but ten metres up earned the title), at the paste of the Milky Way beyond. No sign. Kevin touched my shoulder and I jumped. He pointed toward the technician's tower where Enzo burned the midnight soldering iron, a tall, Faustian shape hunched over something behind the plastic windows of the bio box. Jesus wept, I thought, Packett's not going to do something to the electrics, is he?

Kevin crept up the steps toward the central aisle. Metallic squeaks accompanied every step but he did not appear to care. I followed after a second, taking every third step to reduce my noise. Kevin grabbed my shoulder and whispered close to my ear, 'We'll have to grab him, he's between us and the bio box. He's got bolt-cutters.'

I could see his desert boots through the gaps in the timber.

'Things are happening faster than I expected.'

I gripped Kevin's arm. Enzo's voice, while not especially loud, startled me. Kevin shook me off and craned his neck as if he could hear better that way.

'This evening's episode disturbs me, Enzo. I was under the impression nothing would happen until performance energy was reached.'

Dave's voice. I saw his shoulder. I imagined I could see his long, crooked nose and sharp eyebrows, though the window warped everything inside. Kevin's presence grew more electric as our illusions about this production were rent; mine, I fear, grew more perplexed than ever.

Enzo: 'I had the sensitivity up full at the time. Stanopoulos was actually performing tonight, showing off his muscles to Gill and Sherelle – Sherelle mostly, if you ask me – it wasn't a coordinated performance, though, just plain ego, but it was enough to release a little potential from everyone present, Leywood included. And when everyone came out to clap . . .'

Dave: 'Indeed. I hope you have that under control now.'

Enzo (rather *too* confident, hiding something): 'No worries, cobber. It's storing up right here' (pause) 'and we'll open it with the first real audience, say about a week into the run.'

Dave: 'Hm. Yes. I'm glad Packett is here to bring us an audience quickly—'

Enzo: 'A leak's as good as a wink to a blind bat.'

Dave: 'Our sending power would certainly have been too great had we relied only on the flying doctor's story for an audience. Who knows what would have occurred?'

Enzo: 'Yeah. You see, it's *mental concentration* that's the powerful thing. If this show ran on electricity we'd be utterly fucked for power. Beats the shit out of radio!'

Dave (sighs): 'I don't know why I let you talk me into this, Enzo' (chuckles). 'Well, yes, I suppose I do, you maniac. We really should have done the first transmissions to – a – local audience. I might be dead by the time we get a return message.'

Enzo: 'Think of me as the son you never had.'

Dave: 'I do. That's half my problem with you . . . See that everything's in hand; we don't want to take any risk with the actors.'

Enzo: 'That reminds me, chief, when are we going to tell the talent?'

Dave: 'Nothing's changed. When the play's a success and not before.'

Enzo (with an odd trace of contempt): 'It's going to be a bit difficult to keep quiet if anything stranger than tonight's little spectacular happens.'

Dave (with hobnail boots): 'I thought you said you could keep it under control.'

Enzo: 'I can, I can, but – we're bound to have a few jumps in energy levels as we approach opening night.'

Dave: 'As long as things don't reach the surreal stage we can blame superstition and imagination.'

Enzo (amused): 'You mean Packett.'

Dave: 'Well, ye—'

Packett (off, in a mighty bellow): 'I'M NOT GOING TO BE *YOUR* PUPPET, ABRAHAMS!'

We heard him stumble up the bio box steps and Kevin darted around the corner. I followed him in time to see the wiry character actor wrap his skinny arms about one hundred kilos of blubber. The bio box door opened and a trapezoid of light slid down to reveal Kevin atop Packett halfway up the steps, like a boy riding a hippopotamus.

Without the critic we would already have filled the control booth. Enzo sat to one side of the lighting board, the salamander tattoo on his forearm resting on a VDU showing topologies of different shades in intersection, which lit it so it seemed ready to crawl up to his head and engulf him in flames. Kevin sat on the other side, by the door, his back against the window.

Packett and Dave took the two folding chairs which left me to stand, Kevin's foot in my side. We had calmed Packett with the first threats and reassurances that came to mind. Dave had promised to reveal all. I had lent Packett my hanky. Enzo passed around cans of beer and smelly Gauloises; we were taking the first warm sips (gulps, from Packett) when there came a knock at the door.

I opened it, stepping backward practically into Packett's lap. I stepped forward. Robyn held on to a rail a couple of rungs down dressed only in one of those cheap tartan bathrobes, from what I could tell by looking down her cleavage.

She pulled the robe tighter. 'What's going on? I heard shouting. I *knew* you two were up to no good.'

'Uh – we were only—' I said.

'Come in, my dear,' said Dave. 'You might as well hear what I have to confess as well.'

She walked forward, past me. I could smell her hair, full of the ever-present dust and eucalyptus smoke. Another lovely surprise of the bush. We shuffled around the tiny space, inching chairs, drawing up knees, going 'Ouch' as we squashed past one another until we could close the door.

'Can we expect any other visitors?' asked Dave.

'I was the only one in the bed tents, I think. The others are making too much noise in the Boys' Room. Should I get 'em?'

I don't know why, but at that cramped moment I felt a sudden rush to my head. It could have been Packett's BO but I thought it was love.

'No, my dear,' said Dave. 'I fear this room would burst at the seams if anyone else arrives.'

'Tell me what's going on, Abrahams.' It was the first rational statement from the critic since the scene by the camp fire.

'In good time. You must hear it from the beginning. I may take some while.'

'Fine.'

'Hm.' Dave favoured us with a smile he might have given to a class of infants. Actors lap up that kind of thing. He settled back almost imperceptibly, as though to a morning timed only by cups of tea in bed. He began to speak.

In the late seventies, when Dave held television advertising by its designer scruff but his thoughts had already gravitated toward the theatre, on a business trip to Paris he met Enzo in a tiny bar near the market of St Antoine. Enzo was full of ideas and contempt. The mainstream companies who had enabled him to save for his trip came in for the bitterest vitriol. The two found a great deal in common: cynicism, a love of the fantastic and recently deceased fathers. The drinks turned into a meal, turned into a cancelled meeting for Dave, turned into more drinks, turned into a night discussing outrageous schemes designed to shock and educate and enliven their complacent homeland.

It was here that the fluffy-faced Enzo got drunk enough to give away his darkest secret. This concerned, as he called it at the time, 'the hidden splendours of the mind'. (Enzo did not quite blush at this recollection but flashed a look of affectionate defiance at Dave, almost against his will.) He waxed incoherent about the Soviet research into electronic amplification of mass delusional systems. It sounded like something out of a fifties horror movie of some gothic novel at the time. Skull drills and slivers of precious metals in the brains of 'criminals' – not even the Soviet government knew everything about the more *outré* aspects of the research. They did know that telepathic communication was possible, with electronic enhancement. Most interesting to the drunken Dave (he'd never have believed it sober, he said) was the fact that groups engaged in the propagation of a complex lie requiring a degree of suspension of disbelief in a series of events based on powerful archetypal material, *on the part of the liars* rather than the lied-to, produced the greatest incidence of consistently measurable results. At this point the Russians got bogged down in the political/ideological implications of their experiments.

For Enzo and Dave, as Australians, nearly rolling about by now in a bar in Montmartre, the mind-boggling conclusion was, in simple terms: a play aided in this way could reach directly into the hearts and minds of an audience not present at the time. A play required suspension of disbelief from the actors; a good play was often based on the most powerful archetypes. Enzo and Dave decided to stage that play.

Obviously no actor would consent to the violation of his or her skull – though Enzo cheerfully suggested a few candidates – so the technology would have to improve first. This was fortunate for Dave, who woke the next morning with a black-smith's shop inside his head and a clear memory of the agreement to continue research, but without the credulity he'd possessed the night before. Back in Australia, Enzo went happily back to his experiments in his vine-covered Greenwich attic and Dave let the idea slide.

However, ten years later, Dave Abrahams stumbled across the solution to their problem. Once again, hard drinking was involved. A chance acquaintance, become Dave's 'best friend in the world', poured out his sorrows to the fatherly producer. The man had recently been made redundant. His government team had built a device which measured neuron firing activity at some distance from the brain, but which had blown up inexplicably time after time until the money had run out. To Enzo this was the Holy Grail, the Missing Link. He hacked into the laboratory's computers and bought the designs on five-finger discount. It meant a house full of hardware. It took him three years and some risky hacking to reduce this to the 'radio mikes' our cast wore every waking moment.

During the period when it looked like telepathy would never be more than a fancy, Enzo's fancies multiplied. He had a hard time sucking Dave into his obsession with UFOs, but in the end Dave, too, was convinced that before they tried it on a distant human audience, say Sydney, they should try – elsewhere. Sarah's *Tempest* in the desert would be ideal for both purposes, he argued. Far enough from anywhere to give dramatic results (ha, ha), and it would not take any extra effort to indulge Enzo's idea first. And he had a really likely solar system picked out. And, after all, it *was* his invention . . .

So after four years of chivvying, he had his way. Pioneer's greatest hits would pale beside Shakespeare. They would send direct into alien minds a complete performance, all our height and breadth and depth, our sweat and danger, to the stars.

It was romantic. No message: Shakespeare. Maybe not even an audience!

Dave's voice diminished to a whisper. His listeners' faces showed disbelief, amusement, concern, and hurt at a betrayal of trust; more than one of these on Robyn's and Kevin's faces. Packett's affect was mostly that flat calm tinged with cynical humour you sometimes see after what amounts to a breakdown. Enzo masked what I guessed was intense anger behind a mock embarrassment. Anger at whom? I wondered. Dave?

'What Sarah told you last month at my house is true,' he went on. 'It is an attempt to strip the preconceptions of advertising away from our art. I have not lied to you except by omission. Certainly Sarah – hm – does not even know about our – side endeavour. You must see no harm can come of it, now we have a measure of the power with which we are dealing. Indeed, the greatest risk is to the operator, to Enzo here. Your part in this plan gives you the opportunity to come in on the ground floor of a new industry. A new era. I ask you not to make a decision about staying with the project until you have thought about it. Until you have seen that we have this under control.' Dave looked at Enzo with some appeal on his face, then back to us with a more direct plea. 'Until you have made up your minds, if you could keep this to yourselves – hm – I would be very grateful.'

'You don't honestly reckon it'll work, do ya?' Kevin asked.

'I see no reason why it should not,' Dave responded gravely. 'I myself have felt the presence of Enzo's thoughts alone. Think of a whole choir of thoughts, of emotions and sensations!' He deflated a little. 'Well, it was not the exact content,' he confessed. 'More the general emotional tone.'

'That you could have read from his face,' said Packett. He was calmer now, almost sober; he must have been on the verge of a dam-break for some time and it would have come out in some form eventually, regardless of whether or not the last few days' events and taunts had set it off. We seemed to have done him a favour. He could have picked a worse place to go berko. His words were surprisingly gentle: 'You know young Enzo here so well.'

Enzo, no doubt miffed at being called 'young', said, 'We were several miles apart?' He sighed, which only set off a thousand questions about Dave and Enzo's relationship in me. I had swallowed the whole story. So had Robyn, by the sound of it:

'What did it feel like?' she asked, before I could open my mouth to pry.

'Oh dear,' replied Dave with the look of one passing the portals of Hell. Then: 'It was like a hand had gripped my heart.'

'What – you felt like a real hand in your chest?' asked Robyn, curiously literal.

'No. It was – hm – a sudden feeling of great and inexplicable loss.'

Kevin sat back under the pressure of Dave's blue eyes. Robyn nodded. I leant forward, holding on to the door handle, to catch sight of his face again. Enzo pushed air out in an effort to subdue what seemed like great anger, and sucked in at length. Packett said, without much force, 'Anyone could feel such a thing on their own, Dave.'

Dave said gently, 'Tell them, Enzo.'

The tall, olive smoothie sighed but did not speak. He looked far from smooth now. He looked hard. Positively craggy.

We waited.

'Tell them. You have worked too hard, son, too long on this to throw it away.'

Enzo muttered something like, 'We have anyway,' at his knees. He raised his head. 'I . . .' He sighed again, then shook his head, disgusted. When at last he spoke it was back at his knees, in a sing-song, like a child's grudging apology. 'The message I tried to send was no big deal, "The cat sat on the mat," I think – anyhow . . .' He cleared his throat, an unconscious imitation of Dave. 'My mother died the week before and that's what he received. He never knew . . . I hadn't told anyone.'

'I'm sorry,' said Packett.

'Don't be.' He glared at Dave. 'It was a few years ago.'

'Go away and think about it,' said Dave, with the timing of the Devil himself. 'Think about what this will do for the theatre, for yourselves, and for the world.'

We went.

FOURTEEN

She had changed jobs. Jay Schnarler was tempted to give up on this tack and go to the local CIA, spin some bull about being a private dick nowadays and beg access to their surveillance cameras, small as pinheads and scattered all over every major city, if his information was correct. Naturally, that assumed that the rising hysteria about the visions (ten per cent of the population, according to the latest news) puzzled them as much as anyone. And even if it did, the use of their computers to sort out which images were of Gore and construct a more or less continuous narrative might clue them in, should anyone in the Agency become curious about his 'case'. He'd better stick to following Kevin Gore's trail himself. At least he'd warned Leywood. Although Leywood hadn't believed this was a fight of Good against Evil he had booked himself out of the funny farm and taken a flat under an assumed name with the money Jay had forced him to take.

Jay wheeled himself out of the lobby, past the chrome ashtray full of sand, the pink marble fascias, across the heat-sensitive carpet and into the street. He hailed a cab, which unlike those at home did not drive itself and slewed across a busy lane of traffic, delighting him. No, he'd go and see this Caroline Walsh at her influential new job – he turned the compliments slip over in his hand – at Borovsky Studios. He wheeled himself up the cab's ramp and read the address to the driver. They tore off. It was more frenetic here than it had been eleven years ago. That was either progress or the effect of the visions. Perhaps a bit of both, he thought.

Then he had an idea.

Everyone was looking for an explanation for the surreal turn life had taken lately. The cab driver, a swarthy guy, of Bangladeshi descent he guessed, was going on about it now, how he had been admiring the avocado tree in his back yard one morning and the avocados had sprouted pink wings and flown off into the dawn. If Jay could interest Borovsky Studios in his own explanation for the visions, or even Martin Leywood's one about spacemen, then Gore and Leywood would become public property. Famous, they would be much harder for the CIA to liquidate. It was a risk. It depended on the Agency not having made the connections yet, but Jay took a deep breath of the sultry air and decided to take it.

Just then, the clouds which had been gathering opened up. Rain came down in waves, helter-skelter from several directions at once, it seemed, blown by the wind. The cab driver remarked on it, then pointed across to the emergency lane of the freeway where an armoured van sat with its back and passenger side doors open. A guard was on his hands and knees on the stretch of coloured asphalt behind the van, shaking his head groggily. The van and guard soon passed behind the cab and disappeared in the rain.

'Gosh!' said the driver, and radioed for the police. 'Those bad guys that did this will have a better chance I think to get away in this weather,' he said afterwards. 'I can hardly see to drive myself.'

'Yeah,' said Jay.

'It is always the way: conditions favour the bad.' It was a clear reference to the US's stance on Bangladesh.

In the privacy of his head, Jay begged to differ. But not about the politics of the Greenhouse Effect. The sudden storm had released him from any doubts he had about giving the whole story to Borovsky Studios. Conditions this time favoured the

Good. With the decrease of humidity came a release of tension; Jay relaxed back into the plush seat of his wheelchair, smiling to himself. He ran his fingers through his close-cropped hair and down the stubble on his neck. He was ahead of the CIA. He knew it. The Lord had just told him so with this rain. Leywood, he thought, I'm gonna make you a celebrity, like it or not. You can't buck the word of God.

FIFTEEN

Close to tears, Kevin Gore forced his lungs to empty and reached for the ignition for a last try. The engine turned over once and would not do so again. He slumped forward on to the steering wheel. The rain pelted the windscreen, roof, and both sides of the car; it seemed to come from everywhere at once, whipped by a wind which buffeted the car.

How many years for armed robbery?

He had never thought about it. He hadn't a clue. And all because the doggerel in his head had asked. Oscar's hindsight rules OK. I must be mad. Me and Martin, he thought. We can share a room! He laughed. Where were the saviours of the world now? – having a poetry reading? He laughed some more. Well, now at least he had no significant others, no fighters of the visions, no transformers of his body to blame. He reckoned he knew at last where the voices came from. From himself. I'll avoid prison easily, cut myself and rant on about being more than human and get analysed and dredge up my father who couldn't hack the family life and my mother who clung to me out of lack of love from my father and tried to make me play with dolls to make sure I knew what a man should do for his wife and child . . . But would I ever get out of the madhouse? There was a serious thought.

A car honked. He raised his head, resigning himself to the worst. But the coppers wouldn't honk. Their sirens still wailed, louder now, from down on the freeway. The car parked next to him was a white blur in the rain. Leaning across the bag of money, he opened the door. It was a Triumph Stag. At the wheel sat Gemma Stranger.

Gemma drove furiously out of the city toward Swan Hill.

'What the *fuck* were you trying?' she snarled when she could afford to speak.

Kevin had, by this time, wiped away the last trace of 'George Shearing'. Puck had dissolved when the guard had grabbed him.

'I succeeded,' Kevin said with some pride.

'What? What's in the bag? Money?'

'Yairs. Not sure how much, though, Budge.'

'I don't believe you. What did you do?'

'Knocked over an armoured van. Really and truly.'

'Christ!' She ignored his comedy. 'That's really stupid. Now you're wanted. You've got a gun, haven't you?'

'It's nice to be wanted. And no, I'm not.'

'Oh, come on. I saw the bolt in the cupboard, next to the Wheeties, for God's sake. Didn't you reckon a *girl* would know what it was? That's why I started following you around.'

'I had a gun,' he admitted.

'So it's armed robbery! Do y'know how many years you get for that?'

Kevin laughed. He turned to Gemma to explain but subsided at her grim face. He watched the wipers go *swickshud*.

'You're such a child you know that.'

'Thank you, people don't often accuse me of that. I'd turn right here, Budge, if I were you.'

'Don't call me that.' The turn-off went by. 'What for?'

'I have to do something about my car. It'd get lonely and rust without me.'

'Are you off your head? What am I saying of course you are. And you thought Martin was bad. I have an aunt in Swan Hill—'

'I'm sure she's lovely—'

'What's that supposed to mean?'

'Take the next *right*! If they find me Passat they'll find me as well.'

She took the next right. They curved back toward Melbourne on a wet and narrow road which dipped and swung sickeningly, at up to 140kph. Kevin, paling, said, 'You're a wonderful driver. Mind if I get to see the scenery?'

'There it is.'

'Please?'

She slowed.

After they left the national park behind, Gemma said: 'So what exactly possessed you to throw away the best years of your life?'

'Possessed me. You'd reckon I was lying.'

'Bullshit I would.'

'Well – we need a place where you can give it your full attention. Howzabout the zoo?'

'Christ, Kevin, you honestly are cracked.'

'Maybe.' Kevin made an exaggerated frown, looking inward.

'How'd you follow me?' he said at last.

'With great difficulty. And I might not have, had you come for drinks with me. I lost you when you caught the bus in Dandenong. Another bus came and left at the same time, but I picked you up again by sheer luck when you drove back in. Then I lost you when you went for petrol; I had to stay in my lane, and when I got back you were gone. I drove all over the area for ages looking for you.'

'But you found me.'

'I found you. Lucky for you.'

'Lucky . . . hm . . . Quite a detective. D'you like otters?'

The Friday night rush into the city had not yet begun. Gemma stayed silent, red-faced, narrow-lipped. Kevin checked out the frantic moves of those escaping the working week, and waved and made faces at the children, already bored by their parents, heading out to the country for the weekend. He started to sing once, an old Paul Simon song, but Gemma shut him up with a glance.

As they pulled up beside the railway station Gemma said, 'The zoo'll be closed. I've got a garage you can leave the car in. You can tell your story while I pack.'

'Oooh. Are you coming with me, O saviour, O knight in shining Triumph?'

'My aunt will hardly let you in without me.'

'I've got no designs on your auntie, shweetheart.'

'Don't call me that. I hate that.'

'Okay, but we're not going to Swan Hill, much though I like canned fruit.'

'Where then?'

'My place.'

'It's the first place they'll look, dickhead.'

'Don't call me that. Anyway they're not looking for *me*.'

'What makes you so sure?'

'A little birdy told me.'

'Ah-huh. You should get out of the city, anyhow.'

'Ah-huh. That's why we're going home, señorita.'

'Oh. But how—?'

'I'll tell you while you pack your frillies.'

'Must you?'

Kevin smiled sweetly and got out of the car. The rain had stopped, and the world smelt reborn.

'You mentioned those people who've had visions.'

'It's all over the papers now. People are lining up on all sides.'

'Really? Hmmmm. That's news.'

'There's the religious nuts – well, not nuts, the Archbishop of Canterbury's not a nut – then there's the scientists who believe it's some kind of natural phenomenon and the scientists . . . where have you *been*, Kevin?'

'Ah. Busy.'

'Ah-huh. Anyway. There's the UFO cranks and—'

'Which side are you on?'

Gemma stopped packing and fixed Kevin with a wise look. He brought his feet up on to the bed and hugged his knees, sitting on Gemma's pillow. Her room smelled of wet boronia. There was a picture of Gemma in theatrical make-up on the wall.

'Tell me what you wanted to tell me,' she said.

'What about the visions, first.'

She sighed. Brushing the hair out of her eyes she sat on the bed diagonally across from Kevin. She stared with disapproval at his boots, which were shedding dried mud on the doona.

'It's an epidemic. It's happened to famous people in public places. Jane Fonda saw one during her chat show on prime time TV. John Paul the Third has seen one.'

'Seen what?'

'Oh dear.'

'I want to know.'

'The distinguishing feature of them is that no two people see the same thing. As a matter of fact, none of Fonda's viewers and only two of her studio audience saw anything.'

'But they saw her.'

'Ah-huh. She said later she saw a Jackson Pollock painting. It demanded—'

'What, the painting?'

'—it demanded she devote her life to art, give up talk shows, take up cheap red wine and tortellini.'

'No kidding.' Kevin began to giggle. He fell sideways on the bed. He had to stuff some pillow into his mouth to halt the fit. 'I bet,' he said, but subsided into giggles again. 'I bet she went on TV the next day and had it all *analysed*!'

Gemma smiled. She stared down at her knees for a while.

'So what about the Pope?' Kevin asked.

'Nobody knows. He just looked terrified and went into a coma.'

'Punch and Judy time.'

'Hm?'

'Locked in the cupboard with the Devil. Punch used to do that to the vicar.'

'There has been some speculation. A lot of people think it's the end of the world.'

'Could be.'

'What? Don't hint. I hate that. Tell me or not, I don't care.'

'But you do, Ms Stranger.'

'Yes, I know, or I wouldn't be so furious with you. Good one. But I always get angry at rank stupidity.'

'And how do I rank?'

She grimaced as if sick. 'Most governments are issuing statements trying to calm down the population; we haven't had a lot of trouble here but there have been riots and attempted coups in South America, so the new Pope is being urged to come out with a statement one way or the other.'

'Which way or the other?'

'For instance – are you sure you haven't heard any of this?'

'I've overheard bits and pieces at the pool and that but I haven't thought too much about them. For the past while I've cut myself off from pretty much everything. I don't read the news sheets or watch telly a lot anyhow, and recently I've – I've been preoccupied.'

'Ah-huh. Well, in America the two noisiest movements are the fundamentalists, who think it's the end, and the scientists, who have two main theories.'

'Yeah?'

'One is that a combination of pollutants and increased ultraviolet has produced a hallucinogen—'

'Mmmm?'

'And the other is that it's a psychological reaction to the turn of the millennium.'

'It's a bit late, isn't it?'

'This has been pointed out. They reckon that science itself – well, rationalism – is to blame. A damping effect on the natural predisposition to apocalyptic religion.'

'Ah, yes. The dampening effect of science. So what do you reckon?'

'They compare it to what you and Martin experienced out past Arkaroola Station eleven years back. There's mass delusion, some real physical effects – like rain out of a blue sky. I can't quite bring myself to believe it's some sort of alien *Tempest*, though.' She smiled and bit her lower lip at the same time.

Kevin hugged his knees tighter; he imagined the blue blood pulsing slowly through his body with each beat of some reconditioned equivalent of a heart; he grinned but it soon faded; he gazed up at the photo of Gemma dressed as Ophelia, it looked like, trying to see through the thin costume, but he had not been equipped with X-ray eyes; he realized this hysterical flippancy came out of a continuing tension between his possible insanity and the more disturbing idea that he really wasn't human in several important ways, but that didn't lessen it; he examined the photo of Gemma's father on the cluttered bedside table, a thin, slavic-cheeked man with wild blue eyes, his arm around a stern old Aborigine, standing in front of a beaten-up EH Holden sedan; he looked back at Gemma.

'Believe it, sweetheart,' he said with his most annoying smile. 'It's an interstellar vaudeville and I'm the next act on.'

He told her he needed the money from the robbery to organise the right response to the visions. When she assumed this meant building another thought amplifier he made another flip reply which left her to believe she was right. By the time she figured out that Kevin, no technophile, must be getting help, he might be in a state stable enough to give her an answer at length. They had to be on their way at once. He had made the necessary arrangements . . .

'Finish packing,' said Kevin. 'It won't mean the end of the world, but it *will* make a lot of difference, I can tell you that.' *And the truth would be so unbelievable you might just laugh, and where would that leave me?*

'Can't you give me a weensie bit more?'

'Aside from the fact that there's been a confusion as to what *The Tempest* meant, no. Nothing that wouldn't convince you that I was completely mental.' Perhaps convince me too, he thought.

'Try me.'

'It would be like speaking Swahili to you.'

'I speak Swahili.'

'Look: not one word more, or I leave without you.'

'I really hate that! "Don't you worry your pretty head about it." What do I have to *do*?'

'Wait for the right time. Goodbye, Gemma. Thanks for the help.'

'No!'.

She lunged across the bed and grabbed his forearm as he swung over the edge. Her hard, bony fingers had a strong grip. Kevin placed a hand over hers.

'I don't understand it myself,' he said, which was the truth, if he was crazy. 'We don't have time for idle explanations.' He could hear his mother say to him, *Just like your father, Kevin. If you won't tell me what's on your mind how can I help?* But he got up to leave anyhow.

'Go then.' Her voice was thick.

He left.

Partly to keep himself awake, Kevin listened to every news programme his radio had to offer. What Gemma had said was true: it was like listening to an account of events a thousand years back, except for the public analysis of analysis, and analysis of that as well. It didn't really matter what the aliens were saying to the human race (it was probably, 'Hello, we come in peace'). If the visions were so widespread, then they must be sending from quite close to the earth, perhaps within the solar system already. He drove faster. In Bairnsdale he was forced to stop for petrol so he ate some supper. As he sipped his coffee afterwards he overheard a couple of locals who had taken sides on the vision one of them had seen, part of the main message by the sound of it.

'You wouldn't know where your old woman's *fanny* was if someone hadn't told ya, Johnno.'

'Better 'an you would, Damien.'

''At's what you reckon?'

'Yeah, pull the other one, Damien. I got it straight from the man: sixty-one Cignarse, *mate*.'

'Sixty-nine *horses'* arse more like it.'

'Laugh if you like. I arsed Frank down at the bookshop an' he reckons there is such a place, it's a star an' it's got planets and everythin'. So how would I come up with that if I'd never heard of it before, ay? If it hadn't been rooly rool?'

''S whatchamacallit. Like the way they steal songs without realisin' it. Subconscious stuff.'

'You're bloody *un*conscious if y'ask me.'

'You'll be unconscious in a minute, Johnno.'

'Anyway, I *seen* it.'

'Oh yeah . . .'

Argument between the two seemed an inevitability after a few drinks; they had talked roughly but backed off when it came to a fight. Scrappers. Only it was a vision which had given them the excuse this time. With most stable people this wouldn't be a worry. Yet there were a lot of unstable people around – what of them? And when the message came to everyone, impenetrable information which each person read as they liked, what then? Kevin finished his coffee and left.

When he finally pulled up by the flowering gum next to his front gate a huge orange moon, like a colossal illuminated speed limit sign, was rising over the hills behind the house. Struck afresh by his country's ancient, still charm, he wished he had not been such a dill with Gemma. She would have liked this. Although his body still felt like it was on the road (some things didn't change) he found himself able to think for the first time since before the robbery. In this light, only the bag of money on the passenger seat told him he had not imagined it. I could be going mad, he told himself. 'Insane' does not mean 'stupid'. I could have found out everything myself, where to get the gun and so on, then suppressed the memory and convinced myself the information had come from *elsewhere*. But that would mean that everyone on earth is going mad.

At this thought, though the evening was cool, he felt his skin prickle with sweat. It came to him he had opened the door and put his foot out but then sat in a funk. He stepped out of the car and walked toward the gate. If I am going insane, he prayed, please, don't let me go when I'm alone.

SIXTEEN

from
Charms All O'erthrown

We believed them. We consented. Heaven forgive us. We helped them and shut up about it, trying not to lie. Have you ever betrayed your country? The assurances that nothing dangerous would happen – all at once they seemed like crap and I would want to confess the lot. I would go so far as to collar someone then I'd renege as I opened my mouth and find myself inventing some confession about my feelings for Robyn for the sake of confessing *something*. We co-conspirators took to spending more time together because we couldn't stand the twisting any more, the bald-faced innocence we met in the rest of the cast. We'd get together and worry, which brought us closer, I suppose. I still visit Packett in the asylum now and then; it turned out his wife had left him because he was crackers and not the other way around.

I make it sound relentless. It was persistent. However, *The Tempest* is in many ways a delicate piece and requires more practice than the comedies of mistaken identity to make the characters' motivations credible, they're so cornball; even greater discipline is required to make the effects and conclusion work. And in many ways we treated it as a tragedy, which put a lot of extra pressure on Sam (as Prospero), on Ariel and on me. Rehearsal went ahead, shakily at first, but soon taking firm shape under Sarah's strong, energetic hand. The fact is, I forgot our outrageous purpose most of the time since my concentration was required for the serious business of play. Besides Caliban, I had a reaper puppet to operate, I assisted with the set, dressed those 'other spirits attending on Prospero', and sewed. Although Pete's moment of glory still occupied many mouths, discussion centred on explanations from natural causes. Predictably enough Pete became the Golden Greek and the whole episode a joke, especially when it came to Pete's 'trip'. No other incidents occurred (Kevin's bump, Robert's fall and the food poisoning had actually been accidents, we were assured). An intense and luculent calm filled our amphitheatre. If anyone noticed it, they didn't mention it; the theatre and the Australian Outback can be like that.

By the time work had settled into a less demanding routine of runs, notes, pull-outs and adjustments, my thoughts had largely devolved to other things. One day, Robyn and I found ourselves almost alone in camp with the glaring afternoon spread out before us. The others had yahooed off to 'town' to shop. So we took a four-wheel drive to Nooldoonooldoona Waterhole. Robyn laughed at my jokes, she listened to my stories, but usually she was as reticent about herself as Kevin. On the drive down, though, she regaled me with the story of how her mother and father had met. Her father had been a painfully shy man whose only passion had been geography. He had collected so many physical details about the world in his head it had cluttered his mouth as a teenager. By contrast, her mother had been a poet, already well-known in her twenties for the eroticism of her work despite its breadth of subject matter. (New Zealand is like everywhere else in that respect.) Robert Ho had argued over the distance from the pub he was in to Melbourne with some yobbos, who then had hijacked him on the way home. Robyn's mother, on her way back from a reading at a nearby artist's colony, had seen the fight and intervened, beating up two of the thugs and sending the rest packing. This was the reason Robyn had headed for Melbourne when she'd left New Zealand, 'To find out for myself how far it was,' she said. Because the distance, 'as the blow flies', had become a part of a family legend. Her tale was full of funny and intimate details, and I felt privileged to hear it.

We swam, by tacit agreement, in our underwear that afternoon. Silly, really, since we had seen one another bare oodles of times at work and swimming in groups, had handled each other's bodies daily on stage. Also, her black sports bra and white knickers (tea-stained by the pool) simply aroused me more with each wayward pubic hair and translucent outline. It was lucky the water was so cold.

We lay on our stomachs, face to face.

'Robyn,' I said, trying to beam what I felt into those green eyes that were splashed with brown, 'I really like you. And more, I think.'

There, I had said it. Sort of.

She smiled crookedly, almost winking at me with her right eye the way she did. Her teeth were perfect. I wondered if she used the Equity dentist. 'Martin, I think I know what you want.'

I coloured deeply.

'I want to be with you too, to spend lots of time together. You're like nobody I've ever met before.' She laughed a little mischievously. 'But I've got to tell you right now. If you want to be my mate – two things: my work comes before anything else, *anything*; and I'm celibate, I don't fuck and I haven't for years. So now you know.'

I could see her steel herself for my response, but I was not disappointed. I was relieved. So this was why she had been friendly and stand-offish at once! Half her charm to me was her dedication to her work. Half of the reasons for my divorce had related to my single-mindedness about the theatre.

'That's wonderful!' I said.

'What – that I don't fuck?' She looked miffed.

'No!' I laughed. 'That you actually want to be with me. That you don't think I'm a bore.'

'I didn't say *that*,' she said.

I reached into the cold pool and flung water across her back.

When we had settled, she asked, 'Don't you want to know why I'm celibate?'

'You'll tell me eventually.'

'No, I bloody won't. I don't really know myself. Oh – maybe I've got a low sex drive. I enjoy it but then it's over and I don't even think about it. Takes too much energy from my work, I suppose.'

'And work takes too much energy from sex,' I said.

'Yeah. Maybe it'll be different when I get older. Maybe in a few years? I can't honestly ask you to wait, but.'

I smiled and looked away at the water. Ferdinand's lines came to me and I spoke them with such ardour it surprised even me:

> As I hope
> For quiet days, fair issue, and long life,
> With such love as 'tis now; the murkiest den,
> The most opportune place, the strongest suggestion
> Our worser Genius can, shall never melt
> Mine honour into lust . . .

She swung her knees around, half sat up and clasped her fingers in my drying hair; her lips were soft and cool and felt fuller than in my fantasies of such a kiss; she kissed me with a kind of fury I've never met since, kissed and tore away just as my skin began to prickle. It was as if she had had a premonition of what was to come. Tears made her eyes seem larger.

'As long as it doesn't get too frustrating for you,' she said gently.

'You do like kissing?'

'I do. It doesn't often lead to much, but.'

'I like kissing, too.'

We went on in this way, doing and talking about things we liked to do, until the sun had dried us and I was a bit worked up.

'Oh, I hope it won't get too much for you,' Robyn said.

'Mistress, dearest,' I replied, 'I'll be your patient log man. Besides – we have ways of dealing with that.'

I pecked her on the cheek and rolled into the icy water.

When I surfaced, Robyn called, 'Would you like us to live – to get a tent together? Or would that get too much?'

'NO!' I sank, resurfaced. 'Yes! I mean I think I could handle it!' I sank again. Robyn laughed. From underwater, I could see her happy face, that crooked grin making her slightly oriental eyes definitely banana-shaped. She put her hands to her cheeks in mock distress when I pretended to drown. The sun was behind her short hair and I was forced to look away. A crested pigeon, distorted by the pool's surface, seemed to scoot in jerks across the ferocious blue above. Even the faint sound of Robyn's laughter died away and I was left with bubble sounds and my own heartbeat. I looked back up at Robyn. I have this memory of how she was at that moment: her face was still bright with her lingering smile, contentment replacing it imperceptibly; her head was tilting slightly; her large hands were hanging by her hips past the lines on her skin where her underpants had rucked down; several pieces of grit and twigs were sticking to her white tummy and one was falling off, almost; her whole person was crisscrossed with wobbling ridges of light off the water. All these things and much more I noticed in moments, between one scissor kick and another. For a change I had forgotten myself completely, and off-stage, too.

I bobbed up and heaved out of the pool, filled with possibilities of what we could become together. I had no doubt we would be right, as a couple. Our future seemed to spread in every direction at once; I felt loath to speak for fear of baulking anything. Instead, I sat beside her on the edge of the waterhole and put my arm around her shoulders. We dangled our legs in the chilly water, listening to the various birds' occasional calls in silence.

So the afternoon was spent.

Bastards. As wicked dew as ever your mother brushed with raven's feather from unwholesome fen drop on you all. I suppose

I ought to be grateful for a good memory and some weeks to cuddle up at nights or mornings or minutes away from work. But I am not, the red plague rid you. *All* the infections that the sun sucks up from bogs, fens, flats, on you cream-faced bastards fall and make you by inch-meal a disease! Perhaps you thought we were part of some disgusting alien conspiracy against democracy, in league with hard-line Arab nasties, no doubt; that we were testing a weapon. Our only conspiracy was against our own. Our only crime was to dream.

Who knows who told the CIA about our secret? For some time I suspected everyone who knew of it, and for that you too are responsible. That I should suspect Robyn of anything but the innocent charms of an acting talent is cause enough to hate you. Then I remembered the American voices Pete Stanopoulos had heard suspended above the flames. You had been interfering all along. You knew what you were doing and continued. I hope on a perfect summer's afternoon that you receive the one bright glimpse of how a love returned might quicken your tiny lives and, like us, see that promise slip away.

SEVENTEEN

'Not you again.'

'You should have used the intercom, buddy.'

Martin swung the door all the way open. 'Don't call me that,' he said. 'I accepted your money, I did what you told me, but I still don't believe your story about the CIA being interested in me after so long.'

Jay wheeled from the cracked linoleum on to the beige carpet of Martin Leywood's new flat. 'You took the money, you got the flat,' he remarked, sounding more cynical than he felt. In truth, he felt more than righteous now; he felt touched by a bent to all and sundry he had decided could only be described as love. A window had opened in him, perhaps for only a brief time, which made him feel terrific.

'Okay,' admitted Martin. 'You think that the CIA – of which you are no longer a part – will connect these visions with Enzo's project.' He motioned Jay toward the lounge area and made for the refrigerator. 'And in the same way as they closed doors for me with newspapers and politicians after what happened eleven years ago, by threats and favours, presumably, they'll try to cover up now. If anyone so much as sniffs at the truth they'll shut them up. Beer?'

'Thank you. If you had been listening instead of giving me the stale spleen you have obviously rehearsed for years – and which I might repeat I do deserve – you would have heard the next part: this vision thing is too big to cover up and your *cobber* Kevin Gore has been doing the rounds of producers with your version of what happened; the next step is to shut you up forcefully. To liquidate you, as they say.'

Martin handed Jay his beer. 'I know. Sooner or later someone'll think ours is a story worth following up even without proof, and if I'm not around to talk to it'll be merely another crackpot explanation. So why have you come?'

Jay admired Martin's sense of self-importance. There he sat, in an opportunity shop lounge chair, white-silk suited, fiddling with the knob on his elegant walking stick, fresh out of a mental hospital. The man was probably worried sick about merely coping in the big, ugly world. Yet he conveniently left out the possibility that the greatest danger to the CIA here was corroboration by an ex-agent. Much more credible than an embittered freak. Jay smiled at Martin. Leywood wasn't stupid, so it was some kind of quaint, foolhardy courage which gave him this front.

'Look, Martin, I know my apology for what we did doesn't go any way to redeeming me. I will probably burn in hell for that.' He put an elbow on the wheelchair's arm and thrust his forehead into his hand, massaging his brow. 'But I'm here; and I'll do what I can. If things went the way you say they do, there'd be millions of people believing Elvis Presley is alive and running a Seven Eleven in Idaho. Truth is: not a soul believes your story because it *sounds* like dog crap. And neither your say-so nor Kevin's will make it sound like any more than dog crap.'

Jay examined Martin in the light of his new-found concern. The veins on the polished brown forehead beneath the receding, mousy hair bulged a little. Ears pulled back and nostrils flared and longish jaw clenched with tension, he looked fragile. His long fingers had left the walking stick's knob and now fiddled with the grimy black silk scarf knotted around his neck. Jay wished there were another way of saying this.

'But while I was tracing Kevin Gore, I had an idea. I had it followed up there and then – there was no time to consult with you. The last producer Kevin had seen was one Caroline Walsh, who now works at Borovsky Studios. At her old job she didn't have the budget or power to take on a project like yours. But now she does, and it turns out that Borovsky might have considered *Charms All O'erthrown* as a good idea for a film.'

That jerked Martin out of his sour mood. 'He didn't say anything about that to me!'

'By her account, he doesn't sound too rational at the moment.'

Martin's fragile look returned. 'He seemed a bit distracted when he said goodbye to me at the loony bin, but that's quite normal where I've been.'

'Yeah. Well, when I backed up everything you said in your piece she jumped at the chance to produce it. She wants to buy world rights. The film is already cast.'

Martin made a face as if he wanted to be sick. 'As long as you testify that I'm not a paranoid moron, ay?'

'I've already done that. Signed and sealed.' *And with copies in a bank vault.* 'Believe me, she didn't take my word for it either. She checked me out as well.'

'So now what? Two years hiding from your pals – sorry, *ex*-pals – at the CIA while they faff around and spend the budget on lunches and meetings in Jacuzis? How am I supposed to live?' His eyes narrowed. 'Just what sort of money do I get for world rights, anyway?' he asked.

Jay finally relaxed a little. 'You'll like that part. You'll have to talk to her about the exact terms, of course, but the figure she named to me had six zeros attached. First step, rush your prose version of what happened into print and give some of what I said to the newspapers as a taster. She wants to move fast, not only for your safety, but' – he smiled cynically – 'she thinks the excitement about the visions might not last.'

Martin almost smiled back. Jay began to let himself think this might work. 'The trick will be to keep you and your story in the news while they go into production with the film. If I know the cocksure way the Agency will go into this, it shouldn't be too difficult to make a great deal of mileage out of their evasions and denials. And if my guess is right, these visions are gonna get worse. The public is aching for an explanation.'

Martin took a breath, on the verge of acceptance, but checked himself and let the air out again. Slowly he tilted his head. 'This is . . .' He shook his head. 'This is – unexpected.'

Smiling, Jay nodded.

'What I do not understand,' Martin went on, 'is what you expect out of this. Why the sudden rush toward redemption when you've let it sit for so many years?'

Jay's smile vanished. Ashamed of his complete turnaround, at having to justify himself before the sort of person he had for years believed to be his inferior in every way, at his reluctance to admit to the continued embarrassment over his homosexuality which for so many years he'd mistakenly tied up with a fear that God really did exist, he cast around the tatty room, at its peeling wallpaper and mouldy ceiling, in hesitation.

Martin saw Jay's fear and pounced with an intuitive conclusion.

'You've had one of these visions,' he said quickly. 'You've seen something that's convinced you to your bone marrow that you have been a murderous bastard for most of your life and the time has come to *do* something about it. It's exactly what happened to Kevin and I: when the crunch came each of us saw different things eleven years ago, and now no two people are seeing the visions exactly alike. You saw something very personal, didn't you? Something that changed your life? *Didn't you? DIDN'T YOU!*'

Shuddering, Jay breathed as deep as his ribs would let him. Martin needed satisfaction, he saw that too clearly; his strange new empathy shouted it to him much louder than could Martin. It would be a kind of revenge for Martin. And Jay would not get his cooperation – even if it meant liquidation at the hands of the Agency – without that revenge. In a low voice, he began to tell Martin about his mother and father, about his own homosexuality, about what he had done and not done in the CIA.

Finally, he told Martin of what he had seen prowling through the sky on feet of flames not so long ago, of his abject fear and conversion.

And when he finished, he saw Martin was moved in spite of himself, that he had received his satisfaction yet was not pleased with himself for demanding it. Martin Leywood actually pitied him. Of course he had not thought that he would when he asked. We are all more human than we think we are, thought Jay.

He fumbled his wallet out, took Caroline Walsh's card from it and held it toward Martin.

Martin took it. Now, he would let Jay make him famous.

EIGHTEEN

He dreamt of high-school examinations. That he lay on a cold steel table did not concern him; his veins opened under the examiners' knives, vital organs pumping their blue life away while all around hydraulic Victorian machineries inscribed his reactions to the violation on greasy reams of paper like the product of some decayed Industrial Revolution belonging to a miscreant history. These Heath-Robinson pistons surely did not belong to his own past, the one which segued neatly into a short and comfortable Post-Industrial Era, but that did not matter. What concerned him more was that nobody demanded the sums set him should balance – all they cared about was getting the job done.

He woke in sheets musty with disuse, examination pressure still on him while he blinked and stretched. It was as hot as summer. He was back in his own bed.

Eggs filled the basket by the door and he found croissants in the Coolgardie safe. His neighbour Kirsten, bless her. Inside the generator shed, tugging at the starter (some things never changed), he heard the telephone tinkle. As he crossed the front yard full of rusting baths and machinery, tyres crunched on the drive and he looked up to see Gemma's car rolling toward the house. He stopped, torn between the phone and greeting, then realised he was naked and forced himself to wave casually before he stepped indoors, as if he welcomed people this way every day.

'Hello, hang on!' he said into the phone, then tore up the stairs for some trousers.

Gemma stood at the door, knocking politely, and he waved distractedly as he passed on his way to the lounge.

'Come in,' he called. 'I'm on the phone.'

He thanked Kirsten, assured her everything had gone well in Melbourne; no, he couldn't come around as he would be really busy for the next few weeks; he promised to take her out on the town soon, his treat. When he returned to face Gemma he found her pouring black beans into the coffee grinder; she had dumped her suitcase next to the faded club lounge.

'You must have driven half the night,' he said. Each gesture died half-born.

'Ah-huh.'

'Have you had breakfast?' He crossed to the basket of variegated eggs.

'Unh.'

'Duck eggs. And croissants. I'm having two, poached, on toasted croissants. Sound good?'

She switched on the grinder.

'I'll put the same on for you.'

He went outside to fetch a bucket of water from the tank, noticing as he stepped through the door that she had looked up at him, cracked blue eyes intense and a bit alarmed under her coarse hair, her freckled hands frozen in the act of removing the kettle lid. Her blue, boat-necked dress was wrinkled. Her lips were wind-chafed.

When he got back she was seated on the couch leafing through Banner's *Trees of Eastern Australia*. As he poured the rainwater into the kettle (no wrigglers, the filter seemed to be working for once) he said:

'After I got out of hospital in Adelaide, after the fight with Martin, I discovered I cared more about trees than about most people. It took me a pretty long time to speak to anybody at all. I certainly avoided any kind of closeness for ages after.'

But she was staring at him as if he were a fascist trying to sell a comic to her on the street, so he busied himself with the stove.

She took breakfast with a small smile and devoured it without pause. He admired her appetite. With a second cup of coffee beside her, she reached down to her enormous bag, pulled out a packet of Drum and quickly and efficiently rolled herself a cigarette.

'I didn't know you smoked.'

'What you don't know about me'd fill the proverbial.'

They sat in silence, smoking. In half an hour, Gemma was asleep, curled up in the far corner of the couch. Kevin went to say hello to the ducks.

Kevin scarcely knew what he wrote. It stood to reason that if he were to broadcast he'd need a play. They were making one to measure. The words poured out of him so fast (pausing only long enough for him to flip pages), to read them now would distract him from his location on the paper, he might never decipher it if he wrote off on to the desk or over the same line several times. It appeared to be a comedy rather like *Waiting for Godot*, though its general tone swallowed high above Beckett's miserable masterpiece. Kevin did notice the imagery, the dialects used, and at least two of the characters depended on his own experience, with native landscaping, suburban Melbourne, the size of his ears, with life in Australia as he saw it. So he as a person – at least the bloke he used to be – was necessary to the play. Or could they have taken the themes and applied them to anyone's experiences, out of any place or time?

Kevin left the thought, since his mind held no space for anything but the play which burbled on to the pages of the cheap school exercise books stacked before him.

Hunger came and went. On he ploughed, light-headed. They understood his need to piss, but allowed little time for it. No sooner had he buttoned up than the words drummed again in his head. He rushed back to the desk and took up the biro again.

His back and arse ached from sitting. He stood. His legs

ached, his feet felt the size of balloons. From painful, his forearm passed into a kind of numb, wooden state, leaving him amazed it still worked; likewise his fingers. Anyone could tell he hadn't worked hard for a while. Thirteen years old first day at the shoe factory—

Fortunately the weather did not get very hot. About thirty, lovely. It had rained during the night and the air remained pleasant and light. Kevin's one delight was to glance up to notice the day had changed hue from pale gold to midday white, later to horizontal bronze, tanning his skin further, lightening his arm hairs by a few shades.

Shortly before sunset, though his fatigue and pain reduced the world to a tunnel from eyes to page, he heard a quiet tap-tapping on the normally loud stairs. He cast a quick look to his left: Gemma took a few steps into the room then one step back. A few minutes later he heard the toilet flush. The next he knew there was a presence behind, to the left.

'Sleep well?' he asked as he turned the page.

'Mm. Um – thanks.'

'I'm writing a play.'

'Oh.'

Time passed. She asked, tentatively:

'For the aliens?'

'Ah-huh.'

'Um—'

Kevin turned another page.

'I'll explain later.'

She left. Soon afterward a thin, reddish hand with many more lines and freckles than he remembered appeared to his left, holding a plate of sandwiches. Then there was coffee, electric lights, juice.

Night fell.

Kevin's right hand was an immobile claw when he woke in the early afternoon. He used up nearly all the water in the upstairs tank showering some life into it. His mind felt as stiff as his arm and shoulder; he had no recollection of going to bed, only of finishing. Someone – Gemma – must have undressed him. Despite his fatigue, Kevin felt his penis pump itself up at the thought, on automatic. Water pelted his hard shaft and he felt troubled as well as a little more activated. He turned off the hot water.

Dressing, he realised a great deal of his stumbling about was because of hunger. On his way downstairs the aromas of frying and coffee nailed him to the planks for a minute. He breathed in deeply, trying to work out what was cooking.

At the sound of him Gemma turned her head.

'There's some juice on the table.' She smiled kindly.

'Ta.' He descended to sip.

In a minute she said, 'Here you are,' and dumped a plate of pancakes, bacon and eggs, and a jug of maple syrup on the place mat. She then fetched an equally large stack for herself and tucked in without ceremony.

For some time they clicked forks and knives against plates.

'You must have had a time finding this place in the dark,' Kevin said when she rose to get the coffee.

'Yeah.' She laughed weakly, that hiccough. 'Especially after six or eight hours on the road. And I was mad, which didn't help. There you are.'

'Thanks. Did you see the moon?'

'Mm. It was fantastic. I would have been more lost without it.'

That they had shared the moon dulled his fears a little.

'Guided by the moon,' he said.

'Guided by the stars.'

'Hay? Oh. I will explain. Everything.'

'You weren't in a trance, were you.'

'I'm not sure what a trance is – unless I've performed myself into a trance in the past . . . No, I don't think so.'

'A while ago, over lunch, you seemed to go into a trance.'

'A lot of things were happening to me at the time. I was, uh, sick. I had a fever. Much better now.' He smiled for a bit.

'Um – can you type?'

'Not really. Don't even own a machine. You want to read the play?'

'Ah-huh.'

'Feel free. You can type it, too, if you want. I'll borrow my neighbour's typer, if they have anything so primitive around.'

'You're sure it's okay?'

'Anything that saves me time is all right with me. I've got heaps to do.'

'Actually, I'm a terrible typist. I always get a man in. I'll see how much there is to do.'

'Okay. But if you do wind up typing I've got one request: don't revise as you type. Everything must be as it's written.'

'I promise I won't touch a thing.'

'Oh. I didn't say that.'

And she laughed!

Kevin wanted to tell her everything. He had not known it till now, but the whole business was a burden he had been holding tight to his chest with a kind of sullen glee. The need to tell somebody about things did not go away just because you did not own it, it became something else. He was not going crazy from festered loneliness but . . .

'Gemma, I'm sorry I left you in Melbourne that way.'

'It's all right.'

'It isn't. I was completely unreasonable.'

'Well everything's all right now. Full stomachs make a lot of difference, my father used to say.'

'More than mine did. I – I want to explain myself—'

'I've given up trying to explain you, mate,' she said. 'I'll probably understand a bit more when I've read it.' She stood, gathering her tobacco and coffee.

'So will I,' said Kevin.

With the puzzled look he was beginning to appreciate, she questioned him a moment then went upstairs to get the exercise books.

Kevin made some calls to Sydney and Melbourne while she read. Although it served only as a cover he confirmed the booking on the Belvoir Street Performance Space. He spoke to several old friends he knew could handle the job, some of whom still acted and could do with the work. The rest of the parts he cast on the advice of those friends he had met with recently, trusted, and who remained in the business: he had no time for auditions. He didn't know much about the play or its characters, not having read the thing, so whenever the actors asked him for details he managed to sound confident enough, improvising around the sketchy details, thanks to the telephone. They would have smelt something rotten for sure had he met them in person.

Every so often he heard that goofy laugh from the dining area and turned to check out Gemma. She appeared to be enjoying herself, when she wasn't frowning over the scrawl.

The laughs came less often as the afternoon passed. By the time both Kevin's ears were sore from his old black Bakelite phone he noticed she had not laughed for some time. She was looking puzzled, no longer mouthing the words to herself. Now and then she would flick back several pages to read a line or a whole page again. Kevin made one last call, to a local builder who owed him a favour, then went quietly to the kitchen area to prepare dinner. Apart from eggs and stale croissants there was not much there, so he made coffee and waited for Gemma to finish.

'Well,' she said at last. 'You certainly can write.'

She sounded like she meant it.

'Come on,' he said. 'I'll take you to dinner with my ill-gotten booty. We can talk about it there.'

She insisted on driving. 'I'm just one of those people,' she said. Kevin said he didn't mind, but he worried about the speed at which she took the corners of the gravel roads.

'You'd better not use any of the money. I'll use my credit disk.'

'I was only joking. It's still on me, though.'

'No, I'll pay – it's the least I can do.'

A while later, he said, 'About the money . . .'

'Mm?'

'The bills were on their way from retailers to the bank, so they were sorted but they hadn't been read by any computers.'

'Mm?'

'Anyway, it still might look suspicious if such a large amount went into my accounts, but if I set up a production account or two and put some into my business accounts and savings as well, then put the rest into your fixed-term account . . .'

'How much is there?'

'Bit over a quarter of a million.'

She sighed. 'How much do you want to give me?'

'Oh, a hundred thousand.'

She let out an exasperated laugh. 'I'll think about it. I'm not turned on by money, you know.'

'Huh! Well neither am I. I'll pay for dinner, thank you.'

They bought a bottle of Chardonnay from the local and took it to a restaurant by the ocean's edge, where over lobster (guaranteed clean) under the stars Gemma asked Kevin about 'his' play.

'I don't know what it says.'

'Every writer says something of that sort, but you must have an idea. It is a message.'

'No, really. I didn't write it.'

'You mean you plagiarised it?'

Kevin wanted to tell her but feared where it might lead. Apart from that, he didn't know where to start. He began to speak with no mind for the world's fate, aliens, voices in the head, visions or plays. Instead, he tried to explain his terrible fear of losing her.

'I – I seem to have walked out on you a lot, Gemma. We never began well, and never mind what you saw when we met I don't have anyone I'm close to. Anyhow, the first time I walked out it was because I felt – I felt compulsions that were not my own. I knew I wouldn't succeed at selling Martin's play, but it was necessary to go through the motions, and the timing of that was vital. I had to make phone calls that afternoon or people would not have been there to see me. Why this was necessary I'm still not sure, but I'm told it will become clear eventually. Well, everything that's happened since has only made it more difficult to tell you anything and at the same time it's made me want to explain things to somebody – some one – I could trust. When I left Melbourne that way it was because I didn't want to fob you off with some bullshit that wasn't – that wasn't everything, and had I told you everything, I was afraid you might not – that you might think I was . . . I feel very isolated now. Just at the time when I was getting half-fit for human company again. You should see my ducks. Um. I've been hanging around on this farm for the past ten years . . . And you've been there even when I thought I didn't want you. I don't know anything about you! But – I think – I've got an image of us. I'm not sure if it's borrowed or mine, if that makes sense. We could get along, if I unbent long to see how it'd be. I've really thought I've been going crazy . . . and you just show up and you don't let go . . . I dunno. Is it more than this stuff about the play and the project for you? Are you the kind of person who sees the madness ticking in my eyes and takes pity on people like me? I mean, you like Martin . . . I've been thinking, in this past day or so, that maybe it's more than that.'

She had stopped eating a while ago. She gave a lopsided smile and said: 'I do like you, Kevin. No – I don't like you all the time, you can be obnoxious. But if you're asking what I think you're asking, the answer is yes, the thought has crossed my mind. And, really, I didn't come up here because of my thesis or your communication with whoever, or because I think you're – because you need help. You're *not* cracked, I don't think so. No matter what I might have said. Tell me about it and we'll see. But it doesn't matter if you are. I think we should try. I haven't much experience at this—'

'But you're *beautiful*!'

She laughed. 'Not to most people.'

'So—?'

'So, yes. But tell me about this stuff first. We've both got to know everything before we go – any further.'

Gemma smiled at him encouragingly. Kevin examined her slightly upturned nose, the eyes which always looked ravelled in a thousand cares, the small and thin-lipped mouth, the pixie ears which, like his own, jutted. He could not tell what life with her might be like, he just had this image of her on a towel on the sand, and next to her, wrapped against the sun – he couldn't trust that, no matter where it came from. It had always been the same, this game. No matter what changes had been wrought in him. So she held her head at a tilt, so she did everything, even tied her sandals, tentatively, except for driving the car. So what? He didn't need to know what things would be like. Never had. It had always been his mistake, waiting to be sure.

'I'm being—' His throat was suddenly dry. He swallowed. 'I've been contacted by people from the future.'

Kevin searched her face again, but found judgement carefully suspended. Gemma took a sip of wine, her spiky red hair threw brilliant highlights in the wash coming from the restaurant doors. A light breeze, cool off the bay, rustled the leaves above. The sea shushed. Kevin took a sip from his own wine.

'I don't know how they're doing it,' he said, and took another sip. This was not quite a lie, but neither was it the truth, which annoyed the hell out of him. He went on: 'It's voices inside my head. There seem to be at least three.'

'So for them it's after the aliens have landed?'

'No. It's a time which would not exist if they had landed. They're not going to take over or anything,' he continued hurriedly. 'It's – I'm not sure I understand the ins and outs myself. This is the way they put it: in *their* past, a play was performed which brought people from another planet.'

She nodded.

'Well, these aliens got here. Or, rather, they arrived but decided to talk to us at a distance for a while first. And this is where it really gets weird. These people, who've been in contact with the aliens for more than twenty years – they have some sort of society of players who take care of it – they've benefited from the contact in lots of different ways. Pollution's under control, lots of extinct species have been brought back, there are no famines. Anyway, one thing they've applied the aliens' knowledge to is the nature of time. When they started to look at it they got a huge shock. They discovered that their own time, their present, was not the most likely time. In fact, it was only a ghost of possibilities not yet played out. *And their existence was growing less likely every day.*'

Gemma looked off into the nearby stand of cypresses, as if clarity might lie there, and back again.

'I'm not really with you. You mean you've been contacted by ghosts?'

'No. What it really means, in practical terms, is that their world (to them it's the real world) is falling apart at the seams. The natural laws are ceasing to work. The planet is about to break up. There are earthquakes and floods in which millions of people are killed, and the air is leaking away. They say the end won't be *so* bad; eventually things will fly apart all over, and nobody will feel a thing. They never will have existed; their possibility will have been reduced to almost zero.'

'Ah-huh. So, why is their world becoming impossible?'

'Because we will make up our minds that we want them to land. At this point, now' – Kevin tapped the tablecloth – 'there are two possibilities: when the aliens get close they listen to the faction amongst us that wants them to stay out in space for a while – or they land and that's it. The worst thing that can happen to a people. Genocide.'

With not a little clatter and clumsiness, Kevin got up. The rush and pause of the water was stronger here at the edge of the restaurant's patio, the air more tangy. He listened to Gemma slide her chair back, rise, and come to him. For a while they simply stood, gazing at the vague line of ocean beyond the row of the evergreens' twisted spears.

'You said something at my place about a confusion over *The Tempest*,' Gemma said at last.

'Melodrama.' Kevin did not look around. 'Bad habit of mine. Our play *was* about a shipwreck on a desert island, and nobody – not them, not us – had any idea of what would happen. The investigations into time were a human kind of obsession, based on their theories. By the time they got to within radio distance at least four countries were sending out signals. Greedy about the advanced knowledge the aliens possessed. Come to think of it, "genocide" is only partly right. It wasn't war, but it might as well have been. It was a combination of things. For one, the aliens are not uniformly good or bad, like us. The problem with that assumption is that it comes from using the aliens as a metaphor – I mean, they're not metaphors, they're bloody *aliens*! That's always been the problem of first contact. We don't know how to look at them, they don't know how to look at us, we don't see what we're looking at until it's too late. There you go. In the past it's always been humans with other humans – and look how badly we've fucked it up each time even then. The aliens never saw us as sub-beings, they didn't try to convert us to their religion, but there were other, equally dire, situations. One parallel is when a whole Balinese royal family committed suicide because the Dutch were totally ignorant of their ideas of honour. Well, maybe that's not a good example. The Dutch were being brutal arseholes. Perhaps a better one is the English wiping out whole tribes here when they brought smallpox to the continent.'

'That was only one thing,' said Gemma. 'There were water-hole poisonings and shooting parties and rapes and venereal diseases and breaking up families.' Kevin turned toward her ferocious voice, taken aback at his vast ignorance of her, recalling the photo of her father with the Aboriginal elder beside her bed. 'Everything that could be done was fucking done, over and over. Europeans in Australia still justify hate for Kooris by applying double standards. Rather than feel a colossal lump of guilt on their backs, they hate. We don't have to hate *or* cringe.

We just have to listen!' Oblivious of buttery fingers, Gemma ran a hand through her hair.

'Mm. Well. It won't be quite like that, either,' Kevin said. 'It's difficult to say what it will be like because we won't understand what's happening to us. F'rinstance, the way the aliens communicate is a threat to our sanity. Talking with one personally can kill you and you can kill others before you go.' Facing her now, he scratched his chin violently, leaving red marks. 'Then there are ideas that can kill. They're not made for our societies, but they'll seem so god-like to us people will think: how can they be wrong? There will be a disease, at least one, but it'll be a disease of the heart, a romance that can only take you down, and nobody'll know if it's the aliens' presence or a virus or something else.'

Kevin tried to take Gemma by the triceps, but such was the received urgency in him he could not clench his fingers. He dropped his arms and went back to his seat. Gemma sat opposite him again.

'The most likely future is one where our population is very small, only about a million or so, and scattered throughout the universe in ghettoes, and worse. And ninety-nine per cent of what we are, good and bad, is gone. The ones who are alive are not even human, by our standards. We're a prehistoric tribe by the aliens' lights. Some of them are doing their best to save us, but even that cripples us, sterilises or kills us.

'It's a thousand years of torture. And it ends with extinction.'

His hands fell among the cutlery and scraps. Gemma's small voice made him look up.

'I'm sorry to seem such a dill, but I don't get it,' she said. Her careful lack of judgement had evaporated; she looked sad. 'I mean genocide I understand, as much as any middle-class white Australian can. But this time bizzo – I presume the play you wrote is aimed at stopping the aliens from actually landing, right?'

Filled with fear, Kevin nodded. Her leap to understanding his motives for the robbery had come from comparing him to Enzo.

He wanted to shout: *But I'm not a UFO nut!* He tried to believe it was the hints he had dropped back in Melbourne which had led her to this conclusion. He told himself to assume she thought that way was to underestimate her. He couldn't help but feel dismal at her sad face. He propped his chin on one fist.

Gemma continued: 'If people in the future have contacted you, and the aliens haven't landed, and theirs is the less likely of possible futures, for them you've already staged your play, yes? There's a paradox in there some place.'

'Ay?' said Kevin. He opened his mouth, then pushed it shut with his hand. This felt like a fight for his life. She had to believe him! 'You think – no, no, it's not like that at all.' As if getting nearer to her would clinch it, he leant across the table, pointing four straight fingers at her. 'The only reason there's more than one future in the first place is that the future I'm being contacted by is based on an improbability: how can I put on the play and the aliens not land if nobody contacts me? They're growing less likely as the possibility for my success decreases. In their past I've been contacted, so somebody has to do it in their present. Miss out on one bit and *then* there's a paradox. They're only the least likely outcome *before* they've gone through the process from their end. Then they become the *most* likely outcome. So I've got to do this, Gemma, but – more than that – I can't do it without you.'

She was startled at his change of subject. He was startled that she was startled. To him it was all tied into a furious knot. As her lips struggled with a smile of encouragement, he felt the space across the table widen.

Kevin wanted to say more. He gazed down into the dark below the table where his left hand hung. He searched for his wrist. He imagined the slight scar running across the pink, shining like the reflector strip on a highway's edge dividing the parts he had covered from the territory he must venture into sooner or later. He must go further. It was stupid not to tell her. He stared at the wrist, willing the words into the space between them, but looking up he saw the gap stretched until it seemed a rift no action could span. Even as he tried to make his eyes tell him, 'It simply is not so,' and failed miserably since his eyes backed up and backed up again the strange yawning distance he felt, even as he (from a coldly observant layer of his mind) marvelled at the effect, Gemma reached from what seemed the horizon and placed her palm on the knuckles of his right hand, her fingertips on his wrist. He was, at least, prevented from travelling right out of reach. He turned over his hand, and held on.

NINETEEN

'I don't know what you've been making such a song and dance about. If you're cracked then so are all of us. Half the world is talking about the visions and voices and the other half is getting them.'

Gemma squeezed his hand. The beach was deserted, aside from a couple of seagulls and a big Pacific tern which ran down the sand as the waves rolled out then back as they broke. The moon, past full, was seeping out of unseen clouds on the horizon.

'You see?' Kevin said. 'That's the beginning. There's been violence already and there'll be more – that's just their return message. People are seeing things now that they have no comprehension of and interpreting them in their own way. And what they're hearing about what's going on from their spiritual leaders is not much chop. I only heard voices, human ones at that, and look what a berk it's made of *me*.' He laughed. ' "A man hears what he wants to hear and disregards the rest." '

'What's that?'

'Old song. The point is, I'm not a particularly strange character and *I* found enough trauma and bullshit in my past to have legitimate worries as to my sanity. Think of the world! There's a lot of people weirder than I am out there.' He waved an arm in the general direction of America. 'This is only the beginning.' They walked a way, then, in silence.

'Still, you're not cracked, are you. I believe you.'

'Cracked. Hm. You know, just because everybody else is beresque it doesn't mean I'm sane. We may *all* be going crazy. Perhaps that's why the dinosaurs became extinct. Mass 'steria!' Kevin danced away, kicking up sand and flinging his arms into the air. 'Cracked or not!' he shouted. 'The practical upshot amounts to the same difference!'

'NO!' Gemma chased him, took his arms and forced them to his sides. 'It's *not* the same difference,' she told him. Her breath smelt sweet with lobster and white wine. 'This is at least something you can *do* something about.'

'I don't have any choice,' Kevin said tightly. 'I'm – it's – ' He looked away, at the black and silver ocean. 'I'm the only one who can do it.'

'Who can tell the aliens to wait? Why?' asked Gemma. Then a thought struck her. 'How?'

Kevin wanted to tell her. He began to wonder if his fear wasn't some part of the mechanism inside him, some safety.

'Let's go home,' said Gemma, her voice more hoarse than usual, and delicate.

Oh. God. Kevin sank inside himself with dread. Yet the unnatural fluid pumping through him felt no fear at the look in her eyes; its qualms were strictly mechanical, anything which fitted would do. Gemma reached down, raised his hand and placed a succinct kiss on his knuckles, then let go.

Kevin took a deep breath and forced a smile.

'Now I would be cracked to refuse,' he said.

He fell into the Triumph's plush as if it were his long-lost cradle, letting Gemma's sure driving rock him into a sensuous languor. Through his feet the engine's pulse felt as new and exciting as when he'd first clambered into a sports car, at the age of twelve. The intact bush rushed by their tunnel of light the same eerie way it always did when there were no other lights about; however, tonight the ancient landscape seemed fresh, the spotted gums more massive and the road less defined. To Kevin the land created ahead by their high beam seemed like the product of his private game with city landscapes made real before his eyes. It held an element of the past, but it was not quite what he had thought it would be like. As though history had turned in a spiral rather than in the forced circle of his usual imagination, the broad trunks and fronds which flashed by hinted by their extreme vigour at a *garden*, way beyond the abilities of nature as he knew it. He wondered if Oscar, The Man from the Future (& Co.), hadn't interfered in some fashion, using their knowledge of his mind and his fancies about the land to produce a vision of what things could be like if he succeeded. A comfort at a time when he was troubled about this new body.

Just then a huge white figure swooped into the light – probably a boobook – and out again. A part of him which did not marvel at the spectral beauty of the bird reasoned: if they think I need comforting, doesn't it follow that there is some price to pay, that I've been made some kind of incomplete freak?

As the voice muttered on, the mundane, sinister tape loop of insecurity, this, and clearly no message, Kevin's desires rose to deny the reasoning with luxuriant energy.

'You're quiet, mate,' said Gemma.

'Trick of the light. Been babbling non-stop, actually.'

'We're nearly there, aren't we?'

'Can't you tell by the drool on my chin?'

'Kevin, I'm not very good at this.'

'You mean you're underage? And to think I wore my long pants tonight.'

'Dag.'

'Ah, so you want to talk dirty? Warthogs. Mud-wrestling. Labor Party Conferences. London. Toffee apples.'

'Toffee apples?'

'Yep. I distinctly remember dropping my toffee apple at the Royal Melbourne Show in nineteen seventy-nine. M'dad made me eat it. I've never been able to eat one since – they smell of cowshit to me.'

*

Gemma lit a fire while Kevin gathered bedding from upstairs. There was no need of a fire, but the wide steps down to the hearth made an ideal place for a snuggle, covered with couch bits and scatter cushions. Gemma had found the whisky, poured two tumblers, rearranged everything comfortably and was seated close to the young flames hugging her knees by the time Kevin returned. Her cheeks looked painted in this light. The hairs on her legs shone red. She had taken the pins from behind her ears and her hair curled forward a little.

He dropped the blankets beside him. He looked at the fire for several moments, then stepped down to crouch beside her. He was terrified.

'We haven't even kissed.' He tried to sound normal.

'Well, then.' Gemma cupped his ears with her palms and pulled his face close to hers. He was unbalanced; he fell to his knees. She laughed, pecking him on the lips. They kissed.

She rubbed his stubble with her knuckles affectionately, gazing into his eyes with the slightly manic intensity of one who has been very lonely for a long time. He wondered why. He got up to gather the blankets but she took over. He watched while she concentrated on the task, thinking of the anger she had shown when he'd mentioned the genocide of the Aborigines. That wasn't enough. And she didn't come over as shy. As Gemma wrapped the last cushion, tucking the blanket securely underneath, Kevin placed his hands beneath her armpits; she shuddered; he nuzzled into her hair and kissed her neck. Gemma twisted round to look at him with a small, tight smile that was almost a frown.

'Undress me.'

Her boat-necked blue dress was hooked together. Her back was covered in freckles. She had many sharp angles, eager yet gentle hands, swimmer's muscles. When it came to undressing him, Gemma took maddening ages, pushing his T-shirt above his breasts and kissing and running her hands over his chest and back. Kevin thought she'd never finish pulling down his jeans. All with that small smile.

Holding tight, in briefs, they crumpled together. Kevin on to his back, Gemma on to elbows and sharp knees. Underlit by fire she seemed older as well as smoothed-out-young. As he rolled her pants down her buttocks with flat palms she shone mischievously and responded with fingernails on his lower belly. When she gripped him, squeezing with thin fingers, he cried out. Gemma tugged at Kevin's briefs and he at hers.

They broke apart at last to finish undressing. Like birds' their small breasts rose and fell.

She descended on him with her lips. Then nose and chin and forehead and tongue and cheeks. Even her ears. He fell back, up the steps away from the heat, then sat up suddenly with a startled gasp to run both hands down her spine.

The scar on his wrist caught his eye. His hand turned over, almost of itself.

'Mmmmm, it's gone soft. That's lovely.'

'Gemma – no.'

Kevin brought Gemma's head up to face him. He hugged Gemma tight, staring past her into the fire, but seeing water, hectares of water in a valley below where Gillian Portman-Smith struggled with the current and was sucked down and he could do nothing, nothing ... If only he had said something, told them about Dave and Enzo. He had to tell Gemma now, but he feared losing her. He had been Gillian's best mate, but he hadn't told her anything, let it continue. Do it *right* this time, he told himself. Speak to her. But he couldn't say a word, his throat had thickened, the tears he had stopped up for so many years trickled on to Gemma's shoulder. Kevin wiped them up and held them before his eyes, blinking in wonderment.

TWENTY

from
Charms All O'erthrown

Petras Nicos Stanopoulos

Donald James McDonald

Enzo Guisseppi Paulo Carmoni

David Clive Abrahams

Helen Smart

Samuel Jefferson Schuyler

Gillian-Anne Lydia Portman-Smith

Sarah Jane Witchell

Jennifer Margaret Drape

Robyn Elizabeth Caroline Ho

Opening night. Rain threatened during the afternoon, but passed over without a drop. As evening swept across the clear sky and we swept the stage, I wondered who out there would find a performance crowding into their hearts and minds one day. Would they know what it was to play, to take your passions and foibles and roll them with rough strife through the gathered public for an evening? Enzo was sure someone was out there to receive our message, but I wasn't sure they'd have the sort of minds to comprehend Shakespeare, if they did exist at all. Looking up I had no sense we were about to do anything

momentous. What would cause a fuss was the second performance, which was aimed, said Enzo, at the audience just sitting
down to the Sydney Theatre Company's *Our Town*. But there
was no time to linger in fancy tonight, there were props to
check, costumes to iron, warm-ups to complete, make-up to
apply. My damned hands shook as if an audience awaited
curtain up. So much *make-up* for me, too! Caliban's lumpen,
beautiful, half-twisted face leered at me from the mirror, latex
and art tissue as yet innocent of foundation, but I could see him
already. He was there. I snarled at him, squeezed the excess
water from my sponge, rubbed at the pancake then caressed
myself pallid before shading. Around me were sailors and at the
tent's far end stood Milanese noblemen. 'HmmmmmmMA!
Bah! Pah!' they said.

Nearly six weeks is a fair old whack for preproduction by
Australian standards; we had come to think of opening night as
the end of rehearsal, though most of our audience were emus.
Packett was still the only outsider present. He had left us for ten
days after our night of playing boy detectives, 'to let things cool
down' went the official story. Five of us knew he would leak
Sarah's project and motivation to his paper. The big news would
come as a scoop, after our pirate interruption of *Our Town*.

Despite our group's suspicious over-tranquillity, which I now
believe was an effect of Enzo's invention (if the centre of our
continent is blessed with that quiet glow all the time I can't
explain the barbarity of the first Europeans who never saw it),
Robyn, Packett, Kevin and I actually passed from a guilty silence
to a state of egotism, where we took credit for the revolution in
theatre about to occur. Or perhaps the dreaming rehearsal as
well as our exaggerated sense of well-being, and on top of that
the decision by the group to come out here in the first place,
were all subtle aims of Enzo's machinations rather than only
side effects as the device built up 'potential' like a battery, or
like a dam. Certainly, I was unaware and more full of myself
than ever as I finished my make-up and looked up to find Kevin,
dressed and ready as Antonio, turning decidedly guilty eyes, I

thought, away from Gillian. I gave him a knowing wink, which could have been innuendo about our stage manager; he hesitated, in doubt, then smiled slightly.

The breeze which had cooled us all day gusted and the tent roof flapped about as if skittish. I wondered if Kevin was worried about the wind, which makes an audience restless, then I remembered the emus in the aisle of our deserted theatre and gave a laugh. I shrugged and attended to the stack of ironing beside me.

Gill nodded at Robert, struck Kevin quite a hefty blow on the triceps, then left. Robert said: 'Five minutes, little treasures – five minutes, Martin.'

I pouted. An easy thing to do, as Caliban.

'Chookas, mate. Chookas all.'

It's bad luck to say good luck.

'Places!'

Stationed inside my sea sprite – a bare chicken wire form in which I could be seen as an ambiguous shadow – on the prompt-side audience-effects platform, I felt such a fool! The idea was to rock the entire audience through a clever system of levers, servos and hydraulics, as though they, too, were plunged into Prospero's maelstrom with the King of Naples, Antonio, Ferdinand and the rest. As I worked the handle up and down, side to side and diagonally, I rocked an audience of three: Dave, Packett and Sarah. The emus had not appeared, for some reason best known to themselves. When some paying customers finally showed up I would be an expert, creating nausea at a flick of the wrist. Never mind, I thought, on with it.

After that, I plunged into the thick of the play myself. Like many of the best performances, out of all of Sarah's sprawling, magnificent *Tempest* I remember only flashes:

Prospero's involuntary gasp as I bound from my trap door, Caliban in a fury. How high I leap I don't know, but I remember Sam's upturned face, his mouth an 'O' as I fly.

Laughing till my face runs at Fred Carol as he tries to get to his feet, a butler so drunk he is rubber. I remember to re-enter on time, then Trinculo and Stephano, Jenny and Fred, rope me into an acrobatics class. By our last scene together we have become a trio with (to us) seamless timing and an edge to our comedy. Stephano is a real cutthroat; I really am afraid of him.

Ariel's first glistering flight. It seems as if she has simply forgotten to grasp the next rope. I almost step out on stage to catch my dear Robyn. She floats, bathed in lasers.

Miranda takes control of her gormless spouse-to-be; volumes about their future are implied by her simple domestic actions: a punch at Ferdinand's shoulder, neatening his hair, hands on hips to bawl him out.

Kevin, malign Antonio, and Don, wicked Sebastian, writhe with chagrin when King Alonso wakes as they are about to despatch him, the cowards.

A riot of pagan spirits on roller skates, trapeze, sliding down telescopic fireman's poles, cartwheeling, shimmying to tempt a saint, flinging handfuls of wind-up butterflies and those helicopter seeds.

The toll on Sam/Prospero is palpable. His bitterness as he delivers the lines:

> But this rough magic
> I here abjure; and, when I have required
> Some heavenly music, – which even now I do, –
> To work mine end upon their senses that
> This airy charm is for, I'll break my staff,
> Bury it certain fathoms in the earth,
> And deeper than did ever plummet sound
> I'll drown my book.

The payment he must make for the return of his dukedom seems more than it's worth at that point. Even Caliban's heart goes out to him, though I do not yet know Prospero's true relationship with me. We are such stuff as dreams are made on. *Yes.*

A turn of the wrist expresses King Alonso's true grief when he thinks his son is dead.

Golden shafts of light, pollen-filled and dappling, crown Prospero, Ariel, Nymphs and Lovers with pagan forgiveness. More butterflies and whirligig seeds, now all in white. Blank surprise when Prospero's secret is revealed to me. My sorrow extinguished, I perform acrobatic feats of which Martin thought me incapable. My God, thinks Leywood, that somersault was impossible. Ariel's sorrow and joy as she is released from her bargain: she curls up like a maple leaf in autumn, opens like a wild flower. All our company on stage together.

It began with a cacophony of birds. Leaving.

The galahs gave their grating calls of alarm as they flew into the lights, a whole flock of rainbow birds from a way down the creek gave sickening dull thuds when they hit the lamps and properties; their little bodies fell all around us, on us. There were stubble quail, Bourke's parrot, bronzewings and butcher-birds, spinifex pigeons, plovers, a red-kneed dotterel – my mind named them, matching them to the pictures from Fred's books even as I gulped with horror at the sight. A cattle egret appeared before me out of the darkness, almost careered into me before it swooped up and through the rig, back into the night. A corella, that sad-eyed little fellow, fell next to my right foot, giving harsh shrieks of distress, flapping in circles on its broken wing; both its legs had been driven into its body. I raised my foot over it but could not bring it down.

From the looks of satisfaction at a job well done on the faces of the two who later visited me in hospital I know this was no side effect of Enzo's, it was interference. Later, when Kevin and Packett and I compared what we had seen, we found our stories differed utterly. Some effects were from real things moved by power of mind, like air and water and birds; I must conclude that much of what we saw, however, was illusion. Yet where does one leave off, the other begin? I shall merely relate what I saw myself – which is confusing enough as it is. It must suffice to say that every time Enzo harnessed the energy of our minds, *the weather changed.*

Most of us simply stood there, amid the shrieking chaos of

feathers and claws. There was a lot of shouting. Some raised their forearms or hands to protect their eyes. A couple of us laughed, perhaps recalling Hitchcock's film, but hysterically. It was terrifying. Young Sherelle began to scream and didn't stop. A crested pigeon clung to her long hair and flapped and she could not move to take it off. I started toward her.

Then dawn arrived. Eight hours early. As if Maralinga still rocked under British nuclear tests the horizon flashed brighter than the eye could bear and rapidly faded into a wan morning-type wash. We cast long shadows. *This is the end of the world:* dread filled every part of me as the horizon clouded over with a distant, roiling, bruise-purple mass which *raced* toward us. The flow of birds had trickled to some stragglers and the fluttering dying. We woke from one nightmare into another.

Lashed at first by a single gust of sandy wind we had no warning before the storm had taken us whole. Our immediate group decision was to try to finish the play. Prospero started weakly on his epilogue but Kevin yelled him down, 'Get off, you morons! *Get off stage!*'

Night descended fully, real night, as cobalt and magenta swiped the ghost of dawn, as red and gritty billows killed our lamps. How much was illusion, how much real storm? Kevin bawled and waved his arms above his head:

'GET OFF ST—'

And we were screaming, covering naked legs with hopeless hands and we were screaming, desert air-streams scoured our flesh beneath our flimsy costumes, everybody running all directions but never reaching shelter, there was no place we could run to and no one dared to try the darkness at the stage's edge, screaming, bare arms flailing, some were crouched to keep the stinging sand which whipped us without mercy from their eyes, as in someone else's fever dream we screamed but met with silence in the maelstrom called on us. And the moment did not pass.

A deeper sound arose from underneath the hiss of sandstorm. It soon became a gurgle, the ache of grinding rocks, the sharp reports of snapping twigs and trees, a non-stop wash that lulled me so in spite of half-blind eyes I tried to find its source. An ochre wall of water filled our floodway. A flash flood, built of rains a hundred miles from here. Its tangled foamy surface looked like dusty lead. I staggered two steps backward and kept falling that direction when it hit.

With a slam the flood engulfed the set, which bucked and shifted, spilling actors everywhichway, showering us with sparks. The wave rebounded from the cliff and returned to wash us off the stage. This I know was real. Flash floods happen, whatever the cause.

Petras Nicos Stanopoulos

I saw you run toward the cliff face. You were bashed by a swinging timber. I watched you fall. I hope you were dead then. I turned to run for the cliff, I will admit it, I turned and ran away. Long live your beautiful children, Pete. When I last saw them they were healthy, intelligent, strong.

Donald James McDonald

you raving lunatic cider guzzler. I would never have worked with you by choice, but I liked you. I never saw you go. I'm sorry to say I've lost the urge to talk politics until dawn now. Can't drink cider. My little memorials are pathetic, I know, but at least they exist.

Enzo Guisseppi Paulo Carmoni

they found your charred husk among debris kilometres away. Identified you by your teeth. The deep, nearly animal energies you tried to harness – did they prove too much for your device? That it blew up and took you with it says, to me, that the Americans had their own device and jammed you somehow. Surely the voices that Pete Stanopoulos overheard whilst swinging from the rig above the flames prove they did. But *why*?

What drove you to tell the Americans about your breakthrough and to underestimate their measures must be guessed at, now. I know you were a vain young man, always in leathers, your hair fixed just so, and your technology was its own style. Too clever, you held yourself above the emotional outbursts of 'talent'. Dave Abrahams felt your private grief, without your consent. Letting the CIA know about your invention would, you thought, make you famous in the broader world than Dave's one of theatre. You had more vision, your space project showed that, and the CIA were the ones to take it further still. You would put Dave in his place and be recognised, all at once. This is where my guesswork breaks down. Although you were always cynical about peace protests and so forth, I find it hard to believe you were such a militarist, which is its own form of idealism, underneath. Did you imagine you would do some good for the world through the CIA? Perhaps you were blinded by your vanity. Perhaps you told someone at one of the UFO meetings you attended. The two men who questioned me afterwards clearly implied you had been the one who'd blabbed. You may have thought your device could only cause illusions. How wrong you were. Well, however much I have cursed you, Enzo, I hope your message got through.

David Clive Abrahams

I never saw you again after our last-night chat and no one else did either, except Packett. He said it had been quick for you. Dave, I hope we were good enough to represent our kind. No. Though time has played havoc with my self-esteem, I *know* we were at our best that night. Did Enzo lie to you? Did you know we were watched? Sometimes, thinking of the sadness that often surfaced in your eyes, I think you did. But perhaps you were worried about the play. At the funeral I told Pat what I thought. It did not surprise her. She said it might be best to let it lie. I would like to, Dave, but I can't. It's so tied up inside me I can't sort this from that. It involves too many things to untangle. My one good chance at love; my talent, my only charm; guilt; some kind of justice. I have pounded my head against walls so far, but if I don't go until I drop I'll be stranded in this café staring at my bloodshot eyes in the mirrors which go on for ever, and my life, as much as yours, will be over.

Helen Smart
beautiful Miranda. I never knew you very well. Robyn said you were wonderfully funny. I saw you in that Beckett season and you were great. Great.

Samuel Jefferson Schuyler
you and I leapt for the cliff face together. As we started up you were slammed hard against a bar. Before I could grab you you fell away. I was left with a handful of red mud. I remember your Italian food. Your nasty wit. The odd way you swung one shoulder as you walked. I keep an image of you laughing that afternoon at the waterhole, your head thrown back, the powerful muscles of your neck taut and your wide mouth showing those highly carnivorous teeth. And I can hear you saying, 'Buttocks to you, Kevin. Great, wobbling buttocks.' You were a Prospero with a power in you too great for your body, a manic and bounding Prosper I can never forget. Fred still mourns you.

Gillian-Anne Lydia Portman-Smith
I don't know anyone who knew you who did not love you. Swept away in the first moments, I thought I saw you in the eerie light, swimming toward Kevin, Sherelle and I much later as we sat, covered in mud, on the cliff top. I called your name. A brown wave rushed up behind you and rolled over you and you were gone. At that moment something broke behind Kevin's face; he twitched, eyes widening, jaw clenched. Then his eyes died. I have seen only anger in them since. What there was between you, I don't know. If others knew, they didn't say. On the day he and I fought I made the mistake of saying your name and now he will not speak to me and he does not answer letters. I think he hates me. But I loved you too.

Sarah Jane Witchell
I did not see you either. You, too, were found long afterward. The papers which paid you tribute left out your gentle way with

vain actors, your ability to heal the rifts in any company, at least for the duration of the show, your vision and boldness, your wit and driving intelligence. You knew what we needed at different times and gave it to us. Your laugh was gold.

Jennifer Margaret Drape

my oldest friend. I can't speak of you, so I've left you out of most of this story. I loved you. Goodbye.

Robyn Elizabeth Caroline Ho

I can still see you waking in the morning, still smell your soft difference to the tent's plastic and gum leaves and dust. I have tried to set this down before, but I haven't made it past here yet. I tell myself it's good for me. If I can get it finished I may admit you're gone. It's easy enough to see it. Won't leave me alone. Why the broadcast Enzo made and the effects of interference which were the flood singled out my mate for such a ghoulish show, I cannot tell. And why what Pete Stanopoulos felt suspended from the web on fire had no effect and yet the flood was real, we felt it, and what became of you was real and caused you pain and you cried out and I saw it in your eyes, why all this was so is still beyond me. Was our belief in our performance when perverted by our enemies enough to take us up and dash us, enough to break our set like kindling? And was my belief in our lives as man and wife so strong that when combined with Enzo's broadcast you were not allowed to rest in death but became a marionette? Robyn. I did believe in us, but not that way.

You vanished in the roaring minute it took to bring us down. The flood rushed by, pulling cliff away from under us, but Kevin and Sherelle and I scanned for others beyond the edge. We inched away from the crumbling bits until we found a spot we thought would hold us for a while and there we lay, our heads above the current, searching for our friends. We saw one of the musicians climb to safety on a slender island. We saw Gill go down and not come up again. Abruptly you showed below us, scrabbling up a slope of mud, the red muck just dissolved as fast as you could grab it. You slid back down the slope. I stumbled to my feet and ran toward you, screaming I don't know what, Kevin tackled me and we both went down and slid toward the edge. I hung over you. Bits of set and lamps and bars fell around us while Kevin held my legs and I reached for you, I reached. I watched the iron lighting bar slide off the last remains of rigging, stripping parts of lamps as it descended trailing flex, I lunged toward you and felt my calves slip through the crooks of Kevin's arms till only desperate fingers clutched me. The bar had gained momentum. I saw what was to come and could not close my eyes. The bar impaled you, then slowly toppled. It turned you on your side, then raised you in the air. You fell off with a smack. I could see inside you.

It was like what Pete became, but more so. You glowed in a shade of emerald light that isn't found in nature. Your organs were delineated. I watched your heart stop beating in your breast. And then, though it was clear you had died, you raised yourself above the mud on straightened arms and smiled at me, your crooked almost-wink and smile, and asked me,

'*Was't well done?*'

Ariel's voice. Her last line. Your arms gave way then. You flopped face first into the mud. The water rose to claim you. It sizzled where it touched you. Your light went out. You slid further down. There was bubbling, which ended. You were gone.

TWENTY-ONE

They sat knee to knee, heads resting on one another's shoulders. The steady firelight melted the bony angles of their spines into gentler curves, made unknown ground familiar. The new season brought a wind to whistle lightly in the eaves. The turkeys stirred and were still. Now and then the fire popped.

'Oh. I poured some whisky before,' said Gemma.

'Where?'

'Behind you and up I think, if we didn't knock it over. Yup, there it is.'

Kevin twisted around and scooped up the Duralex tumblers. Gemma received hers with a glance down.

'Happy times,' said Kevin.

'Cheers.'

They sipped.

'D'you want a ciggy?' asked Kevin.

'What – already?'

Kevin nodded humourlessly. He got up to fetch his makings. He offered some to Gemma, then, taking a pinch of tobacco and a paper for himself, he said:

'Well, this is a fine start.'

'I'm sorry.'

'No! You're very – I think you're really spunky, Gemma.'

'Thanks.' As she shoved the hastily rolled cigarette into her mouth her hand shook, and she left it there, to cover half her face while she lit up.

'But you don't believe me.'

'Hardly.'

'You are. When you showed up at Sherelle's, right from then I noticed — I did! — you had a lovely body . . . You're really strong, I like that, and you don't work at a tan—'

'Go as red as ribbon if I do.'

'I mean you don't try to make yourself over for blokes.'

'Oh, yeah.'

'You want me to go through everything?' He checked his anger. 'Your breasts. I couldn't stop staring — through your dress. Didn't you notice? I thought I was being awful but I couldn't help it. Your neck, just at the hairline, when you toss your head I catch sight of it and I want to drop everything, forget this crap we've got ourselves into. All I want to do is to hold you and *chew* on you. God, it's too much sometimes!'

'Well, here it is. Look. And look.'

'Don't do that.'

'But look at you!'

He looked down. 'Gemma, I can't.'

'Do you want to talk about it? I promise not to try to help.'

'I dunno if it'd do any good.'

'There are things we can try . . .'

'It's not your fault!'

She glanced down at her small breasts as if to say it was.

'It's my fault. I should have gotten things straight with you.'

'You're gay?' She forced a smile.

'No.' He stared into the darkness. 'I'm not quite a man.'

'Whoopie chook. I'm not quite a woman either.'

'I'm not a man *or* a woman.'

'Bullcrap.'

'Really. I'm not — human.'

'I'll prove to you you are.'

'I'll prove to you I'm not!' He had said it. But so aggressively all sorts of other things rose to complicate it. There could be no apology when so much frustration leadened him. He was afraid he would prove himself crazy if he acted upon his words. He felt

angry with Gemma, he knew it, because he had worked himself
up so much about this that even a little denial on her part
dropped her into the crowded category marked, 'We Reckon
You're Bonkers'. He wanted her on his side more than anyone.
A part of him did blame Gemma for his impotence, totally
unreasonably, and this provoked a stream of hate for the people
from the future so intense he knew that if he turned back to face
Gemma right now he would do something he'd regret for sure,
lose control. He stared into the fire and steadily cursed Oscar
and his mates, rocking back and forth.

I don't care if they're blown to subatomic particles, he
thought. I hope we all go down—

Kevin straightened and looked down at his bare chest, which
was bronzed with firelight, without seeing a thing.

He had shed tears. He'd never admitted as much to himself,
but he'd abandoned a fairly successful career, retreated into the
forest with his animals, dealt with those people he did meet as
less than human, really. Once or twice he'd been dragged into
bed but he'd never even thought of making a go of it with
anyone – and all this for the memory of Gillian. On that road
of isolation and nurtured bitterness he might have wasted years
more waiting for the circle to close. Only idealists travel in
circles, he reckoned.

Of course, nothing had been erased or mended. His tears were
not a sign of grief. That had settled into its place long ago. Here
is a beginning, he thought. When you plant a seed you've got to
take your time. Stay calm, mate, let it come out naturally.

He put his hands on his knees, and pushed himself until he
stood on shaky legs. He went to find the spare bottle of whisky.

When he got back Gemma was dressed, still hunched on the
middle step of the hearth, face ruddier than the fire could paint.
Her frown was crooked because she had sucked in one corner
of her mouth, her eyes were wide and bloodshot with tears in
check. She moved not at all as he sat. Kevin placed her Scotch

by her foot. A tough and narrow foot. He wanted to kiss her instep.

'When did you start thinking you were an alien?'

He fought back the instant reply. He shifted away from her, as neutrally as possible. They stared into the heart of the embers. Kevin took up the tongs and as he carefully rearranged the fire, he began to speak.

'If I am crazy I will prove it, one way or the other. I'm sorry I yelled at you.' He picked up a hunk of red gum, which he tried out this way and that before balancing it like an egg, on one edge, and wedging some burning ends under it. He still felt on the verge of hysteria.

'I have never been in contact with the aliens, I haven't even had a vision, although I've heard some of the accounts on the ABC. Pretty strong stuff. I can see why people get religious about it, I think. But it is aliens. Everyone will see that soon. 'Course that doesn't mean they'll let go of their religious bent.'

He hefted a full cross-section of pine, but discarded it in favour of another third of hardwood because he liked the smell. His back strained from lifting while seated.

'That's why I'm doing this, staging this play. I am not an alien. But . . .' He swept up the stray embers with the lump in hand, placed the second piece of wood across the first, took up two others in a squat and fell back on to the cushions. As he spoke he rubbed the two together. 'When they first contacted me – I call the main one Oscar, by the way – they used voices from my memory. Some kid's voice. Martin's voice. It wasn't clear then, mostly scrambled snatches when I was nearly asleep. They sounded ridiculous to me, I suppose because they were in rhyme. It turns out that verse – well, all the effective musical elements of language – they have a better chance of being communicated telepathically. Rhyme, metre, alliteration and so forth make what is said more basic and powerful, they're not just there to make things pretty. What am I saying? You know all this, don't ya? Geometry's got an emotional power, which reaches right back beyond words into what you might call a dreamtime. You can use normal, rational statements but you've got to be – *tuned* to it first, and even then it hardly comes through clear enough to be noticed. It's next to impossible to do anything physically to the past. So anyhow, I didn't get what Oscar was saying because it was in silly rhymes, and also because what they were on about was too fantastic to believe.' Kevin banged the blocks of wood together, forcing his next words, though he knew it was wrong. 'And as well—

'As well because I'd done my fucken best to forget about Martin Leywood, and the flood. And Gillian Portman-Smith.'

That wasn't so bad, he thought, and glanced sideways at Gemma. She was watching the fire.

'Therefore it surfaced as impulses, as compulsions to, say, go to Melbourne to visit Martin. Do the rounds of the producers. That part still confuses me. I mean, why do it at all? When I finally gave in to them and relaxed I got detailed instructions, and some explanation. You'll rob that armoured van, get the gun from here, the car from there, you'll get into the safe this way. They'd researched the past in detail. *It all turned out to be correct.*'

His voice grew thick, but he ploughed on regardless. 'You see, the reason I accepted this before it proved to be right and the reason I'm the only one who can get these messages from – from the people in the future is that **I've been made into something not a human being any more!**'

Kevin swung around to Gemma. She turned to him with understanding eyes. She had accepted everything, the smile she offered told him that, and more. He half rose to receive her with his arms.

And then an ugly thought occurred to him. He hadn't finished, he hadn't told her everything, and yet she took it all with ease. It could be she was influenced by something more than what he'd said. It could be his persuader working on her mind. Wildly, he cast around the room for the side effects of broadcast, an odd glow, or even rain. His head jerked, he dropped the wood. He bolted to his feet. Gemma grabbed his thighs.

No glow, besides the fire. This wasn't a performance. But the thought of Gemma's reason bent made Kevin angrier than he could stand.

'I'm – I've got to get out of here.'

He turned, oblivious of her hands, ran out the door and kept on running. Sticks poked his soles, gravel lodged there but he pelted on, unheeding. Another fat moon lit his way, rendering the landscape in the shades of steel and coal. The turkeys nattered at his footfall, their corrugated iron shed soon fell behind; he was into the bush.

A pair of marsupial eyes ducked out of sight. Twigs and leaves whipped and raked his naked body, his face and arms and legs. He ran until he saw no sign of any human, which really wasn't far.

At last, holding a narrow tree trunk with both hands, he let himself slide to the ground. The squiggly gum was smooth in his arms, and solid. He clung there, on his knees.

Gemma's calls came and went. He knelt. Anger took turns with depression. His eyes were fastened on a pool of moonlight on the edge of a small clearing beyond his tree, for something to look at. The lines cut by insects in the pale trunks which gave the trees their name seemed like writing he could almost read. Eventually Gemma stopped calling. The forest was still.

A crackling of stiff leaves came from the dark past the clearing. Kevin looked up. Time had passed, the moon had shifted slightly. A small wombat, about the size of a box of wine, waddled into the gentle wash. Its hair shone silver, its eyes a fierce brass. Kevin was close enough to hear the whuffing of its wet nose, to smell its musk. It couldn't have noticed him. Lucky he was downwind.

As if to call him a fool, the wombat lifted its blunt snout and, twitching its stubby ears, appeared to stare at Kevin with grumpy wombat impassivity. Time became beside the point. The wombat, old enough to have lost the good nature of childhood but too young to have mastered the rolling tetchiness of the full adult, gazed at him for so long he began to wonder if it were entirely natural. Would anything *not* relate to the destiny of the race again? The thought alone was enough to drive you mad. But what better comfort for your freaked-out Frankenstein than a wombat's sturdy pragmatism?

To tell him what it thought of such egotistic rambling, the wombat lobbed a series of tidy vegetarian turds. It walked forward into the clearing, then stopped. It sniffed the air and made a foul-tempered nasal growl. It sniffed again, waddled closer, and (at last) saw Kevin. It turned and trotted off into the dark.

Kevin began to smile. It had not seen into the deeps of Kevin's soul at all. It was a wombat. Just a wombat. Nothing more. Kevin tried to stand, but found his legs and feet, cramped from squatting by the tree, would not support him. He stumbled forward into the gum tree, and took a sharp blow on the head. This was too much.

He laughed. He held himself up by hugging the tree, almost cacked himself with laughter. He laughed till he was weak from it, gasping and pounding the tree trunk with his fist. Soon he found he could stand, almost, and he turned and wove his way back home. Falling into bushes like a drunk, shouldering past trees, he cut and grazed himself quite badly now and then but he didn't give a monkey's.

When he arrived at the open door the lights were on. Gemma sat on the couch, her back to him, watching what appeared to be an old Tarkovsky film on his minute black and white. Kevin leaned against the jamb and watched her watch. The muscles stood out on one side of her slender neck because she'd bent it till her ear was almost on her shoulder. With one leg tucked beneath her, her dress rucked up the other's thigh so far he could see she hadn't put her underwear back on, she looked that relaxed and patient he felt a bigger twerp. He ached to nuzzle that thigh.

Suddenly he felt as naked as he was and awkward with it. He remembered a pair of dungarees he had left hanging on the line for a month. Silent, he retreated.

The tank water was cold. His cuts and scratches stung, but the lump on his crown felt better for a wash. He dried himself with a stiff T-shirt, and returned to the doorway.

Gemma stood in the rectangle of light, waiting for him.

They hugged. Kevin laughed again, just for feeling lucky. He was himself, whatever had been done to him. So she believed him. So what? She liked him. Couldn't he accept that? First you get upset that she won't believe you then you chuck a berko when she does. Honestly, Kevin!

They kissed, then. Breaking apart, Kevin stared into Gemma's eyes and said: 'Whatever happens, be my mate?'

'Of course, you dill.'

'You must be wondering why I ran out.'

'No. If I got all silly each time you did I'd be a bloody wreck.'

'Let's have a drink.'

'Sounds all right.'

'I saw a wombat.'

'I can see a dingbat right in front of me.'

'I did!'

'Ah-huh.'

Inside, it did not prove difficult to show her what he'd thought he might have had to show her earlier. There was a good scratch halfway down his forearm from his stumbling through the bush, which he squeezed, much to Gemma's disgust. A line of bright blue droplets appeared.

'You see why I've been so crazy? This dries like normal blood. Oscar and his fucking technocrats have altered me. See – sending something back in time takes stacks of energy. They're not even sure it's possible to send objects. But they can alter things. They altered a virus, and here I am.'

'Mah Gahd! They gave you a disease?'

'Not exactly. The virus was a way of causing bigger changes within my whole system. I've been turned into a kind of android, from the bottom up.'

'And that's why you can't fuck me? Your bottom?'

'I'm not sure I'm able to have sex. Well, I think I might, but I reckoned you wouldn't of liked a machine inside you.'

'Beats a vibrator, kiddo.'

'You don't know that yet.'

'Ah-huh?'

'Ah-huh.'

'Ah-huh!'

'Ah-huh.'

'I love you, Kevin.'

'Don't say that.'

'I'll say what I like!' She stood and turned to the open door.

'I LOVE KEVIN GORE!' she shouted.

'You'll scare the wombats away.'

'You really saw a wombat?'

'Yairs. He gave me a lesson in melodrama. *It* did.'

She came back. She leant across the kitchen table. 'So why did they do that to you? To fuck up your love life?'

'I am a device to transmit to the aliens.'

'That's a bit far-fetched.'

'I'm glad you said that. You see, although I'm still basically organic, I've got much the same kind of thing in me as Enzo used during *The Tempest*. My nervous system and brain double as the device and the power comes from performance of deep, symbolic structures. It can be used to sort of brainwash people, though that doesn't last. I – I don't want to do that to you.'

Gemma narrowed her eyes. 'You're a *clever man*,' she said.

'Huh. I only want to be able to call you Budge. Whatever that means.'

'No, *clever* in the Aboriginal sense. To be *clever* means you have supernatural knowledge. You might have magic powers.'

Kevin frowned. 'It's not the same. History doesn't travel in circles.'

''Course not. So. Enzo used the thing to convince all of you to do the play in the first place, and probably later to calm you down when the accidents happened.'

'Mind like a steel trap.' Kevin poured generous glasses of

Lagavulin. 'He probably also used it to stop us talking about it after Packett told us what was going on.' He sat and looked at his glass.

'Then why didn't you use it on the possible producers of Martin's play?'

'It doesn't last. Besides' – Kevin took a moment to savour the peaty malt – 'that was necessary to the success of what we're doing now. I'm not sure how.'

'You think the Americans had a thing like Enzo's? It would explain its use as a weapon.'

'Mm! There's another thing that points to that, too, besides the visits we had from the two Jehovah's Witness types afterwards. If Enzo was totally fried, and his equipment was destroyed in the first few minutes of the flood, then why did we get that surreal business when Robyn died? Martin saw her glow and speak to him. I saw her as a moth being burnt on hot coals ... They had their own machine. Probably to block the signal from Enzo's, but the two machines in concert built up such a potential from the performance – which was a doozy – things went full-bore haywire. Remember there were atmospheric disturbances every time we can prove it was used. Those bastards might even have known that and caused the flash flood deliberately, to cover their tracks.'

Gemma had forgotten her whisky. Now she sat down opposite Kevin and took her glass in hand. Leaning back in the creaky bentwood she raised the glass to her thin lips but refrained from sipping. An earnest look crossed her pockmarked face. 'I thought *you* were a bit whack-oh. Those guys must be utterly mental.'

'I don't know. It's possible they're evil.' Kevin took a gulp of his Scotch; he made a face.

Gemma still hadn't drunk. 'If they have a device of their own locked away somewhere, and know what Enzo was trying to do, then is it possible they'll try to interfere with you in any way? There are at least three weeks of rehearsal before you can transmit, aren't there? They might find out.'

'I don't know. You're right, I can't transmit anything but performed material. You have to be really submerged in what you're saying and that might take more than three weeks. I'm glad you think it's a good play. It might shorten the whole thing.'

'Well.' Gemma held her glass out towards Kevin. 'No more stuffing around, ay? And never mind the rules.'

'Yeah. Bugger that for a joke.'

They downed their whisky.

'Let's go to bed,' said Gemma, licking her lips.

'Ah-huh?'

'I promise not to molest you.'

They went.

TWENTY-TWO

The rental firm took one look at the wheelchair and decided to lay on the best disabled vehicle they could muster. He couldn't yell at them for caring. Partly, this was because the boy at the counter had taken a shine to him. His type too. A sociology student at the local university, no muscle tone to speak of, soft voice, big brown eyes, careless with his long orange hair. Jay didn't go for the industrial objects through the nose or lips, though. They'd clang when you kissed. So he waited as patiently as he could and when they couldn't get a car till ten thirty he didn't chew them out, although his final meeting with the Melbourne CIA wouldn't take him past nine. He accepted coffee and chatted with Kim, his name was, about – what else? – Martin's book.

Charms All O'erthrown. An already dog-eared copy of the cheap paperback lay on the grainy force-grown counter beside them, Martin's long, bland, somewhat sorrowful face almost sliced in two by 'Soon to be a Major Motion Picture'. The boy didn't recognise Jay. In interviews his face had been carefully masked by a Joe Bloggs computer image. That wasn't why he felt nervous. You could reason that since he'd already put off seeing Gore for three weeks while he helped Caroline Walsh launch the book, another couple of hours wouldn't hurt; or you could say that as Martin Leywood's notoriety increased so did the danger toward Kevin and something had to be done to protect him, too, before anyone discovered that the stories Jay had spread about Kevin hiding somewhere in Melbourne proved utterly false. Jay's meeting down the road with his old Agency buddy was designed to protect Kevin as well as Martin and Caroline, but no matter how skilful his mixture of lies and negotiation Jay would never trust the CIA to simply roll over on this one. He didn't feel edgy enough to cause hassle here and yet – it took the *fun* out of this Kim's flattering attentions.

The boy had read in *The Australian* that old Noam Chomsky had come out behind Martin's accusations. He hadn't seen a vision himself but knew people who had. Jay changed the subject, asking him if the vegetarian meals at the pub he'd selected for the meeting were any good, imagining wistfully what an evening spent with Kim would be like.

At last the time came for his meeting with Warner. As he rolled down the sidewalk under a streaky orange sunset Jay contemplated the last few weeks' successes, trying to bolster his confidence. This sort of lack had never worried him as an atheist in the CIA; if anything, he'd suffered from over-confidence. He stopped for a moment and watched an Italian widow wash and sweep the pavement in the rich light.

Apart from the delay on his plans for Kevin, things were going fine. People had listened. Caroline had shrewdly held back on any mention of spacemen until the actual release of Martin's book ten days after the first press release. After a series of newspaper articles questions had been asked in Parliament about the CIA gagging of police and newspapers eleven years back. The US government then denied involvement in such a way as to confirm that a telepathic device was the source of the worldwide disturbances. A Senate investigation followed. The Independent Coalition here was screaming for a Commissioner's Inquiry. A few careful interviews from Jay and a leak of his negotiations with the CIA were enough to consolidate credibility in Martin's book. The public read and decided for themselves that the incomprehensible quality of the visions confirmed what had until then been a fringe explanation for them:

Aliens. Enzo Carmoni had aimed at the stars and something was answering back. A few bright sparks even connected the rain or wind which invariably accompanied their visions with the flood which had wiped out most of the cast of *The Tempest*. It had taken a little over three weeks to make Martin a national hero.

Jay realised that the widow had stopped sweeping. At first he thought she was staring at him. No, she was looking past his right shoulder, into the air. Shuddering, her eyes rolled back. A brief shower pattered the widow and the back of Jay's neck, and was gone.

Noticing the silver crucifix between the widow's breasts as he rolled past, Jay wondered what images danced across the old woman's brain. Were the media pundits right? Did it depend on your own make-up? Had Jay *not* seen the Devil after all? If they were right this natural Catholic might suddenly wake a raving atheist.

Jay was not about to hang around and find out.

After some small talk and a few lies they settled down to big dishes of rice and stir-fried vegetables and such. The man was hungry, had obviously been working hard. Not on the negotiations with Jay: that was a negative thing, to agree to leave people alone. Jay decided to leave him be and see if he came out with anything voluntarily. They retired from the counter to a pub table for coffee before saying anything further.

'Well,' said Warner, lighting up a reefer, 'you got it. You agree to testify that the decision to execute Thoughtboost was merely a local one and we do nothing more on the whole deal. Close the file.'

'Okay,' said Jay. The man's marijuana stank. Jay resisted an impulse to look at his watch and continued to smile good-naturedly at the guy's broad face.

'Lord, you should see Burroughs. Although he was only Section Chief for Tasmania at the time and Pinker's long dead,

he is in one hell of a tizz, man. Afraid that Washington's gonna
sacrifice the whole department. There goes his pension!'

'Really,' said Jay.

'Yeah. And naturally, meanwhile, Thoughtboost might be
dead but we've got a whole mess of observation goin' on. This
is too much for Burroughs. All he's good for is butt-licking and
telling stories about 'Nam. And he picked Australia because it
was a nice quiet unit to finish up in. Man, they're tearin' his
balls every which way! Washington haven't really swallowed
this shit about aliens, and they got every office from here to
Iceland checking for home-built Thoughtboost devices.'

Jay nodded. That seemed likely. But there was a lie behind
Warner's eyes which he couldn't place.

'Now we got *this* done I have to drive out to some fucken
hick town in New South Wales to go prowling round for 'em
myself! Some fucken life, ay?'

Jay started with fear. To him, New South Wales meant Kevin
Gore. It was paranoia, he knew it, but you couldn't be too
paranoid when the CIA were involved. His old buddy didn't
notice Jay's fear. He went on to list those still in the office from
the time Jay had worked there, then described Burroughs'
anxiety attacks in graphic detail. Jay in turn pretended to be
astounded at how the evening had flown and just a little bored
with Warner's office gossip. He invented some hot date at a
nightclub, paid the bill and saw off Warner with a refusal of a
lift.

As he wheeled himself down the pub's ramp on to the street,
he heard angry voices from the alley beside him. And one
terrified voice. His first inclination was to mind his own business, to get the car and continue with what he already thought
of as his assignment. Where are your lofty new ideas now? a
part of him mocked, which stopped him dead. Yet he did not
power down the alley to anyone's rescue, he waited, big hands
hovering over his back wheels, to hear more of what it was
about. The words, 'seeing things ya bloody twerp', had popped

out of the more usual abuse. He let himself roll into the alley's gutter, to catch the words.

'Cunt.' A nasal, markedly Australian voice.

'You're a bit obsessed with them.' The frightened voice, an educated younger guy, tried to sound cool. 'That's the seventh time you've used the word.'

'Wassa matta, *cunt*, don'tcha like 'em? Poofter *cunt*!' The first voice rose hysterically on the last epithet. It seemed his victim had struck a nerve. 'What I seen is my own business, gay boy, an' I don't need no poofter psycho explanations of what I seen. Cunt. I been contacted by "a higher form of lifeform" and what I been told is to *get* poofy know-it-all bastards like youse and smash ya bloody heads in! I reckon that's good advice? So don't go tellin' me what it means 'cause I already know, my little snit has told me so. It's a *higher*' – there was a dull thump – '*form*' – another thump – 'of life*form*.'

Jay did not wait for the next blow to land, he was down the alley and ready for a fight before he could think about it. Only when he reached the cul-de-sac did he realise there were three of them lined up against him, big fuckers, and that, combat medals or no, he was just another guy in a wheelchair.

Blood trickled from a cut beneath the boy's delicate nostrils where a ring or a fingernail had caught him, but otherwise he looked fine. He was rubbing his jaw with one trembling hand, and breathing hard. As Jay coasted up behind the assailants he took in the kid's features as if studying a photograph. He would have been surprised to learn that he wasn't gay. Or perhaps it was wishful thinking. There was something in the way the streetlight coated his high, flat cheeks, something in the way he held his large head. A tall, well-built possible student with lank, black hair cut short at the back but with the sidelocks fashionable a few years back. His black jeans and T-shirt hung off him as if he scorned the exercise which would have turned his broad Australian frame into a god-like body.

It was love at first sight. Jay felt the blood rush into his neck and his hands grip the chair's wheels to halt it in a fury at the thought that these bastards had dared to *touch* this beautiful boy.

In training, they had to stop Jay from running into trouble chin first, again and again. 'You got too many balls,' his instructor had told him. 'Someday that gonna get y'all killed.' And it nearly had, in service, many times. It would almost certainly do so here. He checked himself. They weren't aware of Jay yet but would be any second.

'RUN!' he shouted, and while attackers spun toward his voice he launched his wheelchair forward, at the last moment thrusting a clawed hand at the balls of the one blocking the boy's escape route. The poor bastard looked down – too late. Jay elbowed him aside and fled toward the street.

The beautiful boy hesitated like a rabbit, casting this way and that before sprinting after Jay. Turning his head as his powerful arms pumped the wheels forward, Jay saw one of the attackers make a grab at the kid but miss him by millimetres. He heard pelting sandshoes on wet stone then saw the kid sprint past him and turn in the brightly lit street toward the pub.

Good. The kid had brains. Now, if Jay could outpace his pursuers to the corner he'd be okay too. With metres to go, he felt a drag on the wheelchair's right side. One of them had grabbed a handle. *Damn* those things! With as much force as he could muster Jay jerked the right wheel forward. The attacker held on. He gripped both wheels as hard as he could and tried to drag both of them the remaining two metres into the light. Perhaps out there someone would stop or call the police or something. Just a few more feet . . .

He had made it into the light but it did no good. He could see nobody to either side for a couple of blocks.

He would have to stand, as it were, and fight. He grinned without humour as he turned and looked at the hairy fist coming down at him.

Then a black sandshoe and a black-jeaned leg flicked across his field of vision. It connected with the grinning head above and behind him. It knocked the smile off the man's face. The kid had crouched around the corner and come to Jay's rescue. 'Come on!' he shouted at Jay.

As Jay spun his chair and headed up the ramp to the pub doors, he couldn't help but think that, even so urgent, the boy's voice was every bit as beautiful as his face.

'What's your name?' the boy asked simply, a wet bar-cloth held to the right side of his jaw. When Jay told him he said, 'Sounds like *Dickens Goes to San Francisco*.' And he smiled.

The boy's name, Jay learned, was Geoff Barton. He *was* a student, at Melbourne University. And he was gay.

'Guys like that,' Geoff said. 'I didn't think they grew them any more. At least not round here.'

'Like what?' asked Jay, pouring the last drops of lager into his glass and handing the bottle to the barman.

'Poofter bashers. I mean it was true when I moved from Tasmania to Melbourne, but this guy had seen one of those visions and it must have told him to beat up on gay men.' He laughed. 'He must have been an arsehole to begin with, but these visions must be really powerful stuff to get someone to do that.' He sat down at Jay's table, at last, opposite.

'I heard what he said to you,' said Jay. 'That's why I came after you.' He smiled at Geoff. Geoff smiled back. 'These visions are strong shit. I had one before I left the States.'

'Yeah?' Geoff dropped the bar cloth on the table. 'What was it like?' His brown eyes shone with fascination.

'Well . . . I'm not sure if that asshole out there interpreted what he saw correctly if it meant going out and bashing gays.' He rubbed his wrinkled forehead. 'I'm not sure if *I* interpreted what I saw correctly. But it was powerful. God *damned* powerful.' He smiled at Geoff's obvious frustration. 'What I saw was the Devil himself.'

Jay told Geoff about what he had seen. And how it had converted him. It meant revealing his own gay disposition but, hell, if he was straight with himself he took a pleasure in that, in watching the boy's eyes as he said it. This was the second time in as many weeks that he had told the story. When he was finished he wasn't sure if the boy thought he was crazy. But he was sure Geoff was still fascinated.

'I have to go now,' he said, looking at his watch. 'Business to do in New South Wales. Give me your address, Geoff. We can have a drink when I get back.'

They exchanged addresses. Geoff thanked him. He thanked Geoff. And as he turned away and wheeled himself toward the door, Jay realised that for the first time this relationship might go further than a one-night stand. He might be about to re-join the world. Did the terror he had seen stalking the desert sky mean more than a message from God? Perhaps it stood for what he had been himself while working for Uncle Sam: a nightmare figure; a stealer of souls. Or, rather, did it stand for Uncle Sam, a country too large to administrate, concerned with its own perpetuation above all else, insidiously using the ideas of freedom and individualism to promote the exact opposite? Was that the fiery cannibal he had seen?

Well, after he got back from helping Kevin Gore into some hidy-hole, he would call Geoff and together they would look into it. He was a bright boy. And Jay would be delighted to be lent a hand – especially such a graceful, slender one.

TWENTY-THREE

The first real autumn storm thrashed impotently at the windows. When he discovered the windows would not open, Martin's lower abdomen came over all tremulous, never mind the latest thing in air conditioning which graced one whole wall of the hotel room. The air smelt exactly like a camp site at Wilson's Promontory National Park, complete with odours of wet leaves, seaspray, bandicoots and even the occasional waft of camp fire (no carcinogens, of course). In an attempt to quell his dread of enclosure, Martin picked up the list of questions for tonight's television interview on *Two Thousand Seconds*.

'Oh my God,' Martin murmured. 'Oh my God.'

There were alternatives to the ones they thought might prove offensive. Still, there was no way that he could stop them using the term 'tragic relationship' to describe his affair with Robyn. They were trying their best to make him into some story-book anti-hero. Well, Martin *had* written the story book. *Charms All O'erthrown*. Sitting at this ornate snit-cum-desk as near as dammit to the top of the Regent, Martin began to appreciate just how much solace he had taken from the role of ignored madman. Nowadays they nodded seriously, praised the book Caroline had had rushed into print on the tail of her revelations to the press ('Ex-CIA Agent Reveals US Secret Weapon Is Cause Of Visions') and trod daintily around his real and imagined scars. Martin re-read his words (ouch), examined his memories – and felt embarrassed.

It had been another man who'd found it necessary to vent his
obsession in print. A younger man. After the argument with Jay
Schnarler, which both vindicated him and surprised him with
his own lack of bile, he'd let himself out of Salisbury Cottages
and soon found himself a new, screwed-down, drier version of
the old Martin Leywood, built out of others' expectations rather
than out of the younger man by a natural process of growth and
forgetting. The previous Martin had excelled at the Grouchy
Eccentric; how he'd do as the Prophet Out of the Wilderness he
was not so sure. The costume didn't fit. He didn't even like the
man.

He drew neat lines through the worst questions, ticked the
alternatives to which he least objected and fed the sheets back
into the snit, which said 'thank you' in a Californian accent.
Martin yawned deeply. He tapped the sequence on the snit
which would print up a menu. To eat out of boredom repulsed
him. But was it really boredom? You mustn't let yourself be
satisfied with superficial thinking, old son, he thought. Just
because you're rich. The new Martin Leywood didn't have to be
stupid as well as colourless. No, what he felt was – guilt. He
had made a profit from tragedy. When Caroline Walsh had
contacted him through Angie at the loony bin and told him
she'd read his script for *Charms All O'erthrown* and that she
had persuaded her new employers at Borovsky, one of the
world's Big Seven studios, to go ahead with a multi-million-
dollar production of his play as a film, then when she made sure
it'd be successful by releasing the tapes she'd made of her
conversations with Ex-Agent Schnarler, Martin had felt no
qualms about signing contracts for the rights to the book and
the film. After all, he had spent more than two years back when
he had written the book trying to get the thing published. He'd
finished up rather too fond of his Chardonnay.

So what if I am making money out of all this folderol? He
stood, menu in hand, and crossed to the far wall, where he
slapped the plate which would kill the air conditioning. He had
not been so agitated since that first night in the lock-up, when

he'd been thrashed and left to rot by the police after trying to force copies of his self-published masterpiece on passers-by, drunk, poor, wild-eyed and friendless after Packett had died. Is it nobler to be a failure who has to pretend to be crazy so he can stay on social security? I made an execrable alchoholic anyway, he thought. He went back to the snit and tapped out a reasonable order of healthy food. Hot pastrami on rye with everything he could think of; a ginger beer; tofu salad. The new Martin Leywood was beginning to discover his own likes and dislikes. First thing tomorrow he'd ask for a room with windows that opened.

He was going shopping. With neither a hint in the green room over wine and canapés, nor a shadow in the questions vetted only that morning, the afternoon talk-show host had framed the feature with sequences from horror flicks and sci-fi tracts and, using a deceptively tame tone of voice-over, had argued a new line of scepticism regarding the imminent aliens: the spiritual upsurge long expected for the turn of the century had arrived, belatedly, in a form which satisfied a technological, materialist society. So tactfully had the essay been put, Martin hadn't felt offended at the interviewer's refusal to take his story at face value. The argument was not brand spanking new, it had been mooted before the US government had admitted to their 'monitoring' of Dave and Enzo's project. It was, however, original to contend such a thing *after* most people had accepted the visions were from aliens and not from God. And unlike the superficial numbers which had been pulled on him lately (*Two Thousand Seconds* had produced a man who claimed to be Robyn's 'real' father), it gave him pause.

He had not actually considered the meaning of all this hullabaloo. For others. And the consequences. Although the interviewer's scenario involved a spiritual let-down after people discovered there had never been any aliens (no spacecraft had been detected approaching, so far) and it had been a form of collective madness, to refute him begged the questions he now found himself pitifully unable to begin to answer. He had been shown clips of the rioting in the Socialist Federation and elsewhere which indicated that people still looked upon the aliens as some kind of salvation from the ills of the world. There had been interviews with people in Melbourne whose lives had been torn apart by their interpretations of the visions they had seen. The number of people affected was growing every day. From a sensation it was becoming a global issue. And more people every day were coming to accept his own version of the story. Which made him some kind of hero, yes, but also a villain. How do you view your responsibility for the violence your actions helped cause, Mr Leywood? What will actually happen when the aliens land, Mr Leywood? How alien is alien? And if the interviewer's theory was correct, what then?

Is it all a product of our imaginations?

If so, he didn't want to think about where it might lead, or what would happen to him as leader if the aliens didn't show. It was at this point he decided to shop. What would he buy? was a far more pleasant question to answer. Why, everything, dear. By the time he'd been thrown in Salisbury Cottages he'd sold most of his possessions. The suit he wore was his trademark now, according to the printout news, but they never considered that it might be his entire wardrobe. Trademark be buggered. He'd buy one of the bodyguard's suits or something and have a quiet shop on his own. Wearing sunglasses. And a hat.

'Oh *shit*! He tossed his hickory walking stick on to the humungous bed. He would feel lopsided, but there was nothing for it; the stick was an obvious giveaway, and he'd only used it out of vanity. Overcompensating a little, he walked down the hall with Arthur, his afternoon bodyguard. He felt better already. As they emerged from the lift, however, Johnno met them, looking anxious. Lord, thought Martin, what now? This bodyguard thing was such a waste of time. He would give the autographs and be done with it, he decided. He looked at the glass doors to the foyer. There was no one hassling the doorman. The man stood there happily picking his nose.

'I DO know him you bloody NARNA! I dressed him when he was sick, wiped his arse, for crying out loud. Just let me *speak* to him, ya great stupid bastard.'

The energetic abuse spun him like a leaf in the wind. Martin recognised the broad back and small bottom at once.

'Angie!'

'Martin!' Her face, for the second time in his experience, revealed a fragile side so often hidden by her childlike delight and boisterousness. The first time had been when they'd said goodbye at Salisbury. They embraced clumsily: he was not a slight man any more, but she was *very* big. Johnno and the doorman averted their eyes; Arthur grinned openly.

'It's such a relief to see you, my dear.'

'I never thought I'd get to see you.'

They stood holding one another's waists while their faces settled into affectionate smiles.

'Come shopping with me, Angie, *mon petit*, for a stroll. Come for a meal! Do you have any time?'

'Got a week's holiday from Salisbury.'

'Ah – Mr Leywood, ah . . .'

'Arthur, I know you're not to call me Martin, it being against police regulations and that, but you may speak when you wish, you know.'

'Um – is it? Um. I don't think it'd be a good idea to – ah – just stroll out there.' The stocky man, who looked like a surf desperado stuffed into a small suit, thumbed toward 'out there'. 'I couldn't bank on your safety, ah, Martin. Sir.' He looked toward his superior, Johnno, for support, who nodded gravely.

How could he escape these lovable thugs? Martin thought about the things the audience had said about him that afternoon (one had had to be restrained) and decided Arthur's warnings were more than clichés. Well, one good cliché . . .

'I meant to say, Arthur, can I get a hat and sunglasses somewhere? Can I swap jackets with someone? Above all, Arthur, is there a back door?'

This drew a laugh from Arthur, who obviously liked a bit of

drama. 'You can use mine if y'like,' he offered, pulling a pair of mirrorshades from his breast pocket, 'and Johnno's about your size.'

Johnno put his hands on his hips and shook his tiny head, not in refusal but in restrained amusement at his younger colleague. Here was a side to the VicForce Martin had never seen.

'There are shops in here, aren't there?' said Angie.

'Why, so there are.' Martin and the only friend he'd made in Salisbury Cottages still had their arms around one another's waists, so Martin began to steer Angie toward the door to the plaza. Angie, much stronger, steered him in a circle back.

'At least take the glasses and turn the jacket inside out,' she told him.

'But that will look very funny.'

'You don't have to wear it ya drongo!'

Martin complied. They set off for the old-fashioned boutiques which lined the courtyard at the centre of the hotel. The autumn beat itself against the ubiquitous glass, not as cosy as against corrugated iron, but with Angie around it helped take the edge off Martin's isolation and uncertainty. Her presence made the afternoon into one of those long fantasy games played on rainy childhood Sundays.

Arthur made no secret of it that he, too, appreciated Angie Langsam. His eyes and swallows spoke eloquently. Martin wasn't sure it wasn't professional interest, one bouncer to another, but this happily married man's attentions caused Martin to see Angie in a sexual way for the first time. He had seen her as a kind of poker-playing sister; it didn't mean she saw him that way as well – though if she had wanted it she would simply have asked. Of course, he had heard her say before, now he thought of it, one 'shouldn't root the patients'.

They bought a new suit off the rack and some expensive swimming togs for Angie. If anyone recognised Martin in the wood-panelled shops (not a hologram in sight) they were too polite to show it. Then, as they worked up a head of conversational steam, the urge to shop evaporated. When the rain stopped, they ran through the puddled streets to a place recommended by Arthur, who'd escorted other 'bignobs' there.

'The trevally's bloody beautiful and they have barramundi flown in!' he shouted after Angie and Martin as he chased them across the slippery tramlines to the restaurant.

Inside, among the ferns and exotic flowers, by a noisy waterfall which aerated a pond full of bright pink loaches, watched by a blunt stick of a blue-tongue lizard Arthur informed them was named Harry, Martin relaxed. It was the kind of place frequented for the peace it offered. They nattered. He caught up with loony-bin gossip, she sympathised with his plight. Arthur, pretending not to listen, bless him, kept an eye out and ate. And ate.

'Ooh, you poor bunny, rich as fuck, wine and champers for brekky, horses' doovers with the PM, film contracts, adulating crowds, m'heart goes right out to ya. I can barely stand it.'

Arthur glanced around to see if anyone had reacted to her increasingly loud voice, but as though bored with the conversation.

'You know I've given up the demon drink, dear.'

'You never did drink enough to be an alcoholic anyway.'

'You know that wasn't my problem.'

'Your problem was that you actually liked it there.'

'So. Same again?' Martin waved at the wine butler.

'Uh-huh, but with a beer chaser this time.'

'Another lemonade and bitters for you? Geneva and the Belgian lager for the diva, here, and another bottle of light for myself.' He smiled at the waiter, crossing his legs. 'Thank you,' he said, and turned to the bodyguard. 'Arthur, either I have a virulent case of dandruff or the waiter has recognised me. Should we leave, dear?'

Arthur spoke idly, looking as if distracted across the garden: 'Nah. Seems okay here.' He smiled shyly at Angie, then looked away again.

Martin and Angie exchanged looks, grinning.

Then the chef erupted from the kitchen.

A huge, hairy picture of an ogre, fury storming through the avocado trees and orchids toward them. Red-faced and red-necked, his stomach would have peeked from under his smock had he not worn an apron. Martin was transfixed by the curly neck hairs which made a joke of a hairline; he knew they grew right down to his arse. This fantasy made him useless during the confrontation. Before he could stand Arthur placed his body between the fat chef and Martin. Shouting something about his virgin daughter and the devils whom Martin had sent to rape her in her sleep, the chef grabbed both Arthur's upper arms and head-butted him. Arthur fell backwards on to the table. Angie reached the man's arm in time to prevent him from taking Martin by the throat. Despite some wild swings at her head she managed to push him away until he tripped over a rock.

Then she sat on him.

By this time Arthur had recovered enough to pin the chef's arms to the ground. He continued to rant about how his daughter had taken up with the 'hooligans from the flats', but his struggle gradually subsided.

The other bodyguards arrived. Handcuffs were fitted.

'Orright,' said Arthur to the other diners, who had gathered at a safe distance. 'You can all go home and tell ya mums now.'

It was not until they reached the hotel foyer that Martin realised what a beating Angie had taken for him. Such was the unreality of the event, the sound seemed to have dissipated into the ether; he could remember what had been said, that there had been much shouting and grunting, but all he recalled was silence. He looked at Angie and gave a cry. Her shirt was torn down one seam, a cheek had begun to swell and one ear was bright red. He insisted she come up to his suite. Arthur, humbly eager to assist, fetched a T-shirt and first aid kit after seeing to his replacement at the door.

Angie shrugged off the injury, saying she had copped much worse at work. But Martin dabbed and fussed and sent for a bottle of gin. He knew she was right, but here in black and blue was the impact of the visions on people. And not just anyone. Angie. A person whom, he admitted to himself as he wiped the blood from a small cut on her broad white forearm, he loved.

Daily, there were reports of the effects the visions were having. But these were mostly from Africa, South America, or Niugini. Riots, summit conferences, quirky 'human interest' pieces he could always blank out with a movement of a thumb on the snit's remote, write off the increased crime in New York or the bombing of a mosque in Birmingham as the result of normal stupidity, *their* interpretation of events, their own responsibility. Not his. The next step, he thought, putting away the sprays and creams and gauzes, is for someone I know well to go crazy. I can't simply sit around and wait for that. But what to *do*?

He turned on the data centre, programming it for a continuous, minute-long sampling of news. He sat on the edge of his luxurious bed, staring dismally.

'Shook you up a bit, didn't it, chook?' Angie said quietly, lying across the bed on her stomach beside him, drink balanced precariously at her side.

'Yes.'

The screen showed a demonstration by Polish Catholics in the streets of Warsaw, then cut to a crowd gathered around a war memorial in what looked like an Australian country town. A man dressed like an office worker at a picnic addressed the group, gesturing with one fist. He was very good. Martin thumbed the volume control.

'. . . one of the few *other* surviving cast members of that ill-fated production is staging a play. He has written it himself and it's his first production in eleven years, but if this group get their way Kevin Gore will have to find some other method to hit the comeback trail. Following articles in Sydney papers this morning about the play, protesters have converged on the town to demonstrate against the production, said to be an attempt to tell the aliens to go back the way they came. So far—'

The screen cut to news from a different channel. Martin

jabbed the manual override but hit the skip forward control instead. By the time he found the correct station the feature was over.

'*Blast!*'

'That was about your friend, wasn't it? The one who came to visit you.'

'Mm. Kevin Gore. Angie?'

'Mmm?'

'Do you have a car?'

'No.'

'Blast! We'll never get there in time.' He lay back across the bed and spoke hoarsely to her feet: 'Oh, dear. They're doing it again. The bastards . . . The bastards . . .'

'Who?'

'Mm?'

'Who's doing it again?' Angie swung around on her bottom so she sat on the bed facing him. 'Who's doing what?' she demanded.

'The bloody CIA! Didn't you read my book?'

'Nahh. Don't go in for that sort of thing. Conspiracy stuff.'

Martin blinked at her a couple of times. 'That Schnarler *warned* me we'd be in danger once the CIA made the connection between the visions and us. I thought we'd be safe when it all came out into the open! The US government has virtually admitted responsibility anyway, or no one would have believed me still. I thought it was because we had them cornered, but it must be because they're trying to take credit for contacting the aliens or something. How could I be so *naive*? If Kevin's trying another broadcast he would have wanted to keep it secret, but the bastards have found out and leaked it to the papers. Shit. First they do their best to stop us and now, when it looks like there might be some profit in it, they start rabble rousing.' Martin reached for Angie's shoulders. 'Oh, Angie . . . What can we *do*?'

Outside, it had begun to rain again, a fine spray which was blown against the window and dribbled down. Angie spoke, firmly and with some practicality, but Martin did not hear. He felt nauseous. He rolled on to his side, burped and tasted bile. This luxury hotel room, which he had forgotten to change for one with opening windows, this prison, was filled with the glare of sunset, a divine and rich light. It was as if God and all His angels might descend at any minute, trumpets blowing, to declare the Kingdom of Heaven. It drove him spare.

TWENTY-FOUR

The aliens had been detected. Within the orbit of Jupiter, according to NASA. While it would be a fair while yet before they reached the earth at the rate they were supposed to be travelling, the thought of three days of hysteria rising in the streets before enough performance energy was gathered gave Kevin cold shivers each time he encountered it. So he tried not to. Difficult when Kevin and Gemma had met such ugly threats and abuse at the gate only that afternoon, on their return to the farm from the theatre in Sydney. Impossible when the word *aliens* surrounded you in every shop and pub, came out of every screen and speaker. Fortunately, Kevin had enough land cleared on his farm for a huge prefabricated rehearsal shed in which to isolate the cast. Fortunately, too, Kevin had surprised himself when he'd come to direct the play. He was no longer the kind of director who longed to act and believed he could tell others how to do so, right down to the last twitch. It crossed his mind that he had been remade that way by the – silent lately – authors of his new body, but he had decided to put those suspicions behind him. There was no time for idle worry any more. He had become a director who involved himself in every stage of the play's growth, and one whose reaction encourages, often raucously. He blamed this on Gemma whenever one of his old friends, knowing what a dry, ironic type he had been, clapped his back and told him what a nice change it was.

'Not my fault,' he'd say, and make a manic, carnivorous face.

If Gemma was within earshot she would pinch his bum, at once chastising him for lying about their sex life (they had none) and for giving the easy explanation of his personality changes (sex). Kevin would watch her retreat feeling he could race off his stage manager there and then. Although there was still a parcel of uneasiness to be unwrapped, they agreed the first time would take time – of which they had not a skerrick.

That night, after the pair of them had as usual fallen into bed and straight to sleep, Kevin jerked into wakefulness from a nightmare in which the present cast drowned, innocent of Kevin's mad scheme. Gemma held him and murmured inanities, not knowing what to say.

'I woke you,' Kevin said. The autumn had continued pleasantly on the coast. The shadows of the jasmine outside fell through the open window on to their big, wrought-iron bed, waving slightly across their faces.

'You shouted.'

'What?'

'Something about sycamore seeds.'

'Ah.' He nodded as the dream broke. 'I dreamt of a repeat performance of the disaster of *The Tempest*, only it was this play, out here, and I was responsible, alone.'

'Do you think they're behind the demonstrators by the gate?'

'The CIA?'

'ASIO, whatever.'

Kevin sighed, rubbing his eyes. 'Probably. I mean there are as many people who don't want the aliens to land, are scared shitless, and as many again who don't know what to think and lots who are cynical about any new sensation. So I don't see why a few hundred ordinary-looking people should single me out, come all the way from Sydney to hassle us if they hadn't been worked on by someone.'

Gemma persisted. 'What do you think'll happen?'

'Nothing, I hope.'

'They were against you bringing the aliens here in the first place, so you'd think they'd be behind us like crazy this time.'

'Well, they thought we were playing around with a classified weapon, which I s'pose we were, but now they know there might be money or power for whoever claims the right to speak to them, they're right into it.'

'Should we call the police?'

'Who – Curly? Nah. This is Australia. I'm amazed this gang didn't just write to the *Herald*. We'll be right.'

'Are you going to tell the actors about everything?'

'I don't know. Let's sleep on it. Okay?'

She held him until sleep returned. In the morning Kevin realised he still hadn't made any decision about telling the cast, and what with the rehearsal reaching a pitch where it needed his total concentration, and the demonstrators staying on the Crown Land by the gate safely out of eyeshot from the temporary shed in which they worked, he didn't get round to it. Anyhow, it was such beautiful weather and the work was going so well. CIA plots and skulduggery seemed terribly unlikely. Until that night.

Paul, the short and very wide actor who had 'met the aliens already', as he put it, took Kevin to good-natured task about the two hundred-odd people whose banners insisted a utopia of peace, democracy and human rights for all would come to pass if only Kevin would 'LET THE ALIENS LAND'. The other cast members squirmed a bit uncomfortably in their places around the dinner table. Nobody ever mentioned *The Tempest* to Kevin. Sometimes Kevin wished they would. But no faux pas was too much for Paul. No offence was offered and Kevin took none.

'You know I can't swim, mate,' said Paul, grinning.

'How do you mean?' asked Kevin.

'I was always stirred at school, so I wagged swimming classes. Too fat.' He patted his stomach, which seemed rather firm, if enormous.

When Kevin raised his eyebrows and shrugged, Paul said, 'I've read Martin Leywood's book, mate, and if you're up to what those bastards at the gate say you're up to, I want a wet suit. Ask me agent. It's in me contract.'

'We could get a submarine,' put in Dimitrios.

'Or long bamboo tubes; we could walk along the bottom until we got to dry land,' suggested Tracy Little, smiling at Kevin as if to say, hey, I mean no harm, truly.

During the laughter and more silly suggestions, Kevin made a snap decision to blab the lot. He put his knife and fork down on the plate and wiped his mouth on the back of his hand. He waited. Gemma, across the table, did not stop tucking in, but tossed him a look which told him she was proud of him for taking this nonsense so well. He felt a rush of affection for her, remembering her patience and persistence in the face of his anger and self-indulgent fragility.

At the last moment he changed his mind. There was too much at stake to have the actors walk out now, which they might well do if he told them the truth, and they'd be quite within their rights, too.

'This play—' he began, because by now they were looking at him, expecting *something*.

He changed his mind again. A few indistinct shouts had drifted down the hill from the protesters' camp on the shifting wind. These people had not asked for this. They had to be told. He felt queasy with indecision. He remembered the fire that was not a fire, Pete Stanopoulos suspended above the flames, helpless. He remembered the flood that had actually been a flood. But disaster could take many forms. He did not discount simple mob violence, whatever he said. Constable Curly wouldn't be enough to handle things if the gang up the drive got ugly, and the whole police force was stretched to breaking point, if you believed the news, by the various demos in the capitals.

'This play,' he repeated, 'it's – the situation's not what you think it is. Or what *they* think it is.'

His serious face had the cast anticipating more than another one-liner.

'But basically, they're right. I am trying to stop the aliens.'

Paul broke into a knowing grin. 'Good one,' he said, shaking his large head.

Now don't stretch your credibility, son, Kevin told himself. Give them the gist of it and make sure they don't think you're joking. He looked across at Gemma for support, but she seemed distracted by something she had heard and did not meet his eyes. He opened his mouth to explain further – and was cut off.

A huge voice, megaphone chopped and coarse, boomed through the house from outside:

'THE SHOW'S OVER. COME OUT QUIETLY AND YOU WON'T GET HURT!'

It was Paul who broke the stunned silence around the table. He rose and went to the window, drew back the curtains and contemplated the mob at the top of the hill, above the duck house, lit by glow batons and Primus lamps.

'They've got to be joking,' he said. He wiped his broad brow, which was already sweaty though it was not warm. He seemed personally affronted.

'I don't think so,' said Gemma hollowly.

'Well, I'm not going to lie down for *them*, the fascists. It isn't *up* to them!'

'COME OUT QUIETLY AND NOBODY'LL GET HURT!'

The voice was as loud as a pub band now, deafening.

'Ha! What do they think they're playing at?' said Paul.

And with that he stormed out the door.

Gemma, Kevin, Susan and Tom chased him. Tracy, the eldest cast member, stayed seated, grabbing Dimitrios by the wrist as he passed.

The demonstrators were gathered inside the front gate, spilling a good way down the drive. There must have been close to a thousand people, many more than the number present this morning. Someone has to be behind this, thought Kevin as he pelted up the hill after Paul, maybe they've been hired, some of them. You don't just hop in the car and drive over three hundred kilometres in such numbers off your own bat. Not on the say-so of a couple of articles.

Paul had run out of puff and now strode furiously up the rutted track. He stopped about fifty metres below the mob's edge. At this distance Kevin could see they carried more than placards and lamps. There were sticks in their hands, large rocks and tyre irons.

Nonetheless, Paul cupped his hands about his mouth and roared with his best actor's projection:

'PISS OFF, YA MONGRELS! THIS IS PRIVATE PROPERTY!'

He was answered by a rain of stones.

The four behind Paul ducked and raised their arms in defence. Paul stood firm, upright.

The megaphone sounded again: 'THE PLANET IS DYING! YOU MIGHT NOT GIVE A SHIT BUT WE DO! THE ICE-CAPS ARE MELTING, THE OCEANS ARE POISONED AND EVERY DAY THOUSANDS OF INNOCENT PEOPLE DIE FROM INDUSTRIAL ACCIDENTS. WE NEED HELP! LET THE ALIENS LAND! LET THE ALIENS LAND!'

The crowd took up the chant. The PA system battered the eardrums. More stones flew.

'Call the police!' Kevin yelled to Gemma. As she ran off he added, 'Keep you head *down*!'

A rock hit Paul on the shoulder. He swore and bent to gather some stones himself but Kevin took his wrist. 'It will only make them worse!'

'I don't give a shit!' Paul shouted, shaking, some kind of mania in his eyes. The vision he had seen must have provoked this extreme reaction: this shot through Kevin's head as Paul shouted, 'The Bastards! Bastards!', any theatre skills forgotten. He was almost inaudible above the din.

Slowly, the chanting died away; they appeared to have run out of stones, for the moment. Kevin saw his chance. He stepped forward.

'Let me speak to you!' he called.

There were jeers.

'This has nothing to do with the aliens!'

'THAT'S NOT WHAT THE PAPERS SAY.'

Kevin spotted the man with the PA system. He stood in the shadows to the centre and in front of the crowd. Kevin addressed himself to the speaker, a flat, white rectangle.

'You don't believe everything you read, do you?'

'You're just jealous of Martin Leywood!' came another voice from within the mob. There was murmured agreement.

Kevin spun. 'I'm *not*! He's my *friend*! I tried to *help* him!'

This gave them pause. Martin had thanked Kevin publicly for his efforts, several times. But Kevin knew his position wouldn't hold. Sure enough:

'You left him to rot, you mean!'

The truth in this hurt, but there was no time for that now. Kevin started to answer the accusation, but the loudspeaker cut him off:

'ENOUGH OF THIS. YOU HAVE TEN MINUTES TO GET THE ACTORS OUT. IF THEY'RE NOT OUT BY THEN WE'RE COMING IN AFTER YOU.'

Paul ran a few steps toward them.

'FUCK YOU, YA FASCISTS!' he boomed.

Then a heap of things happened at once. A whopping rock flew over the heads of the crowd aimed at Kevin, who ducked and by the time he'd straightened again he saw Paul falling sideways into the grass at the track's edge, blood dripping from his nose, bright in the lamplight. As Kevin stepped toward him through the hail of stones, out of the corner of his eye he saw someone rolling down the track in a wheelchair, and someone else behind him taking aim with a gun-shaped shadow. Kevin, the wheelchair man and Paul reached the same point at almost the same time, Paul and the wheelchair man by rolling and Kevin by what seemed like levitation sideways. The handgun cracked three times and the man in the wheelchair dropped on top of Kevin, who was bending over Paul's head, spilling out of his wheelchair with a look of pain and surprise and a plea for something, Kevin wasn't sure what, wrinkling the brow beneath the man's grey crew-cut.

The gunshots had silenced the crowd and the rain of stones had subsided. Paul struggled to his feet, looking as if he wanted to be ill, and staggered down the slope toward the house. Tom approached. Together they half dragged the man who had saved Kevin's life down the slope to the house. Arterial blood seeped from the fellow's chest, bubbling, spattering Kevin with tiny droplets.

'My God,' said Tracy at the door. 'Another one. Is he all right? Paul's out for the count.'

'I don't know,' said Kevin.

From up the hill the megaphone sounded for the last time, unnecessarily, without much conviction.

'TEN MINUTES, GORE.'

They lifted the man over the porch, into the light.

'It's over, isn't it,' said Tom.

Kevin nodded. He could not take his eyes off his rescuer's face. He recognised the bloke from somewhere. By the time they got him on to the couch in the lounge, the man was dead. His surprise and pain had relaxed, but in his blue eyes there remained an unasked question. Kevin knelt by the side of the body, too shocked to wonder what the bloke might have been asking for but held there all the same. Kevin wondered what had driven the man to sacrifice the promise of thirty years or more of life for him. Gemma approached from behind and placed her hands on Kevin's shoulders. When she saw the dead man she whispered his name, amazed, irrelevantly.

It was over. Everything was over.

TWENTY-FIVE

Dead, they would be of no use to anybody. So Martin sat on the urge to tell Angie to drive faster. The new car they had rented would take a great deal more abuse than Angie was giving it, and they would probably survive most accidents, but Martin did not want to test that. Angie joked about such prangs, and the police, their easy escape from Arthur and Johnno; she played with the excessive number of accessories, winking at other drivers with the headlights, programming the car's minisnit to whisper, 'Baby, give me head!' whenever they broke the speed limit; she even sang. Martin gave in to laughter eventually, but would lapse into silence again. This happened several times during the day.

With sunset's magpies and bellbirds singing and ringing as though nothing of greater importance could ever occur, they whirred through the hills dotted by designer 'squatter's huts', windows retracted to keep them alert. The bush smelled wet and fresh. Although the room-service food had run out a few minutes ago, the beauty of the past two hundred kilometres pushed exhilaration through them. Spotting the unmistakable silver-grey back and red head of a brolga (almost unknown about here), bobbing as it picked its way through the shallows of a billabong, Martin's heart lifted in spite of the dread which had settled there, and he turned to Angie with a smile.

'What d'you reckon's wrong?' he heard her ask. She had said

not a word. For that matter he had kept away from the subject for the entire trip and she had noticed that.

He studied her face as he answered. It was broad and slightly pudgy with grey-blue eyes and lips so full they satirised lasciviousness. She had a large head which was made to look small by her swimmer's shoulders and tied-back blond hair. The overall impression was of one about to lash out with concentrated vitriol, probably because of the permanently widened eyes and down-sloping eyebrows and the uneven lift to one corner of her lips. As soon as she opened her mouth the idea went down the gurgler: she had a childlike though deep voice, usually tight with amusement.

She took it in her stride when he answered a question she had not asked, maybe because she was so tired. (To drive a car which mostly drove itself wore you out more than the old kind, she maintained.) Martin should have been the one to keep her going with conversation, he knew it; on this last leg she needed buoyant chatter, not food for thought. But she did not get annoyed or ask him to do her thinking for her, she thought as she rambled:

'I never could really credit aliens. You know, great hulking latex things covered in gloop or giant vaginas with teeth or that. I tried reading a book about them once, but it seemed like the writer was dressing up what made him awkward about humans.

'What always got me about the movies is they're about fearing the unknown. And the positive ones are about that, too. It's a kind of reassurance: there's nothing to fear out there in the black.

'And the really big unknown' – she pronounced it unknow-en – 'is death, isn't it?

'I mean, what I see day in day out is loonies – well, in our bit, mostly derros. I can't talk about other sorts of loons, but the ones I've met in Salisbury are there 'cos they can't hack it when, say, their wife dies. Or leaves them. They don't wanna die alone, and why should they fear that if they've got a crack at heaven, if it's not the end when they cark? Maybe they're taking their religion the wrong way, but they've had their hopes squashed again and again: their prayers are about as good as a paper condom.

'Anyhow, what gets me about this stuff you're up to your neck in is: we've all been shit scared of this or that disaster for ages now. Nuclear war, overpopulation, all kinds of stuff. And now here's a way out. Or someone to point the finger at.

'But things don't really happen that way.

'I mean, they're not gunna be walking fannies, are they? But it doesn't matter if they're intelligent toe rags, *some* government's gunna wanna own what they stand for and someone else's gunna do their best to croak 'em. There's a lotta people scared to talk to the plumber, let alone aliens. And governments, being full of people – well . . . even the CIA are people, right?'

Parts were right and parts were not so right. Martin tried to sort it out in his sleepless mind and found himself wandering. They passed a sign which told them Tathra was 108 kilometres away. The sun had painted the evening salmon. The night began to cool the rushing air.

When Robyn died he had been doubly shocked. She had left him alone so unfairly to deal with a life which had worked its way into a corner long before *The Tempest*. He had counted on her. She was the perfect actress to match his perfect actor. She was dedication. His very few friends and numerous business acquaintances, a Filofax tossed in the bin, would have been able to say, smiling with unrestrained affection, 'Martin? He's mellowed since he took up with Robyn Ho, ay?'

The only other way out had been down.

For a few more years he had struggled on with country tours and pantos, then he'd latched on to writing *Charms All O'erthrown* as the stylish way to fall. Passed beyond the theatre, darlings, into literature. It was the virtuous way down. And out.

He had known nobody would publish it. He had not been able to face his own selfish reaction to Robyn's death. Nor the responsibility he felt for the lurid manner of her going. For everyone's going. He'd gathered his survivor's guilt and rage at a world not so delicate as he would have liked it to be (a rage, he saw now, aimed partly at his father), and dropped it all on the nasty CIA. When finally he had confronted Schnarler at Salisbury it had been an anticlimax, perhaps because the man had been in a wheelchair and slightly crazed from a vision. He had found himself almost consciously working himself into a righteous wrath, then woken up to himself and subsided. Too much time had passed.

He brought himself to say at last, 'Nnnn, your idea's a lot more understanding than what I went on about in my book. The CIA as baddies, evil creatures who'll stop at nothing to thwart the true and the good.'

'But it's fear and greed, anyhow, ay,' said Angie. 'Evil enough in *my* book.' She thumped the steering pad. 'The fuckers!'

'You like Kevin, don't you?'

'Yairs. I told you what happened with me and him.'

'In grisly detail, my dear.'

'In his own way he's even more precious about the past than you – yeah, he's okay. Not for a lover, mind you, but we could be mates. He's your mate, isn't he?'

'Yes. I guess he is my mate.'

'Well, then. Punch up the map, will ya? I think we gotta turn off somewhere soon.'

Night had fallen. In the amber wash of their headlights a southern boobook, its white-streaked belly splashed with blood, lay on the highway's gravel shoulder. The great night bird sprawled on its back, wings wide, as if banking out of a very low dive. Martin's head followed it as they passed. He glanced at Angie. She nodded, yes, she had seen it. He leaned forward and tapped out the page number on the snit.

They kept getting lost. There was a sign which directed them to Lily a few kilometres before the correct turn-off and it proved to be a road not marked on the map. Which led to Lily, but degenerated into wheel-ruts in waist-high grass. They turned back. With some difficulty. When finally they found the right road, Angie slowed and almost stopped several times because the arrows projected by the snit on the windscreen kept pointing ahead. There were too many intersections and none of them on the map. The correct farm, however, proved hard to miss.

A group at least a thousand strong lined the drive on both sides, jeering and shouting abuse at the four cars on their way out. The demonstrators beat the cars with their placards and glowbatons, they kicked and thumped the cars as they crawled to the gate. Martin could not make out much by the Primus and baton light, save his own name and 'LET THE ALIENS LAND'.

Dire things had happened here. There was an air of sullen victory about the thumping and jeers. Whatever Kevin was up to had been harassed to death. They were too late.

'Take the car a bit further down the road,' he told Angie. 'I'm going to see what I can do.'

'I'm coming too. Maybe we shouldn't have ducked the bodyguards after all.'

'No. It'll look better if I walk up on my own. More of a show for them. They won't attack me.' He gave a sour laugh. 'They're my fans.'

But nobody recognised him. Martin climbed on to the gatepost and, holding on to a tree, shouted down the hill:

'Stop! Don't you see? You've been manipulated! These are not the ones you should be demonstrating against, it's the people who want to *use* this whole thing for their own ends!'

A few faces turned, ugly with underlighting, hate and a certain guilt. Some were grinning as though they were at a footy match and their side was winning. Several of them had brought their children. Most were dressed in designer Dryazabones, an office worker's idea of clothes for 'a night in the rough'.

Martin felt the hairs rise on the back of his neck. His toes tingled – he imagined from the physical exertion after the long journey. And fear.

One man tilted his lamp at Martin's face, and the small group looking at him twitched with the recognition of someone they had seen before, somewhere.

Martin let go of the flowering gum to gesture until he started to fall off the gatepost.

'I AM MARTIN LEYWOOD,' he shouted, beyond false modesty. His toes felt like they had been atomised by some pop art painter by now. He fancied their bits were colliding around, brownian fashion, inside his shoes. Peculiar. 'AND I DEMAND YOU STOP.'

They laughed. They didn't believe him.

In the nearest car rode Tracy Little, a distant friend from many years ago, though they had fallen out of touch when she'd moved to Sydney. Martin would have shouted himself hoarse, voice training or no, had she not wound down her window without fear of sticks or fists and against the best efforts of the driver, to call, 'Martin! It's Martin Leywood. Stop them!'

'What do you think I'm trying to do?' he called back, though he wanted to leap down to buss her on the lips.

Arguments started between those who believed he was Leywood, and the rest, who either could not see him clearly or did not believe it actually was their hero hanging up a gum tree in the middle of nowhere. Martin listened to the arguments for a moment, his legs pulsing strangely with what seemed like growing pains, coldly amused by these people who knew what he looked like better than he did himself. But he knew he must speak quickly into this vacuum. Feeling distinctly odd now, he continued:

'Think! Who are you attacking? *Think* about it! This is the home of Kevin Gore! The only friend who stuck by me when I was put away! You should be *thanking* him for what he's done, not trying to do him in!' He hoped they hadn't. He couldn't see Kevin anywhere.

He looked briefly down at his aching legs – and almost lost his balance. They had begun to radiate a wan light, like the hands of those old radium-dialed watches. It was unearthly.

Unearthly.

'He came all the way down to Melbourne to find producers for my story when no one would believe me. The newspapers wouldn't print the truth, the radio stations laughed at me, television put my calls on hold! And why?'

A sizable number of them were listening now. More were staring at his glowing body. Martin, despite the weird sensations his body was delivering, felt something old and comfortably familiar come alive in him, an excitement which had lain dormant for years. Even if he was contemptuous of those so easily manipulated he was thrilled by the dynamics of the crowd's attention. Angie had made it plain that their fears were his fears. It was not so easy to hate the mob; he was prey to death and hunger just like them, though he certainly didn't look like them right now. He raised his arm to gesture: it seemed to be of molten gold which had just happened to flow into an arm shape.

'WHY?' His voice raged out of him, almost too large for his body. More heads turned. More lights shone at him, unnecessarily. He dropped his voice.

'Because people you never elected, who are not answerable to governments or judges or even audiences had an interest in gagging me.

'*THAT'S* WHY!'

He had them now. All of them.

'If you want to see your way through the mess we're in, refuse the voices among you urging you to cap one violence with another. I don't know if it's the CIA, or ASIO – or even the BBC! It doesn't matter. But I do know that the agents of those whose greed and short-term thinking has got us into this mess are right here with us, among us, tonight. Look around you. Who was it who said it would be a good idea to come out here and stop Kevin? Who was it that told *them* to tell *you*?'

An angry questioning spread through the crowd.

'Don't look at your leaders! It's those standing in the shadows to the left or right of your leaders . . .'

'We'll take care of them!' shouted a voice.

'NO! Let them go back to their bosses with our message: WE WILL NOT BE FOOLED AGAIN!'

The clichés flowed from his lips, but for the moment Martin himself believed them. It was not that they were untrue. The truth was just more complicated than this. Oversimplification was a good part of the world's problems, Martin acknowledged underneath his rage, but he told himself he wasn't lying, urgency was all.

'Throw down your sticks and your rocks!' he bade them.

Their sticks turned into fishes, their rocks into hairy huntsman spiders.

Martin gasped. The crowds shrieked and flung down their weapons, which flapped and scuttled in the dust, and turned back into sticks and rocks. For the first time, Martin felt afraid of the power which had been used here, which might be unleashed in greater measures. It was time to cut and run, before anything weirder happened. Kevin had somehow built a tele-pathic transmitter, Martin knew that much. Quiet now, he thought.

Then the ridiculousness of the thought struck him. Quiet! When looking down he could see his bones a-glow through his trousers, the blood pumping through him like some alchemical fluid? He saw his intestines slowly convulse, his stomach wash the food he'd eaten in the car that afternoon. He was humming all over, it was like his only experience with amphetamines, writ large. Was his luminous translucency a truth about perform-ance? Did it lend more credibility to see his sphincter contract when he began to use his voice? Quiet! he thought hysterically. How can I be quiet? He fought to control his emotions, reminding himself, This isn't an audience, it's a mob, and you're inventing the script as you go along. So invent an ending.

Martin tried. Everyone was waiting for further information, but it only served to make his mind go blank. The humming built, he was sure the crowd could hear it, it drummed so in his ears, it became a whine and the whine a burbling choir of tin cicadas, more penetrating than on summer nights when the insects would not let you rest — and they *lifted*. He was urged into the air. He let go of the sturdy gum tree and floated above the faces bent back to watch him rise. Their mouths were pits of gaping wonder.

Martin's mouth was open too. How in God's name could he get down from here? In panic he flapped his arms like wings. It always worked in dreams.

Desperately, he scoured his mind for the logic which had lifted him on these thousand ringing voices.

He had held back. That was it.

But where had he been in his speech? What could he say? It hardly matters, dear, he thought, just speak.

'Stay,' he said, in an attempt to find a dramatic whisper. It came out almost as a squeak. He could hardly hear above the damned cicadas.

'I don't expect the police will let you go. Stay here. Show your good intentions.'

It was working. He had dropped by half a metre.

'I'm sure my mate — my mate Kevin will let you watch the play he's working on.'

Another half a metre down.

'And he will tell you *why* he's doing what he's doing, and what it's all about.' *I'd like to know myself.*

Martin drifted downwards to the crowd. Their placards had long since been discarded. A pool of pale faces, hands and murmured captivation followed Martin's slow descent.

'Then judge for yourself what must be done, and who you think you'll picket.'

The singing buoying Martin was distinctly softer now. The prosaic fear of an awkward fall occurred to him. The crowd grew near.

'Go back to your camp. Eat, and get some sleep. I'll speak to you in the morning.'

He landed softly. At least fifty pairs of hands and some heads and shoulders bore him back to his gatepost theatre. They helped him balance there again. The voices had gone and he was an ordinary man again, in the arms of his fellows. And already he missed flying; a pang struck him, so sharp he nearly toppled from the gatepost, bearing the force of childhood fancies, all the held-back pain that had powered the dreams of levitation he had slept through as an adult.

The crowd awaited a finish, he realised.

So, one hand tight around the branch above him, with as much dignified appreciation and gravity as he could muster, Martin bowed.

'Thank you for listening,' he said.

The applause began slowly. They had been through a great deal in a short space of time, and while it occurred to them that clapping was an odd response to what was after all a miracle, they needed to express themselves in a positive way beyond the reach of words. It was quite loud applause for an audience in the open air. It continued for some time.

TWENTY-SIX

Kevin looked like the man who awoke to find he had survived a hanging. His gaze wandered around the lounge, pausing briefly at the coffee table where Schnarler's body lay, the couch on which Paul received Angie's ministrations, the door which was closed at last, the telephone in Gemma's hand (she still couldn't reach the police), and back to Martin Leywood's brogues. They were fascinating shoes, expensive-looking, the colour of over-ripe raspberries.

Kevin worked his hands back and forth on the worn arms of the club chair in which he sat. Its stray threads felt reassuringly real. A part of him reasoned quietly: Now if the police don't stop us working we can do the broadcast right here . . . Part of him fought to stay awake, another wanted to cry from sheer relief, but most of him sought the comfort of warm and friendly skin against his own. Failing that, he would look at and touch the objects in his house.

Martin had temporarily taken charge of the cast of Kevin's play. After a wave to Kevin he'd found himself busy giving detailed instructions; the actors had been every bit as susceptible to Martin's artificial charm as the rest of the audience, but none of his performance had been for them. They had sat in their cars a little sheepish and dull until he'd gone over and asked them what they were waiting for. They hadn't known. Were they to go home or back to the house? A bit frightened by this power over what he regarded as the most wilful kind of people on earth (actors), Martin worked out where their beds were and led them away, like a father gentling sleepy children after a nightmare. When he got back to Kevin the man was slumped in a chair in the lounge, looking as if he'd powered the broadcast by pedalling. Well, there *was* a body on the coffee table ... Martin's neck prickled – was it someone he knew? Yet the actors had said only one person had known him, and then slightly. Martin needed a hug from his old mate and a cuppa, but everyone seemed – occupied. He shuffled his feet in the doorway.

Angie turned from Paul. 'This bloke's not gunna be doing any acting for at least a week,' she said, to anyone who cared to listen. 'Hey,' she said to Kevin, who jerked his head up from Martin's shoes, 'did ya see who I brought ya?' She thumbed over her shoulder at Martin.

Kevin snapped out of his stupor. Martin closed on him with open arms. Kevin stood and fell toward the bigger man. Martin was given a pounding on the back that was almost cruel. Kevin turned to Gemma out of Martin's rather smelly embrace (new clothes and sweat) and grinned.

Gemma gave up on the phone. 'Hay, you two,' she said, approaching. She made herself smile for them.

Kevin laughed to see Martin's puzzled look as he recognised Gemma. Then he laughed just to laugh.

'All right,' Gemma said in a tone of sad command. 'You realise that if we're not going to make your spectacular out there in the tree merely another climax from a Spielberg film we have some explaining to do. When the police get here they'll want to question everyone. It means we have a captive audience if they don't sneak off during the night, but will we have a performance?'

'We're short two actors,' said Kevin, stepping back from Martin, 'maybe three.' His bout of elation died away.

'Only two,' said Tracy Little, from the doorway. 'I know I was the one who said we should knuckle under and leave, but

I've changed my mind.' She grinned at Martin. He remembered her bravery in the car and gave his best back. 'And Tom may be persuaded to work on his sprained ankle.'

Gemma slid an arm around Kevin's waist. 'Oh, I don't think we need to do that. We've got two actors who'll piss it in for the job, right here.' She poked a couple of fingers into Kevin's ribs.

Martin and Kevin said, almost in unison:

'No!'

TWENTY-SEVEN

The heavy dew evaporated into trails of mist, rising from the tattered bark which hung in strips and from the tree trunks underneath them, from fallen logs, the occasional liana and from the olive grass amongst the littered leaves. You didn't often get such a chilly sunrise here, in this season, at this altitude; but the climate everywhere was more than unpredictable these days. It was ill.

Those stirring out of sleep – letting go of dreams or sitting on the edges of their beds in their temporary huts, coping drowsily with the cold, one already parked on the electric lav out back of Kevin's house – had no idea that the exchange they would begin the following night would lead to help for the ozone layer. To them it properly remained a play. Angie Langsam rubbed her eyes like a delicate bear, looking through the flywire window over Kevin's kitchen sink at the hill which rose between the farm and what was left of the beach, and decided as she woke that here were a few days out of town she could write to her mum about in full, not chock-a-block with sex and raging but exciting all the same. Martin still lay fast asleep on the settee Angie hadn't occupied that night, deep in a dream about a play before a group of policemen in which he couldn't make his normal acting work but in which a style more technical and deliberate romped it. Upstairs, Gemma lay inhaling the wet refreshment of the morning, only absently enjoying it, her mind fixed on a wetter fantasy involving Kevin. Kevin Gore was already up and, wide awake, he was single-mindedly shovelling duck shit out of the duck house door into the first pale rays of sun. The duck shit steamed.

'You sucked it into the *vacuum cleaner*?' squealed Kevin. The laughter he had stifled snorted out of him. Soon it was an almost soundless wheeze that doubled him up on his chair. Gemma thwacked him on the shoulder with her newspaper. She stood with one hand flat to her chest, chin pulled down, the patience trickling from her eyes. 'Oh, no!' Kevin whispered. 'Plucked alive!' – at which she forced her own grin into something like a frown.

Martin advanced toward them, unsure of what he had heard. About halfway to the table he stopped. Gemma rolled her eyes at Martin. He gave her a short smile. Kevin paused and mugged at Gemma. 'Poor birdy,' he said, shaking his head. Again the laughter welled in him, killing sympathy.

'You promised not to laugh!' said Gemma. 'It was an *accident*!'

Kevin stared helplessly at Martin. He spread his hands, and gasped for a moment. Battling hysteria with every word, he said, 'Ask—' He wiped his eyes and looked startled at the wetness on his finger. 'Ask her why she's called *Budge*!' And off he went once more.

'If you tell anyone I'll rip your legs off and stuff them up your bum,' said Gemma. She stormed out on to the front porch, into the sunlight, brushing past the policeman stationed there.

After a couple of false endings, Kevin controlled himself. Martin waited, then asked, 'Is it a nickname or something?'

'Mm,' said Kevin, his upper lip pressed down by his lower one. 'But I better not call her by it.'

Martin sat down across the corner of the table from Kevin. He felt the coffee pot, then poured himself a cup. Kevin sighed. Martin flipped the towel draped over his shoulder on to the chair beside him. He sipped his coffee. He made a face and spooned sugar into it. Stirring, he said, 'So. She likes you.'

'I don't hate her either. 'Course, we infuriate each other.'

Martin watched his coffee go round. 'You realise,' he said, 'although performance is necessary to make this gadget work, we'll have to fight to keep things in our hands. I mean, a play this negative should make the aliens pause, given they don't *mean* harm. But we'll have to go on . . . You and Gemma will have to be in it.'

'Hay?'

'Well, the only transmitter is, uh, you.'

'You're rich enough to build one and I can get you the plans from Oscar. I'll help you till then, but I'm jack of the theatre, mate. Drive me mad, it would.' He poured himself coffee. 'It'll be politics, and that's more your game than mine.'

'What about Gemma?'

'That's another story. She's right into it. I reckon we could handle her commuting to Sydney. It'll have to be based in Sydney initially, because the actors here are from that way. Anyway, what about you? Is there, uh – are you and Angie – are you rooting?'

Martin laughed. 'That's something we haven't gone into yet. Probably, we never will. You know me, a tad jaded these days. Ah! Just a minute. I found something that sums up my attitude to the subject perfectly.' Martin jumped from his chair and on to the couch, where he balanced precariously, searching the bookshelves beside the window. 'Since I've been sleeping here, I've been taking the opportunity of devouring your books. I hope you don't mind.'

'That's what they're for,' said Kevin, amused.

'Ah. Here it is. Fabulous book. Have you read it?'

Kevin squinted. 'Auden. Nup. Haven't read most of those books. I keep meaning to.'

'Here we go.' Martin turned and, still standing on the couch, he read:

> Dear, I know nothing of either,
> But when I try to imagine a faultless love
> Or the life to come, what I hear is the murmur
> Of underground streams, what I see
> Is a limestone landscape.

He jumped off the couch. '"In Praise of Limestone". Don't know why I never read this man before. Fantastic, absolutely brilliant man, sums it up to a T . . . Kevin, what's wrong?'

Kevin was staring into space. 'Huh? Oh – nothing.'

'I've wasted so much time feeling sorry for myself these last years, I feel I should be – Kevin, what exactly is going on in that tiny head of yours?'

Kevin's brow wrinkled as he strained to remember. He nodded. 'Listen,' he said. He nodded again a few times. 'Right,' he said at last. 'Do you know this?' He recited:

> The Goose, the Calf, the little Bee,
> Are great on Earth I *prove* to thee,
> And rule the great divide – *affairs* of Man,
> Explain this riddle if you can!

Kevin slapped the table sharply. 'Well? Do you know it?' he demanded, pointing an accusing finger at Martin.

Martin had no idea what was going on, but decided to humour his old mate. 'Yes, I do. I think it's from the West Country of England. My mother taught it to me when I was a kid.'

'*You're* Oscar!' said Kevin. He spread both hands.

'Don't be silly,' said Martin. 'What makes you think that?'

'If I had half a brain I would have known. I assumed you used voices out of my memory, and when you finally explained the technical details of what you were up to I naturally discounted the possibility that it was you because you've never had the faintest about science!'

'That's quite right. I don't.'

'But don't you see? No, of course you don't,' said Kevin
excitedly.

'I assure you, dear, I have never called myself Oscar in my
life.'

'No. You wouldn't, would you? But you *will*, you bastard.
Don't you see? We were talking about it a minute ago. If you're
running the society of players you'll be in just the position to
find out about the weakening fabric of reality, and you'll also
be in the position to get the information from the aliens to turn
me into a walking broadcast unit. It was you! You're the one
responsible . . .'

Martin raised his eyebrows. 'So you think because I know
Auden I was – I will be the one with the silly codename. But
why not "Big Buddy" or "Nigel"? Why "Oscar"?'

But Kevin was off on his own track. 'So if the voices were real
people, and you were Oscar and maybe I heard Gemma once or
twice before I met her, then the kid was—' Kevin jumped to his
feet and ran out the door shouting, 'Gemma! Gemma! Listen,
where are you? I've got something fantastic to tell you. Gemma!
Gemma!'

Martin stepped down from the couch. He picked up his coffee
and sipped, although it was stone cold by now. He sat in
contemplation for a while. The prospect seemed rather unlikely
to him, at first. Oscar. He would never have picked that name
for himself. Oscar. He turned it over in his mind. A *nom de
guerre*. Oscar Wilde. Oscar Kokoshka. Oscar Hammerstein
II . . .

'Hmm,' he said.

The rehearsals that day had been a real treat for Angie. She
didn't usually go to the theatre because it was on at night and
she often had the wrong shift. Besides, she was mostly a dancing
person, and so were most of the blokes she went out with. But
the theatre was more fun when you got to be in it. Sort of like
the most entertaining parts of working at Salisbury Cottages
without the hard yakka of keeping the loonies under control or

having to clean up afterwards. And, as Martin's friend, she was privileged. Although the actors had been told why they were doing a play about interfering neighbours and broadcasting it to the aliens, for their own safety they hadn't been told where (or rather, who) the transmitter was. Angie would've reckoned nobody would swallow the bit about Kevin's friend from the future telling him the earth was going to become the sort of Third World of the galaxy – she had heard a lot of lunatic stories in her day, and this one didn't even attempt to sound credible – but they'd all just nodded: the effect of Martin's speech in the tree, Kevin had admitted a bit guiltily to her and Martin and Gemma later. 'I don't know why you feel bad about it,' Angie had said. 'It's for our own good, isn't it? I've seen men grow boobs from the drugs they've been given, and much worse things for their own good, so don't give it a second thought.' It was then Gemma had made her temporary assistant stage manager. 'You need logic like that,' she'd said to Angie. 'Actors are like bloody sheep, sometimes.'

But after two days of rehearsal, Angie didn't agree. Everyone worked bloody hard. They were fair dinkum professionals, you could see that, and what she'd managed to see of the acting – while hurving all over the joint after this and that – was all right. The biggest pleasure, though, was to see Martin Leywood up and off his bum. He was a good actor, once he got going. Not as good as he'd told her all those years in Salisbury, mind you, but then nobody could be that good.

Angie moved her head over the edge of her pillow to see if Martin had fallen asleep yet and, finding him deep in a book, told him as much. 'At least you didn't make me teeth stand on end,' she said.

Martin yawned. 'Thank you, Angie,' he said, as if it were the greatest compliment in the world. 'I shall always treasure that remark.'

'You're being sarcastic,' she said.

'No, I could never be that!' He rose up slightly under his blanket on to one elbow. 'I love you too much.'

'Don't be stupid,' she said.

'I'm not being stupid *or* sarcastic,' he said, miffed. 'I might have been when I was younger, but I'm not now. Well, hardly.' A thought struck him. He put his book down on the floor and reached across the corner to Angie's couch. 'Angie, would you like a job?'

'What, being your floosie?'

'I don't mean that. I said I love you because I do. Do you want a permanent job, working on this play for the rest of the run, and on the next one as well?'

'Most people say they love you when they want a root. I never knew you thought of me that way ya randy bugger.'

'I don't! I mean – I don't know. Anyway, do you want the job or not?'

'It depends. Do you want a root or not?'

'I don't know. Will you work for me if we have sex – or does it depend on whether we don't have sex?'

'Nut it out for yourself, bub. Think about it. I'm not a very complicated sort of person.'

'You never made a grab at me in the loony bin.'

'Don't fish. Besides, you know I'd never touch the patients.'

'Well,' Martin said slowly, letting his hand fall from Angie's pyjama-clad shoulder, 'if it were up to me . . . the thought has crossed my mind. If we slept together and you didn't work for me, I suppose we'd still be friends, and then it doesn't really matter if you work for me.' Abruptly, he made a decision. 'Angie, I do love you, and I suppose it shouldn't matter if I thought you wouldn't work for me if I had the hots for you. Nothing else should matter. I mean, I'm not very good at this and I never was very good at it and I haven't done it for some time. Suppose I say I'm interested, but that I think it's more important to be near you as much as I can, and if that means we don't sleep together, well let it. Okay?'

'That sounded like a proposal of marriage to me, mate.'

'It did, didn't it?'

'Yup.'

'Well?'

'Come over here and give us a kiss.'

He scrambled out of the bedclothes and bent over her face. She pulled him down and planted a wet kiss hard on his lips.

'You've convinced me.'

He stared at her.

'You've convinced me to work for ya. Let's talk about marriage some other time. Maybe over a bottle of gin. Whaddya reckon, boss?'

'I reckon you're smarter than I ever was, Angie.'

'You're not far wrong there, bub.'

He kissed her then, tenderly. He went back to his couch, tucked himself in, took up his book again and stared at the words.

Angie sighed. Now she *would* have something to put on her postcard to her mum. 'Turned down a proposal from a million-aire today, mum. PS I'm chucking in my steady job and running away to the theatre.'

The old dear'd have a bloody heart attack.

The second time had surprised them both more than the first. Sluiced with the scents of their wild enthusiasm Kevin and Gemma had dropped back on to the pillows with their legs locked together in an awkward fashion neither could be bothered to untangle. It had been fast, explosively spending and, as Gemma had half expected, dissatisfying. Gemma could see Kevin would have been happy with that since she'd proven to him she really, really wanted him, no matter what he might have been. Then, as he had smiled his way to sleep and she had watched him, they snuggled, the snuggling had turned into body-drying caresses, an extended prelude which drifted without finishing into lovemaking. No climaxes this time. Sometime during that suspended number of moments Kevin had found the wit to whisper, 'I'll regret this at rehearsal tomorrow,' at which she had laughed and raked her lover's lower back with her once-bitten fingernails.

Now, side by side, the sweat drying in a near-chilly breeze, inhaling of eucalyptus smoke and dinner from the audience's fires up the hill, Gemma whispered:

'We don't need the sleep, really.'

'Hunh? Oh. Mm. No.'

'Nervous about tomorrow?'

Ever so gently, he put his lips to her cheek. It tickled on her furry bits.

'It was the right thing to do, warning the cast about what might happen tomorrow. You and Martin would have been saved so much agony had Dave Abrahams been up-front from the beginning.'

'Don't I know it.'

'Do you reckon there'll be fireworks tomorrow?'

'What – because I'm a human broadcast engine? Nah, only a pleasant glow. And since the cops arrested that CIA bloke for Jay's murder there won't be any other kind of fireworks either.'

'Nice to hear you say you're human.'

'Someone wonderful's just proved it.'

'Don't get gooey. Besides, *that* doesn't prove anything, kiddo. I mean, it's just one more thing. You are what you were before, you think and laugh and shit like Kevin Gore. Real enough for me.'

'You've been peeking.'

'Gahd! What's the difference? Now don't evade the question.'

'Didn't laugh so much before.'

'Ah-huh.'

'And could I make you pregnant?'

She spoke his name and held him tight. They kissed.

'Do you think she'll be human?' he asked.

'Who?' she asked. Knowing who he meant.

'Our daughter.'

'You really think we'll have a baby girl?'

'The voice I heard saying the kindergarten rhymes was a girl's.'

She didn't want to dash his hopes. He'd been that worked up

this afternoon, it had naturally spilled over into their first attempt at sex since the night he'd told her he was a kind of organic thingamybob. And it had worked. He could do everything a human could do. She swallowed and said it anyway. 'Kevin, how do you know it will be *our* daughter who'll be working with Oscar – I mean with Martin – on the project, on you.'

'Ahh,' he said in tones of superiority, 'never you mind! I *know*.'

She growled through clenched teeth and groped below his waist for tender portions. 'I hate that!' she said.

'I know.' He stuck it out for a while then gave up. 'Okay! Okay! I'll tell you.'

'You better.'

'It goes like this: there's a lot of stuff I've imagined and heard and perhaps seen that I haven't known was planted there by Martin. Martin-in-the-future, that is, Oscar. I told you about the wombat.'

She nodded.

'When we went out together to the seafood restaurant, the night I told you about all this, I had a sort of vision of the future. We were on a beach and you were lying on a towel, and beside you, wrapped up against the sun, was a baby girl. Now, don't ask me how I knew it was a girl. She wasn't dressed in pink. She had a little sun bonnet and an emerald green outfit with white trim. It was like in a dream. I knew it. I knew it was ours. I didn't trust myself to hope at the time so I did my best to forget it. It might be my imagination, but I think it was a gift from Martin.'

Gemma was silent for some time. Finally, she said, 'Be nice, wouldn't it?'

'Yeah.'

'You know what?'

'You're mad and I'm not?'

'After we had lunch together the first time, I went off the pill.'

'Hay?'

'Well I didn't think, He's a bit of all right, I'd like to have his love child. I just did it.'

Kevin spoke her name and a lot of nonsense besides and held her very, very tight.

No matter what he'd told the interviewers, Kevin felt decidedly nervous. The media carnival outside the gate had diminished after the police had left, but with Martin staying on the season of *Just Dropped By* at Belvoir Street had been booked out and its performance tonight would have gotten out of hand had Gemma not thought of issuing tickets to the former demonstrators the morning after Martin's speech on the gatepost. As it was, journalists and other gawkers were offering ridiculous sums for tonight's 'Special Preview'. While he hadn't liked to do it, Kevin was glad he'd given the audience the impression that the broadcast was for sometime during the first week in Sydney. Should anyone be out to stop him, it would be too late by then. The demands on Martin by the press had been bad enough (Martin wasn't seeing anyone), and Kevin dreaded to think what disturbances might happen in Sydney outside the theatre. To keep the journalists happy, Kevin had held a long press conference that morning and had given two interviews, one to CNN and the other to the ABC. He'd joked about his nerves. He'd always said that if he ever felt stage fright he'd give it away.

Well, he would be giving it away, after this.

He slapped his skin with pancake and tried to bury himself in his part. This was no way to put on make-up and if he hadn't come to grips with his character by now he never would; still, he'd only had a few days to rehearse. I suppose every bit counts, he thought.

He played an old man named Norbert, an interfering but well-intentioned veteran of the Second Boer War. He was the one who used the line which gave the play its name each time he visited the young couple who'd moved into the flat next door to his. He had an imaginary dog named Jaffa, whom he'd lose in the couple's flat during the first act. His best friend – played by

Martin – was another duffer named Bilt. The two had a comedy routine before the action turned nasty which had to be funny or the business about the baby dying afterward would lose all effect. The routines had worked okay in rehearsal, but it had to be entirely improvised and so depended entirely on the energy level each night. It was a worry. Basically, the piece warned the aliens off by an allegory about subtle interference, unintentionally beginning with the invisible Jaffa scaring the daylights out of the young couple, and escalating from there. But it wouldn't work if Kevin wasn't submerged in his part. You had to *believe* for the transmitter to function. Kevin's portrayal of Norbert came from his memories of his mother's father, as well as a little from his own father, with bits from lots of other sources – the fragility of a bloke who drank at the local, the walk of a character he'd played fifteen years ago, for crying out loud. He had the moves and the lines down pat. Nothing much happened plotwise in the piece, so there wasn't any crucial timing or revelations he might forget to deliver.

He just didn't have the confidence he had once possessed. And it meant more than merely personal humiliation if he proved a lame duck tonight.

He glanced around at the other cast members, surprised. Kevin had been so rapt in his worries he hadn't noticed the others come in and quietly begin to get on with it. Their professionalism gave him heart. He smiled across at Tracy. She had made him fall about with laughter during rehearsals. Martin looked as if he was enjoying himself hugely, contorting his face in the mirror to find the right lines for shading. Susan and Dimitrios, who were playing the young couple, were both fresh out of NIDA, but Kevin knew they had it, he knew they believed.

If he kept picking at his insecurity, there was a point at which everything would fall apart completely. He gripped the edge of the trestle table in front of him and forced the air out of his lungs. From her ironing in the corner, Angie looked across at him and gave a nod of encouragement. Kevin had seen people use this kind of nervous energy in their favour, to urge them to greater heights. Kevin gazed into his own eyes in the mirror. He seemed steady enough.

Gradually, his flutters passed. In the distance he heard thunder. He looked at the flywire stage door, wondering if the potential built up inside him would cause rain. It was too bright inside to see a thing. It didn't matter. The rehearsal shed they'd hurriedly converted into a theatre was on high ground and had a stout tin roof. Loud in a storm, but cosy.

He returned to his make-up. Gentler on his face, now.

He contemplated the audience gathered on mattresses below the stage, children and all, like some performance of religious tales in the Indian countryside, accidental witnesses to a major historical event. Bit like me, he thought.

They *were* like him. An affection for these people gathered in him as the time moved on to curtain-up. The memory of Jay Schnarler's face returned to him, as distressing as when it had happened, but it only served to increase his fellow feeling for the families (and police) beyond the curtain. Jay had become a decent cove before he died. He had risen above the mangling forces around him. Not a bad epitaph, that. Yet Kevin couldn't blame the ones who were still possible victims of those forces either. After all, there had been a time when Kevin, too, wanted to get his hands around someone's throat. They had been deeply moved, many of them, by stuff which reached back into the most primitive part of them and triggered incalculable changes in their minds, more or less by accident; Kevin had heard voices telling him to do seemingly irrational things, and had feared for his sanity. Everyone here needed to begin the slow process of healing. This lot were every bit as insecure as himself about being valid as human beings, never mind that they'd decided the aliens were some kind of gods, never mind a couple of pints of blue blood. If Kevin lobbed his acting right at them and forgot about the other lot in space, his affection would carry him for sure. It was as sturdy as the flowering gum by the gate. Fire might hurt it, but it'd never kill it.

'Five minutes, folks,' said Angie. She winked at Martin, then left.

Kevin had been doodling on his face with his make-up while thinking. He set to with the final strokes and a powder down in a kind of ecstasy.

As he stood in the prompt side wing beyond the spill of brightness, he peeked out at the audience, who were already hushed. Kevin saw the expectancy on the faces nearest the stage, a readiness for laughter or tears or shock or whatever emotional play might come at them this evening; he suddenly saw them as the children they had been or still were, every one of them separate but capable of being moved past the reach of words and so brought together for some moments. He smiled.

'Okay, mate,' whispered Gemma as she passed. 'Ready?'

Kevin nodded. No problems. He walked around in a tiny circle, and couldn't help but drop neatly into character. He began to lick his chops, and wheeze. No problems at all.

Turn. Wait for his cue. And—

On.

EPILOGUE

The surf smashed itself against the beach like a people's revolution. One day it would win permanently but for the moment the land was safe. Bubbles disappeared slowly into the hard, steep slope of sand, only to be thumped into being again by the next wave. Further inland, before the grassy dunes began at the old tide line, under a slightly gentler sun than had reigned five years back, lay a family.

The wiry brown father twiddled an ancient transistor radio. Good news burbled from every station: the inexplicable earthquakes and storms had ended. Was it permanent? Did it have to do with the aliens in orbit these last five years? The father wasn't interested in the news. At last he found some music and lay back on his towel.

Beside the father lay the mother. She wore a boat-necked blue shift which reached to her knees. Every other exposed part of her glistened with sunblock. Even so, after only hours of holiday, her freckles threatened to merge. She was asleep. She had earned her rest.

Far from asleep, wearing a look as cheeky as a bandicoot, a redheaded four-year-old was making a man out of sand. Its bucket-shaped head slewed dangerously close to falling off, its body was an uneven lump and bits of driftwood served for limbs. But the father could tell it was meant to be him – the seashell 'bolts' in the 'neck' were a dead giveaway. An old family joke.

As the father watched the four-year-old apply the final touch, seaweed hair, he knew he would soon be assaulted. Sure enough, his daughter slapped her small hands together like a grown-up, wiped them on her emerald green dress (she had grown out of the white-trimmed type of dress a few months ago), turned and raced inland.

The father knew his role in this well. He put an arm over his eyes and pretended to sleep.

Suddenly a voice shouted in his ear. 'GET UP, MR METAL-HEAD!' Small sandy hands gripped his arm and he was blinded by the sun.

Kevin stood. You had to listen and respond or you were doomed.